The Perfume Beyond the Veil

Sally McShane

AP

AXIAL PUBLISHING
Vancouver

Axial Publishing
2-675 Victoria Drive
Vancouver, British Columbia
V5L 4E3 Canada
www.axialpublishing.com

Canadian Cataloguing in Publication Data
McShane, Sally 1955 –

The Perfume Beyond the Veil

ISBN 978-1-988457-03-1
1. Mystery 2. Supernatural I. Title

Text layout and cover:
Alberto Luna Martínez
James Gerard Duffy

I have been given the most precious gift of a wonder-full family. Philip, Jamie, Stephen, David and Grace, in your own way, each of you has been a genius of wisdom and love. You have often inspired me. To my grandsons Matthew and Noah; may you never doubt you can fly.

My sincere gratitude to our friend James Duffy for the inspiration and the support and to Bob, Brenda, Sandy, Maryal, Corrine, Peter and Ruth for not saying, after reading the manuscript, 'You wrote this!?'

To Tommy and the three who join us at the party: love.

A rediscovery of the supernatural will be, above all, a regaining of openness in our perception of reality. . . . it will become an overcoming of triviality. In an openness to the signals of transcendence the true proportions of our experience are rediscovered. Infinite care abides and abounds.

Peter L. Berger
A Rumor of Angels: Modern Society and the Rediscovery of the Supernatural
Doubleday, 1969, p. 12.

~ Prologue ~

Where do butterflies go at night she wondered. Where do these fragile creatures seek refuge when darkness conquers the light? Leaning against the window in her sitting room, Genia watched their peaceful fluttering as they sampled the flowers she had planted for them. The timeworn lead glass slightly distorted their bright colours. The sun was bright today; blissfully radiant. Genia wanted to open every window in the old manor; to pull that radiance into the rooms; to fill the dark spaces of her new home with warmth. She was aware that despite the soft palette of fresh paint and the lighter furniture choices in the rooms behind her, gloom still reigned. She had naively believed that the paint, the bouquets of bright, tall flowers, the laughter and her determined positive energy would dispel the shadows she had thought to be superficial. She had been defeated. The shadows remained.

Eleven months before, when the heavy front doors had been opened and she had taken her first step into her new home, a light breeze had flowed around her in the foyer, ruffling the heavy velvet curtains, disturbing the moths and the dust. She had stood thoughtfully then, as well. The manor, on the coast of the Irish Sea, had been empty for ten years. It was hers now. This was her new home. The spaces had been grey, sour smelling. She knew she could bring joyful energy into the many rooms as well as the perfume of polish and love. She had already decided much of the design work she would do herself and with every design choice, every brush stroke, she would sing the songs of her childhood especially the Gaelic tunes her grandparents had taught her. Yet, she would eventually realize, too many of the Irish lyrics depicted the loss and suffering of generations of people and seemed to feed the dark energy of the space rather than dispel it. She had added some bright show tunes from her career on stage.

Today, a quieter Genia had subconsciously turned from the delightful view through the window towards that same foyer, seeing the soft buttercup yellow paint on the walls as well as the flowing blue curtains on either side of the oak doors. The marble floors were still in place. The marble was not what challenged the warmth. There was a density in the air, a defiance that mocked her attempts to kill it.

She turned back to the window, seeking the lightsome scene outside. The sun was lower in the sky. There were fewer wings fluttering among the flowers. With the shadows came anxiety, crawling over and within her. She did not anticipate the night.

Tomorrow her nephew Daniel would arrive. One more night and he would arrive.

Chapter One

John ran through the woods, gaining speed by pushing his feet solidly against the dry leaves on the path. He was moving into a swift, smooth stride. He was sweat and deep breaths. There was a foul smell to his left. A scuffle in that direction caught his attention. A brown bear came out from the bush causing John to stumble, losing his pace. His face revealed great fear. Horror. He turned to face the threat and began slowly backing up, making no sudden movements. The bear had stopped to watch him and then almost gently, hypnotically, it moved until it stood on its hind legs, higher than John by more than a meter. A growl rumbled upward from its lower claws, shaking its belly, moving up to its teeth. A dramatic optic of wild magnificent power .... until the bear tripped, crashing on the path in front of John.

"Cut, cut, cut, cut, cut, cut, cut, cut, cut!!" the director shouted. Looking down from the height of the camera crane Daniel yelled, "Why is there a leash on that bear? If it decided to go off script and savage the actor would a tug on the leash get her attention?"

The trainer gave the leash to her assistant and came toward Daniel with attitude. Looking up at him on the crane she yelled back, "Yes, Mr. Director, sir! It's called training. Years and years of specialized training. Days and hours of patient trainer and bear communication. Dorothy responds to tugs."

"Well go back and give little Dorothy a tug because she's harassing my actor. Again!" Samantha looked back to see the bear, on her stomach, creeping towards John, the star of this film. Samantha began to laugh as she ran back to her assistant to stop the beast's progress towards John who was unaware of the action behind him as he consulted with the makeup people.

Daniel shouted after her, stressing his words, "This is not a comedy. I need tension. And take the damn leash off her or keep it away from her feet at least."

He said to the cameraman, "Maybe I will get some tension if our star sees there isn't a leash on the bear."

The response was a sneeze. Not everyone was appreciating the appeal of spring-fresh pine and fir.

The short scene had to be re-shot. All cameras had to be repositioned and lighting reset. The morning hours had been allotted for this single shot and now they were experiencing the hunger pangs of lunch. The delays had been the fault of the bear. The rescue bear had spent most of its life among humans. As a small cub, she had been found alone, beside the skinned remains of its mother. The cub had been shot many times and left for death. She had survived because of the dedication of so many experienced and loving people. But it had not been a full recovery. There were scars, wounds that could not be healed. The nerves in its left hind leg had been damaged by the many bullets. She was afraid of bright sounds and people and sudden movements. In the midst of all this movie chaos, she had found love. For John. The one hundred and fifty kilograms of bear had to be reminded to stand on her hind feet for a menacing effect; to growl at John.

"That's what we call star power," John was told when he complained. "Think of this as a great story for your autobio."

John cursed.

"OK. One more time people; without the leash thank you." In response to John's look of terror Daniel said, "Don't worry John. Dorothy loves you. She won't hurt you. Exactly as you have been doing it John. Same run, same movement and emotion. Your portrayal is brilliant."

Daniel O'Donovan settled back behind the camera in the director's seat and waited for the assistant director to call the scene.

"Action."

Same running, same bear advancing, terrific roar and now a close up on the bear's teeth and then John backing away on stilted legs. OK—some good interaction between John and the bear. Menacing. Fierce. The sound effects people now provided the gunshot from behind.

The bear fell down whining; a belly flop into the dust.

"Cut! Cut!! Why didn't the bear respond to the cue? Samantha, what is she doing now? Where is the savage growl? This bear is about to kill the main character and end this damn film shoot. Dorothy is not convincing anyone."

"The gunshot scared her. She just needs a moment to recover."

"Of course, she does," Daniel responded with repressed impatience.

Daniel looked over to Norman the cameraman, "If we stop now do we have enough to splice and edit? Can the bear go home?"

Norman had been sneezing. His answer was muffled by a handkerchief. "We need a few more close-ups of teeth and claws, a little more drooling. John's reactions can be shot later sans bear. We'll be good to go. If we change to a mobile camera we can get those shots."

"Let's take a break, give John some distance from the beast and feed us all." The assistant director called out the plan and the morning ended.

As the camera crane lowered, there was an easing of tension in the shoulders of the crew.

Daniel stepped off the crane platform. It had been a long film shoot already without the antics of the star bear. This was the last week of filming and the human energy was low. The expectation of an end had clearly diffused creativity. They were all tired of the story and less tolerant of each other. Shooting in the mountain town for this particular week had involved extra logistical challenges. A production shot in a city such as Vancouver provided some relief in the evenings; socializing with friends and a private space called home. Endless trees, melting snow and old damp motel rooms, less so.

His agent had flown up for this last day of shooting. He approached Daniel, "One more day of shooting, Daniel. Soon you'll turn it over to the effects people and editing. It will be great. No worries. Why didn't you use special effects instead of a real bear?"

Daniel looked down. His 6'2" height had always given him an intimidation advantage. His face showed strength of character and integrity. Daniel was a man someone could trust. Quietly he said, "Samuel, why are you here?"

Samuel's response was jolly, "For support Daniel. I know the last days are the most difficult."

"I received an email from your assistant, Samuel."

"Oh?"

"Oh, yes. The answer is no. Once this film is complete, there is a four-month hiatus ahead of me. No new projects Samuel."

"But Daniel this will take a short time."

"No. Lunch is ready and I am going to eat. Now."

~~~~~~~~~~~~~~~

"Samuel, I said no." Daniel's response to his agent had become a bark in reaction to the agent's strong insistence. It was two weeks later and the idea of a proposed project had emerged again, this time via telephone.

"No."

More chatter, more wheedling.

"No. Samuel, I am leaving for Ireland tonight. I will not be delaying the trip again. I will not be staying to meet your new playwright. I will not be available at all. Think four months. No,
~~~~~~~~~~~~~~~

better yet, don't think of me at all for the four months." Daniel had his cell phone wedged between shoulder and ear as he threw clothes from bureau to bed where his suitcase and duffel bag lay.

The agent spoke again.

Daniel interrupted, "Samuel, I have directed two films in the past eleven months, neither one was a comedy. I am sure you will get another director to ..."

A groan interrupted his sentence.

Considering his love and appreciation for this man Daniel relented slightly, "Samuel. OK. OK. OK. Email me the script. I will look at it but don't expect me to agree to anything before October. Forget my phone number for these four months. Good-bye Sam." He laughed as he disconnected knowing Samuel abhorred the shorter version of his name.

He really needed a break from the movie business and his ever-persistent agent. His taxi would soon arrive.

Chapter Two

Daniel took a deep breath of Ireland as he flexed his hands out before him, feeling the muscles pull. He rolled his head, hearing the resulting cracking in his neck. It had been a long, long flight from Vancouver. With more flexing, his body was coming out of a cramped, groggy state.

He collected his bags and walked upstairs to the rental office to pick up the four wheel drive he had booked for the journey south. It was his intent, while he visited his aunt, to explore the rough tracks and to walk the history of Ireland.

His focus for these past months, had been on the murder mystery he had just finished directing. The film shoots were over. The editing and music teams had taken over. Complications had delayed his arrival in Ireland. Genia had sounded anxious about the delays.

A brief time later, he eased into the driver's seat and adjusted it for his length. He rubbed his back against the fabric of the seat. He reached, with his left hand, for the gear shift and felt for the clutch with his left foot. He fitted himself into the luxury, feeling the anticipation of a drive through a glorious countryside. He pushed the ignition button.

The maps of Dublin and the south-east counties of Ireland Genia had sent him lay on the seat beside him. She had outlined his route and then detailed the last turns to her new home.

He planned to avoid Dublin centre and travel the less crowded roads on this Sunday morning. Hopefully most of the population would be relaxing over Sunday breakfast instead of crowding the ring road.

Twenty-five minutes later, leaving the ring road, he reached the spring green of the countryside. He rolled down the windows and let Ireland into the vehicle, into his mind. He could smell the salt in the air when he passed the turn off for the Bray coast. He knew Genia's was another sixty minutes. Her choice of personal space was on the edge of the Irish Sea, past Wicklow. 'Fortunately, it is just distant enough to give privacy but close enough to stay in touch with the modern stuff,' were her words.

Daniel knew her years on the stage had always warred with her need to 'just be Genia'. Often, in the past, she would flee to a distant place on the globe between acting commitments and settle into a routine. She would let her creativity guide her days as she regained her sense of centre, her sense of self.

Genia was a notable theatre and film actor. She embodied a character to a degree that she could not easily separate from it when she was away from the theatre. The evil of Lady Macbeth or the sad, manipulative Maggie played against the indifference of Brick in "Cat" would leave her gasping for 'Genia', especially after a long engagement.

Her last role as a grief-stricken mother, a refugee from a war savaged country seeking justice, had depleted her. It had been a new play telling the story through the mother's love. Genia had resisted introducing a new character to the theatre world. She had felt this woman's pain was too near her own suffering; her recent loss of loved ones.

'I need something light,' she told Daniel when she visited him in his home in Vancouver. 'I need laughter not loss.' Then she had read the script. Her soul had been touched by the soul of this deeply spiritual mother's plight.

He laughed at her look of chagrin when she spoke of her change of heart. 'Daniel, I am inspired. I need to portray this grieving woman and reveal her dignity and her courage.'

It had been an important and yet consuming experience for her.

Daniel saw the turn east from the highway. He shifted the car into a lower gear. Each kilometre had added a degree of relaxation. His map revealed a left turn ahead, a right, another left, a three kilometre stretch and then her driveway with the stone arch. The thick metal gates were open when he reached them.

When he made the turn into the long tree-lined driveway, he felt a huge sigh of release. 'This place,' she had written, 'will give life and joy'. Genia was a strong personality although often described as fey due to her deep sensitivity of the world around her. She walked in a serene awareness of mystery, expressing wonder at a flower or an ocean wave. 'Creation,' she often said, 'could keep one enraptured every moment of a day.' Never had he heard her be critical or negative. She believed everything in creation was unique and connected.

As he passed through the privacy barrier of trees and followed the pebbled curve towards the house, Daniel felt another relaxed sigh; this one coming from deeper in his soul. A fine-looking three storied stone circa 17th century manor house, stood tall before him; its back to the Irish Sea. It was not as grand as most estates because the side ells had been removed, yet it still retained a quiet magnificence. He discerned a Palladium influence with large venetian windows with a flat façade. He knew there was a barn, a separate cottage and a garage tucked in behind the house on the south side. The ruins of a stone chapel were almost hidden behind two old oak trees and loose brush to the north of the manor.

Today, the actress, Genia Adana O'Donovan, his *Ainteen*, was outside, among her flowers. As he pulled the car in front of the graceful steps of her home, she left her flowers to walk towards him. He got out of the vehicle, a smile already in place, as he waited for Genia to come closer. She was a petite, vibrant woman with a mature beauty and a dignity in her walk. At the moment her face was red and sweaty and her clothes held remnants of her garden.

When she reached him, she lifted her hands to his face and looked into his eyes with a loving aunt's gaze.

"Daniel, *a stór*, you have the vigour of satisfaction about you. Is the film finished now?" She had begun addressing him occasionally by this Irish endearment, after the death of his parents, her brother and sister-in-law on a dreary evening two years ago. She had said, within the exhaustive grief at that time, 'The love they planted within you needs to remain as your source of strength. *A stór* means beloved. I hope the endearment will remind you of your mom, your dad and your Irish heritage.'

He put his arm about her shoulders as they stood in front of the house saying, "Yes, the filming is finished."

"And the final result? Will you be proud of it?"

"Proud? I don't think it will be a piece of art but I think it will be a success. The formula of adventure, mystery and big-name stars is all there. Shots were fired and a car chase took place in the first five minutes." They both smiled at this memory of his father who often advised, 'If the action doesn't start in the first scene of a film it isn't worth watching further'.

"It will also pay the bills and fund the next venture," Daniel was still smiling as he spoke.

"And the next venture will be ......?"

"I have an idea in mind I want to pursue. It might involve some research, some writing. I sent all mom and dad's ancestral research here. Did it arrive?" At her nod he continued, "That will be interesting to pursue. And my agent Samuel will be sending a manuscript to ponder. And there are the eventual promotion plans for the just completed film and then...."

"Yes, all work, etc. But first a long creative pause."

She turned him around to survey the gardens.

"What would you like to do first? Look at my beautiful gardens? Settle into your room and explore in your own good time? Food?

Sleep? Remember this will always be your home now as well, so seek your comfort."

"That is a huge gift Genia. Thank you. I think my room first. What do you call this place? A house, a hall or a manor?"

"I'm not sure. It was sold as a manor but I haven't had time to look through the books in the library to do any research on the building. I'll get to it but until then I guess it's a manor. I could create a name such as Rose Manor or the O'Donovan Estate. Something to think about."

They turned and walked up the broad steps to the double front doors and stepped inside. A burst of wind enclosed them in the foyer, disturbing the curtains.

Before Daniel had time to survey the foyer and the wide staircase in front of him, the doors behind them slammed shut and a painting fell off the foyer wall. Genia jumped, startled. Daniel, his arm still around her shoulders, looked down at her and saw an unsettled look on her face. "I guess a door stop or a stronger hinge might be needed here. Can I use my handyman skills while I'm here?"

Her usual response would have been a laugh and a joke. He lacked any handyman skills but today she simply said, "Yes Daniel and more."

"More?" Daniel picked up the painting and leaned it against the wall.

"We'll talk at dinner. We will be eating in the kitchen at the back. Follow that hallway. Fel is with me as well as Dimitri. We find the kitchen warmer than the dining room. Let me show you the rooms I have made cosy for you. Remember these will always be your rooms to return to when you need a home. You can explore the rest of the house later."

Daniel saw to his right a sitting room and to his left a library. Both large square rooms with impressive fireplaces. Both elegantly appointed. Genia had created inviting sitting spaces using cushions in jewel colours against neutral backgrounds; a soft dramatic flair that reflected the personality of his aunt.

At the top of the staircase along the landing to the right and left there were several rooms. She turned right. "I have set aside two rooms for you; one for your computer and this room," she opened the last door, "is for rest. I decided you would prefer a view of the wild Irish Sea instead of the pastoral view at the front of the house."

The room was spacious but dark. The sun had moved over the house.

The manor, which had served as a historic hotel before it was abandoned, had been somewhat modernized when Genia bought it, only needing the last ten years of updates to be completed. She had chosen to decorate his bedroom with a soft colour of slate, adding accent colours to harmonize with the view of rock, sea and clouds beyond his windows. "That door leads to a small sitting room for your work. There's a wild view to inspire you." Genia had thoughtfully provided him with creative privacy. "And this door leads to your bathroom and closets."

He leaned down and kissed her on the cheek. "Thank you, *Ainteen*. It looks like a haven; a good place to write and think. Especially a great place to always call home. I will run down and get my gear, then change and jog out towards that view. How much time do I have before dinner?"

She walked over to the window and pulled the drapes wider. "You have about four hours. I will ask Dimitri to feed us at seven to give you more time to run. Feel free to explore the kitchen and pantry if you're hungry before then." Staring out the window she said in a quieter tone, "Daniel, I am so glad you are here."

The quiet voice caught his attention. "Is something wrong Genia?"

She didn't answer immediately. She just stood staring out the window. Then she turned towards him with a bright smile and said, "Tonight we will talk. Right now, your head is fuzzy and you need a chance for your spirit to catch up with your body."

She hugged him as she passed him on the way to the door.

Chapter Three

Daniel entered the kitchen that evening, having followed the sound of an aria sung in tenor and the smell of roasted lamb. Dimitri was serenading his soup. Dimitri Constantinides was a long-time friend of Genia's. They had met as students in London while studying their craft. Genia and Dimitri both described their friendship as kindred spirits. Nothing more. Dimitri was born in a southern part of Greece. He was Daniel's height at six feet two. He had thick black curly hair worn a little low on his neck, matched by a tamed curly beard. There was some silver in the beard. Daniel had a great affection for him, having met him many times over the years. Dimitri could easily be described as an old soul. Or more properly a dramatic old soul.

A final flourish of notes, another whisk of his spoon and he turned. "Ah, Daniel, my boy, your single malt has been poured. It has been breathing for twenty minutes. No ice, no water." He motioned with his elbow towards the table, "It sits there awaiting your pleasure."

Daniel lifted the glass as a salute, "Dimitri, a true welcome." He let the first sip linger on his tongue. "Hmm. Yes, a great welcome. I'm delighted to see you again. Not that I can actually see you very well. Why is it so dark in here? Let me add some lights."

"All the lights are on Daniel. She even installed extra. Doesn't seem to help. Welcome to the dark side."

Genia came into the kitchen followed by his Aunt Fel. Fel, Genia's younger sister, often looked disapproving.

While Daniel greeted Fel with a nod and a hello, Genia said, "Dimitri, my friend, the smells you have created came up into my room, lifted me from my repose, spoke directly to my stomach and invited me here."

Fel said, "I hope there is less garlic this time. I hardly slept after your last attempt at lamb."

Dimitri ignored the comment. "Ladies your drinks await. Sit, sit. Fel, your usual; a bold red wine. Genia, the same as Daniel; a warm sip of whiskey." He raised his glass of sparkling water with lime, "First we acknowledge the love that surrounds us."

Everyone answered, "Amen."

"And a toast. To Daniel, may your presence bring," he paused with his glass still held high as he savoured his next word, "sapience to our present enigma."

Fel responded sharply, "Enigma? There is no mystery here."

Daniel looked around at the three faces before him.

Seeing his question, Genia forestalled it, "Yes, a toast to Daniel and a hope for rest and renewal." After the sips were taken she said, "Let me light some candles for more warmth and light. Everyone, sit and relax, enjoy your drinks as our master chef stirs his soup. Dimitri, I await a Greek experience."

Fel sat beside Daniel, "Master chef, is it? I would challenge the designation of master."

The squabbling between two long-time enemies fell into the usual pattern of serve and return, interspersed by Genia's questions of Daniel regarding his work, his love life and his writing plans for the next few months.

Setting down her spoon, Genia turned to Dimitri and said, "The soup is delicious."

"Surprisingly." Of course, the churlish voice of Fel needed an audience.

Genia sighed.

Dimitri grinned.

Daniel ignored.

After the dinner of lamb and a dessert of cream and fruit Daniel looked for fresh glasses and filled them with ice wine: a sweet wine from the winter grapes of Canada.

"I brought this bottle for this moment; to celebrate Genia's home, the meal, the company and the wine. Heaven on earth."

"Daniel," Genia had a fond smile on her lips as she began to respond, but at that moment the flames of the candles flickered.

"I see Madame has joined us," said Dimitri.

Fel snapped, "Dimitri, don't start that nonsense again."

"What nonsense, Fel?" Daniel asked with a puzzled frown on his face.

Daniel's question brought silence. He waited.

Fel giggled and sipped her ice wine. She often became giddy and lost control of her mouth and emotions with too much alcohol. Daniel thought this made his Aunt Felicity more likeable.

"Have more wine Fel," Daniel said, picking up the bottle, "before you answer."

"I don't need more wine," she snapped. "Let Dimitri explain his own nonsense. He is the one who has been magnifying the problem, making Genia uneasy. Let him sort it out."

Dimitri shifted in his seat and turned to face Daniel. "Thank you. I will. Daniel this house has a history, a story that began before we were born. It has known tragedy and menace, laughter and pleasure."

Fel pounced, "Oh, just tell him and stop the opera."

"My darling Felicity, it's no simple story. It cannot be thrust upon the listener. Delicacy is required."

Genia said quietly, gently, "Daniel, I think we have a ghost."

Daniel looked into the eyes of his aunt as Fel stuttered a rebuke and Dimitri laughed. Daniel saw Genia's fear.

"Genia, it's not a happy ghost?" Daniel mentally squirmed at his inane question in the face of her announcement. But after all what do you say in the face of such an announcement?

Dimitri answered, "There is definitely an aggressive bully in our midst. More wine Felicity?"

"Daniel," Genia began.

"Daniel," Fel interrupted rudely, "it is all nothing. An old house, some strange sounds and two stage actors with too much imagination. Nonsense."

"Daniel," Genia continued softly, "I don't seem to be able to warm this house."

"Drafts everywhere," Fel countered.

"The light does not penetrate the darkness," Genia said looking away from Daniel to the room around them.

"More windows are needed, that's all," Fel declared.

Genia looked back at Daniel. "A dank smell comes into the room as though someone carried the smell on their clothes."

"The house needs a good cleaning."

"Singing can be heard at night."

"Dimitri gets drunk and sits outside with his bottle serenading the universe." Fel looked over at him with derision. He did not meet her gaze or respond. He was intently watching Daniel as he listened to Genia's fear.

Genia said, "Daniel, someone cries at night."

Fel began, "It is......"

"Woman," Dimitri complained, "stop your words. Let your sister finish."

Holding her hand up to block Dimitri's face, Fel complained, "Daniel, I have been the single voice of reason within these walls for some months. Yes, the initial atmosphere of this place was uncomfortable but some white paint and some brighter lights have made a difference. Then Dimitri arrived and spooked us all with his emphatic, 'I can feel spirits' claptrap. I have been stuck in this place with these two actors and I have been the only rational voice until you arrived."

"Daniel, there is a sadness here," Genia continued in a quiet voice.

"*Ainteen*." Daniel began hesitantly, using the Gaelic. He respected this woman before him. He had seen her battle giants, challenge irrational tirades within the theatre and cope with a younger unhappy sister with love and charm. She had given him immense support in his own career. Yet he knew she was emotionally burnt out. He knew her 'Genia time' had been long overdue. How much of her experience was affected by the nagging of a jealous sister and the emotionalism of Dimitri?

"*Ainteen*," he repeated, matching her voice in delicacy, "I..... ." He stopped, not actually knowing what to say to her.

"*A stór*," she smiled as she responded to his hesitation. "I can see the arguments in your head. They are almost written on the tired lines of your forehead." Her voice changed in energy. "Why don't we leave this conversation for now and talk about it again in the light? The darkness makes us too susceptible to thoughts of spectres and phantoms."

She continued talking over Fel's mocking snort, "It's late and you need a good rest and a dreamless sleep."

Becoming practical in tone, thus diffusing the mood, she stood up. "Dimitri stays in the cottage near the beach. At 8am the maid will let herself in this back door, which won't disturb you since it is on this side of the house under Fel's room. Your rooms are above the dining room and the morning room. The morning room is a great place to sip your coffee as the sun rises. Or take your coffee to the gardens. Or the gazebo overlooking the sea. The maid will make coffee as soon as she arrives, clean up the dishes and begin the dusting."

Daniel stood up, relieved. Sleep was needed before tackling any supernatural possibilities in this corner of Ireland.

Genia led him upstairs, leaving Fel and Dimitri's antagonism in the kitchen. "The gardener will be arriving before the dew dries but he keeps to himself. You won't notice him about the estate. You might meet him in the kitchen since he sometimes comes in for a tea break. Very sociable man. Thick accent."

They arrived at his bedroom door. She had led him along the hallway and up the stairs to his room pretty quickly, conclusive in her need to change the atmosphere. He felt as though he had let her down but he was too lulled by wine and excellent food to know if he was right.

Genia continued, "In the morning there will be warm rolls and cereal in the kitchen. The fridge has eggs and bacon if you want more. Anything else just ask Fiona, the maid, to make it for you. Or cook it yourself. Fel's rooms are on the same side of the house as mine so she won't disturb you when she finishes arguing with Dimitri.

She paused at the open doorway and looked at him, "I am so glad you are here. Good night Daniel. I hope you sleep well."

"Thank you Genia." He gave her a hug and watched her small figure walk down the hall to her own rooms.

Moments later, as he slid his feet between the sheets, Daniel was thinking; his aunt understood comfort. No doubt an expensive new mattress supported him. Soft sheets surrounded him. He turned, pressing his back into the firmness of the mattress. His windows on either side of the bed were slightly open. A breeze from the sea brought briny fresh air into the room. He closed his eyes and felt his muscles sink into comfort. A blink of time and he was asleep. A practical man, he seldom dreamed.

Chapter Four

He woke up saturated in sweat. He was dazed and fearful. He jumped out of the bed, which now lacked any comfort, and staggered towards the breeze coming in the window. He braced his hands on the casement and breathed deeply. His throat was tight, sore, choking with sadness. What the hell had just happened to him?

Daniel never had nightmares; not even in the most stressful times in his life. His heart was racing. What was the emotion? Fear? Anxiety? What had the nightmare been about? There were no details. No lasting fragments. He had a sense of loss and a need to weep. The emotions were not fading although the sweat was now drying on his face and the rest of his body. Had he dreamt of his mother and father, dead now two years? His grief had been buried in work. Was it emerging now? Had the familiar love of Genia and the caustic presence of Fel reminded him of his loss? Was the family dynamic raising memories?

God, how he missed his mom and dad. Daniel walked over to the bed and pulled off a quilt to cover his shoulders. Back by the window, he leaned against the sill, listening to the waves he couldn't see. A fog had descended while he slept.

His dad had loved this old building Genia had bought just before his death. His expressions of enthusiasm had begun with phone calls when he found the manor for sale on a trip to Ireland while researching family history. He had believed there was a connection to their ancestors. He encouraged Genia to come see it. She fell in love with it as well. The house had been vacant for a decade. It needed work. As the structural changes on the house were planned, Genia consulted with her brother and sister-in-law about every inch. Hundreds of photographs had been taken.

Eventually his dad would have convinced his wife that they needed to be with Genia in Ireland when she began the final aesthetic work. Dad would have been in heaven researching the history of the place; examining every book in the library. He probably would have found excuses to leave the chore of decorating to his wife and sister. His dad had been full of love and laughter. His mom the same.

A drunk driver had killed them, ending the laughter, ending the secure, steady love in his life. Daniel had been in Vienna on a film shoot; Fel and Genia had been in London. Genia was in a play. The horrific call had come from Samuel, Daniel's agent. Samuel had stuttered through the words, those horrible words of finality. His dad had died immediately, his mom had lingered in a coma for a week. He was able to hold her as she had held him as a child. He whispered his love to her as he cradled her. Genia had arrived and shared the prayers and hope. Fel had organized them and protected their privacy. His mom had never known of their presence. She had slipped away, one slow breath at a time.

The driver, who had caused the deaths, had not been hurt. She had lost control of her expensive car after leaving a Sunday night party. Her car had hit his parents and two others at high speed as they came out of a theatre. Although she had been charged with manslaughter, her many lawyers had quickly surrounded her with a thick wall of defence. He had been filled with frustration and sometimes rage during the trial as their arguments foiled any form of justice. In disbelief he had watched her walk out of the court that final day: free and unrepentant. The last he heard she was still driving. The death of four people had not caused a glitch in her entitled life.

Still heavy with sorrow and remembered rage he looked at the murky dampness outside the window. The three siblings: his dad the oldest, Genia only two years younger and Fel, ten years later, had grown up in Canada. Daniel's great, great, great, grandfather,

Daniel Irial O'Donovan, born in 1828, had journeyed to Canada 170 years before, leaving behind the horror of Famine hunger; seeking survival. His courage and his love of his homeland formed the backbone of the life he would build in Canada; of the family he would grow.

Daniel's dad had come to Ireland in his youth, inspired by the family history. He studied Irish history and Irish culture at University College Dublin, becoming an amateur linguist along the way. He had married a "wild Irish girl", his father often teased. A woman who stole his heart with her wisdom and wit.

Fel, the baby of the family, had stayed home with their parents and grandparents on the family farm in Canada when Genia left to study theatre in London, encouraged by her brother's sense of adventure. Eventually he returned with his bride to a teaching position in Vancouver. Fel would follow Genia after the death of their parents and grandparents. Her sour disposition towards Genia had settled in by this time. She resented Genia for leaving despite many opportunities of her own to explore life off the farm.

His dad had been able to temper Fel's bitter nature with humour. He once said his youngest sister lacked courage and this had prevented her from experiencing joy. And finding her own value.

She had become a companion to her older sister in recent years as Genia worked on the stage and in film; protecting, admonishing and often attempting to diminish as she sought control over Genia. She weaponized herself as a victim, using guilt and sympathy to control people. Genia endured it all with great heart and understanding. Genia was sunshine and Fel the shadow cloud. His dad had been the refreshing breeze.

Daniel looked back at the bed. By the clock he could see that only three hours had passed since he had first snuggled into it. More sleep was needed.

By way of defeating the mood he began to focus on his morning. He could set up his computer and books in the next room. Or he could explore the county. Or he could start on his father's research to trace his great, great, great, grandfather's life journey from birth to the new life in Canada. A journey that had begun somewhere in Wicklow county.

Sleep was needed.

He moved towards the bed, a tad warily.

~~~~~~~~~~~~~~~~

Hours later Daniel woke up tired. He lingered in the bed and breathed in the fresh breeze coming in the open windows. The smell of spring and the sound of seagulls over the sea waves invited him out of bed. He showered off the dried sweat, got dressed and headed to the kitchen. There he found a beautiful Irish lass with bronze curls like his own, a tentative smile and a subdued manner. Fel was sitting at the kitchen table with a cup of coffee. He had interrupted her litany of chores for Fiona the maid. It was an uncomfortable atmosphere but then again Fel radiated negative energy as she sought some power, some identity in her life. Her voice was harsh, condemning. Daniel barely said hello to Fiona before Fel dismissed her by telling her to go clean his room. Then she focused on him. She stood up.

"Sit down. I'll get your coffee and tell you some of the practicalities of our routine because I suspect my sister didn't bother. Breakfast and lunch are on your own time and pleasure. The kitchen is well stocked. Just put your dishes into the dishwasher and wipe up so we don't get mice. Old houses like this have enough problems without adding more. Dinner is between six and seven. We take turns making it and the time depends on the cook. If you don't want to make it ask Fiona to prepare something
~~~~~~~~~~~~~~~~

you can heat up later. She insists on leaving the house by four." She paused a beat and then continued, "Fiona will change your bedding every third day and clean your room every third day. Arrange those times with her. She is impressionable so don't flirt."

Daniel kept smiling politely.

Fel set his coffee in front of him and returned to her chair across from him. She said, "The stone steps to the beach have been reinforced but the crew who did the work seemed shifty. Be careful when you use the steps. Even though it seems to be a flat pathway there is an incline and a strong wind off the sea can blow you off balance into the rocks. Don't go in the barn. It needs some structural supports replaced. The same shifty characters were hired to fix the barn but have not come back. Genia is too trusting. It seems every aspect of Genia's latest pet project is shaky. The doors, the windows, the roof, the walls all needed some help. Her ideas about ...."

Daniel interrupted her, knowing the road ahead would turn to carping about her sister. As his dad would say, 'Warning. Stop it now. Hazards ahead'. He decided to change the subject. "I am hoping to drive around the local area. Any suggestions?"

"You just got here and you're already restless? I thought you came to visit us."

Patiently he took a sip of his coffee. He smiled, trying to avoid a defensive tone, "I will be here for four months, maybe more. My dad raved about Ireland. I think he took mom on every trail and inspected every tree in the garden of Ireland. I want to explore some of the areas they explored."

Fel stood at the mention of his parents, "Just don't get all maudlin. They have been gone two years. No need to dredge up grief. We could use your hands here helping out with some of the work." As she started out of the kitchen she said, "I need to see if the maid is cleaning or on her phone. I think she has a boyfriend and she sneaks calls to him. Mind what I said about flirting with her."

Daniel watched her walk away, an island, separated from all who would love her.

Daniel bowed his head and sighed. "God love her," he whispered, echoing the oft whispered words of his father after a conversation with his sister. Daniel needed more coffee and maybe some bacon with toast, jam and .... .

Chapter Five

His bags unpacked he headed outside to find Genia. He went out the front doors knowing she would be somewhere in her gardens. He walked across the driveway, along the front lawns and then around to the rear of the house. She was working in the garden that held the morning sun. He saw she was intent on a group of sunflowers, supported by a trellis. A pile of bamboo sticks lay at her feet. Without looking away from the plants she called to him.

"Daniel, over here. See these sunflowers? I planted them four weeks ago from seed. I think they are at least a meter tall already. The stalks can reach to three meters. They're called Russian Mammoths. Their faces will turn with the sun, seeking their life energy from the radiance. I'm adding some more support for them so they won't snap from the weight of their heads. You can see the buds."

His response to Genia, as always, was a smile. He joined her beside the sunflowers.

She turned to greet him, pressing her lips against his cheek. "How did you sleep? With an eight-hour difference it would be bedtime for you now. Are you still sleepy?"

"No. I adjust fast. Do you need some help here? Some 'limited' back breaking effort is being offered."

She laughed at him, "No, not today. Niall, the gardener, is out and about. He has spent the last year reclaiming the gardens. Now he comes two days a week to give me wisdom about local plants and suggest chores to keep me busy until he returns. Always diplomatically, of course. He was with me when I planted these seeds. When I placed the sunflower seeds too close together, he scratched his head and patiently gave me a brief gardening lesson by offering me three good reasons why more room would improve their growth. There he is."

She led him over to the barn which Niall had just entered. "I have to remind him the building is not safe. I have some workers contracted to improve the supports but they've not shown up yet, although they keep assuring me it will be any day now." She laughed.

Genia poked her head in the doorway of the barn and called, "Niall, what are you doing in there?"

A muffled voice answered, "I saw some rakes back here. I won't be a moment."

"Come out Niall, before it all collapses and I have to explain to your good woman why you will be late for your evening meal."

Niall appeared with a rake in his hand. "The old barn is sturdier than you think." He had the healthy complexion of a man who spent time in the sunshine. His age was indiscernible.

"Let's not test it though. Meet my nephew, Daniel O'Donovan. He will be staying here for a few months." With an elegant wave of her hand she introduced them, smartly and briefly, "Daniel, Niall Crowther."

Daniel reached out for the handshake and asked, "Were you named after the King who kissed a hag and won a throne?"

"Me missus would argue that," Niall said as he nodded at the reference to the ancient King.

Daniel gave an embarrassed laugh. "Sorry, I was showing off my limited knowledge of Irish folklore. I wasn't implying your wife was a hag. Of course, I have never met her so why would I think that......" He stopped awkwardly. Maybe the lack of sleep was twisting his mind and his tongue. He simply said, "Jet lag."

Niall nodded his head again. "I have never travelled by air so I don't know. But I do know a tired head. Pleased to meet you."

Genia said, "Niall, I'm going to show Daniel about the property and the house. I'll see you later in the week?" At his nod she said, "Is there any area I should work on until I see you again?"

"I'll be working on the hedge along the pathway and motorway for the rest of the morn' and I'll be looking at the stone arch along the road. It might need some structural support. It would be a good thought for you to look at it and tell me if you want some shrubs added for more privacy." He nodded to them, picked up his tools and walked away.

Genia led Daniel away from the house towards the sea. "Niall impresses me. He is the strong silent type who listens well and hides such depth. But he is right. I don't think you had enough sleep. You look tired."

"Strangely, I had a nightmare last night. A new experience."

"Oh no, Daniel. Do you want to talk about it?"

"I don't remember the details, just an overwhelming sadness mixed with fear."

"Odd," she mused. "And no images, people?"

"Nothing that comes to mind."

"Hopefully it won't happen again. It might relate to the long flight and the letting go of your latest project."

They walked silently, their thoughts united in this idea. Genia pointed over to their right at the old stable, now a garage with a small apartment above it. A cottage was next to it.

"The cottage belongs to Dimitri. He insisted he buy it when the work began last year. He wanted his own personal getaway. He keeps to himself, usually showing up in the evening. He is working on something I think. I don't ask. He'll tell me when he's ready." She smiled, "I'm just happy to have my old friend here."

She pointed towards the sea, with her left hand angled away from Dimitri's cottage. "See the large stone near the top of the path? Of course, you noticed it when you took your run on the beach yesterday. It's a provocative mystery to me. It's large and it looks impossibly heavy. I can't imagine how much is buried below ground. I assume it had a significant meaning when it was placed here. The meaning is probably lost to us. Niall says it's the same type of stone as the chapel ruins and the manor. Possibly Wicklow granite. It has a crystalline feature. You'll notice the granite sparkles in the sunshine."

The single stone was three meters tall and one meter wide. The rectangular shape had been smoothed by the weather, especially the side that faced the sea.

As they drew near, Genia reached out her hand to it. "The stone has some faded Gaelic markings on both sides, which I will have deciphered soon. Your mom took a rub of it. It's probably in one of the boxes of research papers. Your dad thought this side was a prayer yet some of the words are worn. He wasn't sure."

Daniel rubbed his hands over the stone thinking about his mom and dad standing here in joyful consideration of the stone; probably arguing about how to 'rub' the stone. He shook off the sadness. He put pressure against the stone to see if it would move but it was solidly set in the dirt. The surface had rough and smooth patches. Looking at the carving he saw the script was elegant. The letters were not a casual or desperate scratch in the stone but obviously an intentional, time consuming project. Maybe fifty words in neat rows.

Daniel said, "This stone seems out of place. It could be a convenient marker to the path to the beach but it's so large. Maybe a marker to the graveyard?" He stood in front of it and looked back towards the chapel. "It also seems to line up with the large chapel window. Same shape as well."

Genia said, "I am quite curious about the words carved on the other side of the stone, facing the sea."

Daniel moved around the stone, "This looks like an amateur attempt at carving. Was someone carving an image as well? Is this a face? A figure?" Daniel rubbed his fingers over the lines in the stone.

"Hmmm, maybe. I suspect many hands have added to its character over the years. A mystery we get to unravel in the next months? Maybe your dad did some research about it."

"Yeah, possibly. I'll sift through his stuff this week. I haven't opened the boxes since we packed them after their funeral."

Genia touched his arm and moved their thoughts away from a topic neither wanted to address at this moment. She pointed towards the sea and the sand dunes. "There has been some erosion of the dunes over the decades. These stone barriers here along the edge have slowed it. There's a curve along the coastline to the south. Once you get past the curve there's a thick cluster of reeds in the sand. It's roped off because the birds that nest there are almost on the protected species list. If you go near, a few angry birds will chase you away. Don't run too close."

"I think I met the highly protective creatures yesterday on my run. A noisy bunch."

They turned away from the water and looked towards the back of the manor. Genia said, "I'm curious if the waves ever made it over the beach to break near the original house. I suspect if the wings were still on the house today they would be in danger of flooding. I am guessing there has been a century of erosion from the wind and waves since it was built. A house built on sand."

Daniel looked at the manor, "Was the house a "u" shape originally?"

"Yes, there are still some foundation stones under the hedges and flowers back here. Niall used some of them to create the garden paths."

"Do you know about past owners?"

"Yes. We know it was a hotel for a few years. It had gained a reputation for slovenly service and closed ten years ago. I met the owners when I bought the house. Interesting couple. I'll invite them to dinner some evening soon. They told me they couldn't keep staff. Before they bought the manor, it had been vacant for many years. It had been a commune and before that a privately-owned home. The ells disappeared during the commune years. I suspect some of the stone was sold or 'borrowed' since little remains. That is as far back as I have researched. Miriam, your mom, found the name Loth and a breastplate carved into the stone over the fireplaces in the library and the sitting room. I had the stone blasted so the breastplate is more obvious. Nothing on the fireplaces in the other rooms."

She turned. "Let me show you the old chapel. It's along this side of the house, hidden in the trees. It is possibly my favourite place on the entire estate and the one single reason why I bought the whole package. Other than your father's .... hmmmm, let's call it persuasion."

Daniel laughed at the memory of his dad's 'persuasion'. "I would have used the word 'pleadings'. He didn't know all he had to do was send you images of the chapel."

Genia smiled remembering those conversations and emails. "Yes, with the roses flowing over the ruins. They'll be gorgeous when they begin to bloom." She increased her pace. "Although I call it the ruins it's actually fairly intact. I am having it redeemed. It was made totally of stone except the roof. There must have been a fire at one point which caused some of the roof to fall in. What's left of the roof is rotted. There are scorch marks inside. One wall has partially crumbled but I think many of the stones are still there but covered by years of dirt. The old stone altar and the steps are still solid although the structure around them is not safe yet."

As they neared, Genia pointed to the tall grass and bushes near the ruins. "That's the graveyard. Niall and I haven't touched much of that area. Dr. Brandy Bothwith, a historian who specializes in the restoration of stone ruins, is around for the summer. She told us to leave it. We need to appeal to the local historical society or some society for guidance before we can make plans for it. You will probably bump into Brandy occasionally. She works independently and uses the rooms over the garage as her working space. Sometimes she stays there overnight. As you can see, she has already started the restoration. That's the reason for the markers on certain stones. Like a puzzle she is putting the pieces together. A student from the local college is helping her. It was your dad who hired her and together we made a plan to restore it. Well, they made the plan. I just nodded my head a lot." Genia laughed at herself. "I'm in a hurry to see it restored."

Daniel walked around the structure. Genia followed. The grass was deep.

He said, "I see there are windows; the two on each side and the large one that faces the sea. The morning sun would beam into the interior during early worship. How will you replace the window panes?"

Genia laughed again, "Write those sorts of questions down for Brandy to answer. It is her happy place and she will love you for asking. She's a talker. Most of it very interesting."

Daniel laughed, "Do you know when it was built?"

Genia shook her head, "Another Brandy question. Brandy is full of ideas and information. A smart young woman. We have speculated about the age and I believe she has done some initial research. The library papers will give us some more answers I hope."

"We can devote some rainy days to a library search. Is it Catholic or Protestant?" Daniel asked.

"That was your mom's question as well. I have found little evidence of either. It could be pagan or Celtic for all I know. Although I think the structure suggests Christian. I am sure there are clues that Brandy will find as she starts moving the stones around inside. I am also not yet sure when the house was built or who the original owners were. Your dad had speculated about dates and maybe there will be some information in his notes." Genia shrugged. "Who knows? I need a cup of tea and a place to wash my hands. Let's raid the kitchen."

Entering through the kitchen at the back of the house they found Fiona rolling out pie crust for the evening meal.

Genia raised her hands in gratitude towards Fiona. "Thank you dear. Yes, it is my turn to make dinner and I had forgotten. You are saving me the shame of opening a can of soup." She went to the sink to wash her hands.

Fiona responded with a nod, causing her bronze curls to bounce. "I am going to be after asking for a favour. I am using my best Irish tricks to do so. My da says Irish charm and home cooking, used sparingly and appropriately, can be pure gold."

They laughed with her.

"I have a date next week with the village rogue. The one with the green eyes and black locks? The one I described as having potential? Would you mind if I leave early Friday week? At three? I need to put some extra effort into getting ready; get my nails done and maybe a facial."

"Of course, my dear. Just remind me the day before. Oh and remember I have some friends coming to stay soon. The date is marked on the calendar. If you could make up the time then I would appreciate it. We'll make some plans closer to the day. So, what else am I serving for dinner this evening?"

"Well, this chocolate pie for dessert. I'll make some cream for it."

Daniel interrupted, “Can we begin with pie?”

Genia teased, “That reminds me of you as a little boy standing on a chair by your mom stealing the mixing spoon.”

Fiona chuckled. “No spoons today for you, sir.” She tipped her head towards the counter space near the fridge, “Although there are some oatmeal cookies cooling on the racks.”

As Daniel immediately turned towards the cookies, she said to Genia, “For the main meal I have shepherd’s pie in the fridge. Put it in the oven at 350 degrees for 45 minutes. Then a few minutes on broil to give it a crusty top. I put some grated cheese in a dish in the fridge for those who like that added touch on their dinner. Fresh bread in the bread closet. A kale salad in the fridge. Some pre-dinner nibbles in the bowls by the fridge.”

Genia clapped her hands lightly. “Well done. Thank you so much Fiona. Daniel, away from the cookies. Some sandwiches or soup first. Let’s scrounge.”

Chapter 6

He woke up angry, saturated with a sense of injustice.

'Something must be done.' The urgent thought was echoing in his head. 'Something must be done. But how, who? Who will help? It is impossible.' A sense of hopelessness was increasing his anger. He was feeling desperate grief.

Daniel slowly woke up into this confused state of consciousness. He rolled restlessly on his bed trying to shake the strong emotion. What is wrong? Wrong? Nothing. It's a dream. Let it go. Let it go. Go back to sleep.

Another dream he couldn't remember. Another night waking up struggling with strong emotions. But he felt he needed to track this particular dream down. There was an urgency that lingered within him. Maybe a new film script was emerging in his subconscious. Maybe his anticipation of opening the files of his dad's translation of the great, great, great grandfather's letters was the cause. Whatever it was it had to stop.

Slowly he rolled off the edge of his warm bed and headed to the window, seeking again the soothing rhythm of the waves of the Irish Sea. He stood, forehead against the window pane, breathing deeply. It was a clear night. He couldn't see the moon, but he could see the bright reflective trail it left behind as it moved overhead. Beyond the water he could see stars. The word freedom was hanging in his head. Freedom? Freedom from what?

He turned abruptly, decisively, looking for a towel and shorts. That's what he really needed. A run along the sand, or maybe a brisk walk would clear the illusory emotions. As he relaxed he might remember the dream. A splash in the sea could ease the tension in his shoulders. He quietly opened his bedroom door and headed down the stairs, lit from below by the hall night light. He could hear a murmur from Fel's room. She talked in her sleep? Maybe she's on the phone. Or watching TV.

An hour later as Daniel walked back to the manor, following his brief splash in the water, he felt refreshed. Chilled but refreshed. A few clouds had appeared but he could still spot individual stars. His mind was lingering over the fragments of emotions left by the dream. Though a slight anxiety still haunted him, the urgency had faded. He noticed a dim light at the back door. The kitchen door. Someone must have fixed the light over the door. Maybe the gardener? Dimitri? But why start with the men? He smiled to himself, hearing his mom's voice in his head. Equal rights. Any of the women could have fixed the light. Now, as he got closer he realized the light was not coming from the top of the door but from the stone step. It was a concentrated glow covering some figures. He could just barely discern the figures as he approached. A child. No, there were two children and he could see a woman was standing beside them. It was hours past midnight. Why are they here? They looked miserable. Maybe an accident nearby? He walked faster and he called out to them.

No response.

They disappeared.

~~~~~~~~~~~~~~~~

Later that morning, with the bright encouraging sun shining in his windows, Daniel began to set up his working space in the room Genia had set aside for his work. He cleared the writing desk of all ornaments and pulled it over to the east window. He put his laptop in the centre of the desk and using the international adapter, plugged it in to charge. He set up the internet so he could do his internet searches. He found the most convenient chair in the two
~~~~~~~~~~~~~~~~

rooms to use while typing. In his luggage he found his favourite music.

After an hour of puttering he admitted to himself his reluctance to open the boxes containing his parent's files. Both boxes had been closed since their deaths. He turned and stared at them now.

He began by removing the packing tape and postage labels on the smallest box. As he emptied the box on the work table he began to smile. His dad, being a meticulous kinda guy, had colour coded the files and the memory sticks as per subject. The files reminded him of the many family jokes about his dad's finicky bent. All the green file covers were designated as the Irish files. Of course! The green file with yellow diamonds on the cover held the photocopies of the original letters from mother to son 170 years ago. The green file with yellow squares held his father's translations of the letters from the Gaelic to English. Canadian English his dad had insisted.

His father had told him, 'The translation will be tricky because the Gaelic will be affected by date, class and place. For example, the Gaelic alphabet was written in a different script before 1960. A language might look and sound the same but the historical and cultural nuances are what matter when trying to understand the meaning within the words.' As a historian and amateur linguist his dad had loved every minute of the task. Unfortunately, these translations were his first drafts.

The red files were for his father's research of the Canadian years of Daniel's great, great, great grandfather's life. His parents had played with the idea of writing a family history. The file contained those notes and scribbles. He set those files aside for another day.

The files for the backup subjects varied in colour. The file folder with the maps was blue and the three bulky purple folders contained his parents' Famine research. Following his father's reasoning, purple represented divinity and his father felt the files depicting the horrors of the Great Famine should be held within this sacred context. All the file folders had notations on the covers written in his dad's handwriting. On the Famine files he had simply written, '*An Gorta Mór*'; the Gaelic for the 'Great Hunger'.

In the bottom of the box he found a sturdy green box containing Daniel's great, great, great grandfather's letters from his mother in Ireland. The note paper was fine and delicate, protected by special tissues. This box also held various items such as a boat ticket, the original deed of the farmland in Canada, newspaper articles from Ireland, Britain, France or Quebec and early Canada. There was a separate file he noticed, in yellow, with photocopies of the newspaper articles. A large envelope held the rubbings his mom had done of the stone by the beach pathway.

He laid all the files side by side on another table Genia had provided. He turned to the second large box. It contained books about Wicklow, genealogies of Ireland, research on the Famine and early Canadian history. He looked around the room for a bookcase and a place to tape up some maps.

But his mind had become distracted. The image of the children and the woman on the back steps troubled him. He had not slept after seeing that apparition. After they disappeared.

Wait a minute, he thought. They? Had his subconscious jumped to a phantasmal explanation? What of fog? A tired mind? Light through fog? Does fog disappear immediately? The vague shapes had been indicative of human forms. The halo of light around the forms outlined or suggested human forms. What was the source of the light?

Really the question I am avoiding is simple. Do I believe in ghosts? Certainly, Genia does and maybe my judgment, my interpretation, is influenced by her fears, her beliefs. Did I believe in ghosts before I came here? He shook his head. He had never really thought about it.

He realized he had stopped working and was standing looking down at the floor, lost in these impossible thoughts. He decided to just wait. Wait for what? He frowned. That was a troubling question.

OK. Stop. Think bookcase. He needed a bookcase for his parent's books and research. Where? He went looking.

Chapter 7

Dimitri was the chef again this evening. He had pushed Fel out of the kitchen saying she looked tired and needed a nap. That comment, while true, gained Dimitri a spiteful response. And yet she left him to the task. Dimitri had what he wanted: to rile Fel, make dinner and because the acoustics were excellent in the kitchen, sing. Dimitri was singing a Greek folk song when Daniel entered the kitchen.

Daniel went to the sink to wash his hands and then moved to the cupboard where the bottles of alcohol were stored pulling down a whiskey bottle and some glasses. Genia would probably want a pre-dinner whiskey as well.

They exchanged some thoughts on their day. Daniel had explored Wicklow County in the afternoon, impressed by the diverse beauty of mountains and valleys: fertile and sparse.

When Genia and Fel entered the kitchen, Dimitri was telling Daniel a story from his early theatre days. He didn't pause in his story, simply pointing them towards the plate of cheese, pears and apples on the table.

He continued with his story, "Anyway, this old man, Fergus Sanople was a wealthy lonely bachelor. He became our biggest fan and greatest benefactor. He often came on tour with us. He always chose a seat in the front row. Yet half way through a performance he would fall asleep and start snoring. Not a light snore but a snore worthy of a theatrical setting. The audience would sometimes nudge him awake or in one case someone 'nudged' him so hard he toppled right out of his seat. He was a forgiving soul. Without his pots of money we would have been destitute. We had to decide between poverty and adapting to his snores. The challenge helped me perfect my voice range. The people in the small village communities were great audiences. Without artifice they came for the pure enjoyment of the music. We were inspired in our desire to please them."

He looked over to Genia and asked, "Remember the fun of your early days?"

Fel imposed her thoughts before Genia could answer, "You attempt to make poverty and struggle a romantic adventure? Our parents worried about Genia all the time." Her voice was harsh as she mimicked her parents, "'Why hasn't Genia called? Where is she now?'" She smirked. "A letter from Genia would be the central topic for days." Her voice became acerbic. "The time you got your first part in a London play there was dancing in the corn fields. I think they were celebrating because they didn't have to send you any more money."

Two deep breaths of uncomfortable silence followed. Fel sat smugly watching to see if her shard of ugly had cut into Genia.

Genia turned to face her friend Dimitri who was leaning back against the stove, wine glass in hand. "I cherish those days, our rites of passage. Some of my greatest life lessons came out of those struggles; the tears and aggressive woes of those days taught me about myself. That's how we perfected our craft." She was smiling and shaking her head as she added, "Our bellies growling from hunger motivated us and challenged the strength of our ambitions."

Fel interrupted, "Was that gem of wisdom a shot at me because I stayed home with the parents, the grandparents?"

Genia turned to her sister, her smile still on her face, and she answered, "Fel, I have enough trouble with my own life without judging yours. We all grow as we deem important."

Fel leaned forward and the look on her face was not pleasant. She began to respond.

Daniel interrupted her toxic intent, "I saw a ghostee last night. Three of them."

Dimitri gave a bombastic shout of laughter.

Daniel stood up from the table and went to the cupboard to refresh his drink amid the exclamations from his aunts. Daniel was smiling knowing his father would have seen this shift as a masterful attempt to change topics and diffuse a landmine.

Dimitri responded first, "My, my, Daniel, you definitely upped the ghostly ante. Three ghosts?"

Turning back to face his audience Daniel was surprised. Fel's expression was derisive, of course. Dimitri's expressed glee. Well that wasn't really a surprise since Dimitri enjoyed anything that would take a poke at Fel's scepticism. Fel's downright denial would be a better description since scepticism allowed for possibility. It was Genia's face that surprised him. She was angry.

She slowly rose from her chair saying, "Are you mocking me? Have you all been mocking me?" She looked at each of them. "You think my fears are to be mocked, open to derision by all of you over a friendly dinner conversation?" Her face was tense. Hurt.

Fel laughed.

Dimitri started to sputter.

Daniel answered quietly. He had become still in his body and in his facial expression. Keeping his tone neutral he said, "No *Ainteen*. I would never be dismissive of you. I trust your instincts, your sensitivity. I really did see a ghost last night. Three ghosts."

He approached her and poured a finger of whiskey into her glass. He handed it to her. She took it and sat down. Her eyes on his face held a slightly desperate appeal. Her posture showed vulnerability, revealing more strain than he realized she was holding within her. They really hadn't had a conversation about what was causing that strain.

He sat across from her and put down his glass. Appearing casual he picked up some of the smoky cheese chosen to complement the whiskey. "I was walking back from the beach last night after a two o'clock swim."

Genia interrupted him, concern lessening the desperation in her eyes, "Daniel, alone at night? What about the rip tides?"

"No, no rip tides last night and I stuck to the shallows."

He leaned back in his chair. "As I approached from the beach I noticed a light at the back door. I thought someone had replaced the bulb." He paused and smiled ruefully, "Though now that I think about it, it wasn't working when I left for the beach. Who would be changing light bulbs at that time?" He grimaced. "Anyway, there seemed to be a halo of light around three people on the step; two children sitting on the step and a woman beside them."

Fel didn't allow reflective space. "Were you drinking?"

Dimitri interrupted, "Wait, save the deconstruction for one minute. Let's get some food on the table before we answer Fel's insightful response to spectral events."

As he moved the bread, the stew pot and the condiments to the table, Genia stopped staring at Daniel. Shaking off whatever thought was bothering her she moved to get plates and silverware.

Steam, scented with sweet basil, rose from the Thai green curry as Dimitri filled their plates. He turned back to get the papaya salad. Settling into his chair, he lifted his glass of wine and said, "May God be pleased with our paltry attempts to give thanks. Amen."

Everyone raised their glass in response.

"So, were you imbibing too much last night Daniel?" Dimitri asked, looking sideways at Genia.

Daniel shook his head. "No, just recovering from another disturbed sleep. Imagine. I had all the fundamentals for a perfect sleep; a beautiful bed, cosy and warm sheets and a peaceful space with a fresh sea breeze. Despite that I wake up."

Genia asked, "Why do you think it was a woman on the step?"

Fel asked, "Did the fog have breasts?"

Daniel sighed and said, "No, I didn't see breasts. I think it was the long hair, the posture."

Genia asked, "Did you feel any emotions?"

Daniel said, "No, just surprise. It or they disappeared before I really had a chance to respond. I thought they were people who had been in an accident and had come for help."

Genia asked, "Did they see you? Respond to you? Did you speak to them?"

Daniel got out a brief negative response before Fel took over the questioning, "Why did you think it was human other than shape?"

Daniel took some salad, a sip of water and moved his food around his plate before answering: in fact, stalling. "Besides shape?"

Fel smiled sweetly at him and started to twist the screw. "The real question is, if Genia had not set us within this context of the supernatural, would you have thought it was a ghostly apparition?"

After a few beats of awkward silence, Dimitri jumped in, giving him space. "My, my, the curry is delightful. The bold flavours within the papaya salad complement it so well."

Daniel laughed.

Dimitri gained the affirmation he sought from them and the brief distraction. "Tomorrow night it's your turn Daniel to prepare the meal. What are you thinking? What delights will you supply? What succulent morsels will we taste?"

Fel said, "Good try Greek man. Why did you think it was a ghost Daniel?"

Dimitri again, "Well, why not? Why not a ghost? Why is your world limited to what you can see, touch and smell? There is much evidence to support the reality of the supernatural. There are lots of first hand accounts of people seeing ghosts. I have heard of spectres announcing their presence with smell; the scent of a perfume your mother wore or the tobacco smoke of Dad's pipe. Did you smell anything Daniel?"

Dimitri didn't give him space to answer, "Or touch. Some people say in times of stress they can feel someone stroking their hair. Oh, remember that great film 'The Uninvited'? It took place in a grand manor overlooking a wild ocean. The steep cliff on the edge of the ocean was as much a character in the film as the actors. The main ghost's perfume always flowed into a room announcing her imminent arrival. Of course, initially they didn't know it was a ghost or a her. They thought it was the scent of flowers outside. Ray Milland played the hero and he was putting the pieces together slowly as the male hero always does." He laughed. "It had macho depths or lack thereof. That great stage actress Dorothy Stickney was in it. Oh, and the lovely Donald Crisp. It was made in Hollywood sometime in the forties."

Fel said, "It was make believe Dim-metri." Fel liked this verbal punch of stressing the first syllable of his name. "This is real life, Dim. Come out of your make believe and come live with real people. Ghosts do not exist."

Dimitri ignored her and continued, "It was based on an Irish novel that was written to challenge an outdated identification of women as only domestics. The Irish government of the day was incorporating that archaic idea into their constitution. The author of the book, Dorothy McCrindle, was a friend with the president of Ireland and she wrote it to make a point about the equality of women. Apparently, he got the message."

Fel was not distracted, "Ghosts are fantasy."

Genia entered the conversation, "It's getting cold in here."

Dimitri responded, jumping up, "Oh, I left the window open a bit to manage the steam. I'll close it." Over his shoulder he said to Fel, "So this is all there is? Is there no hereafter? No heavenly choir

I can join when this corporeal body is no longer able to house my very magnificent self?" He winked at Fel when he sat down again.

Fel snorted, "If you are talking about heaven I can't see you getting beyond the pearly gates."

Dimitri stayed on topic. "But really, are you saying there isn't a hereafter? Will you just end? Will your soul end?"

Fel sputtered a little and responded defensively, "That is a question for theologians."

Dimitri said, "One of the early Greek thinkers, my countryman, you might have heard of him, Plato, thought there was a hereafter. In fact, he thought there was a Before, a place of beginning where we all had a sense of Presence." His voice became a tad high, as though he was uncomfortable speaking of his topic. "He wrote that he thought our sense of dissatisfaction with life was because we yearned always for that beautiful and powerful love which we had known and had forgotten in the trauma of birth and while adapting to the limits of the corporeal. The closest we can get to it in life is when we feel wonder."

Genia responded, "I think that makes more sense than to think we just end. That reminds me. There is a wonderful description of death in one of Emmet Dalton's accounts of Michael Collin's death. Let me see if I can do it justice." She paused and looked down. When she looked up again her face was distant. She was looking at another reality. Her voice had a story teller's rhythm, "Emmet Dalton had been a close friend and supporter of Michael Collins. The war with Britain was over and a limited freedom had been obtained. A limited freedom with a possibility for more freedom, Michael Collins had insisted when he returned from the meetings in London with Churchill. But passionate disagreements escalated into civil war. Months into the civil war, Dalton and a few soldiers travelled with Collins to the area of Ireland Collins loved; the place of his childhood. A place of rolling hills and verdant green pastures."

Her hands moved gracefully through the space in front of her outlining a hill and a valley. "The convoy was ambushed in one of those valleys, possibly a place he had roamed as a child, known as the Mouth of the Blossoms or Flowers or Buttermilk." She stopped and looked over at Fel and smiled. "Our brother, the language scholar, would cringe at me for not having the correct translation."

Fel briefly shared this smile.

"Michael Collins insisted they get out of the cars and respond despite the call by others to drive like hell. There was a barrier in the road. Collins was shot while kneeling on the road. His rifle was still in his hands when they found him. His head was lying on his arms. He was breathing but the damage to the back of his head was so great they knew he would die in seconds. Someone leaned over him and spoke the words of contrition."

She whispered the first sentence, "'My God I am heartily sorry for having offended Thee'. They pulled Michael Collins off the road behind one of the cars."

Genia pushed her chair back from the table slightly and made a cradle of her arms. "Emmet placed Michael Collins' large head in his arms. He tried to stem the blood and grey brain matter seeping out of the gaping hole in the Big Fellow's head while bullets continued to fly around them." Genia looked down at the 'head' in her arms. "Emmet said he couldn't imagine that a life so vital, a life so strong and intense could end. How could intelligence just end? How could the merriment and song of a person just end? And yet it did. The face of his Chief, this big guy he admired and loved became pale and still. His eyes closed. It was over. He was over." She paused and then repeated the simple statement, "He was over."

They were all looking at the 'head' she cradled in her arms. She paused with them. "How is it possible we just end? Like turning off the TV? Like shutting off a water tap? Plato was pointing us towards a greater reality than what limits us here. We can turn off a water tap or a TV screen but even though the vessel has been limited, the water still exists and the air waves still flow invisibly around us. If we can think past our corporeal limitations there is so much more."

She held the thoughtful silence and then looked up at them with a winsome smile, "Such as ghostees."

Daniel said quietly, "Certainly scientists are starting to take life after death arguments more seriously. I recently read there are some who consider our consciousness as separate from our bodies. In fact some believe what we call consciousness is actually our soul."

Dimitri stood up. "I need more intoxicant. Oh, and there is a dessert. Chocolate cake and ice cream. Not of my making. The maid left it."

Fel stood up. "Ghosts and death. This party has become too gloomy. I'm taking my cake to my room to watch some television. A comedy. Daniel you aren't off the hook about the question of ghoulies and spirits. To be continued."

Chapter 8

Following Fel's exit with her slice of cake and ice cream, Dimitri set the remainder of the dessert on the table. As he cut slices he urged Genia, "Now tell Daniel what has been happening."

Genia looked uncomfortable. "I just don't know any more. I might be going crazy." She deflected, "Daniel let's talk about what you saw last night. Was it a human form? Or forms?"

"Like you, *Ainteen*, I am not certain now what I saw. I didn't think I was seeing ghosts last night. I thought, 'there are some people in trouble standing and sitting by the kitchen door'. When it, or maybe 'they' disappeared as I approached my assumption disappeared with them. But I can't leap immediately to ghost."

Dimitri said, "Perhaps we should define what we mean by ghost."

"Say more," urged Daniel.

"The instant media often informs our understanding of most topics unless you're someone who has a particular interest and you do some deeper research; enough to form your own opinion beyond what the news dictates to you. Otherwise, as related to the supernatural, the horror scripts of today affect how we perceive the topic. Often scripts are written by reductionists within a secular point of view focusing mostly on exacerbating emotions. Angels are depicted as people, like you and me, with the same motivations and weaknesses but they have wings, some cool powers such as smiting and they stare at heaven at some moralistic judgmental authority. The hungry, vindictive ghost narratives feed the audience's ever-increasing need to feel something. Fear distracts them from their own poverty of ideals or dreams or possibilities. Fear is an excuse to suppress their own potential. A ghost dragging a woman by the hair down cellar steps to the dark unknown is a metaphor of their own fearful lives. The story then needs to have a resolution, a defeat of the evil, to soothe the fears of the audience. Which has little to do with ghosts or reality."

He paused. "Sorry I am digressing."

Daniel answered, "But not wrong."

Genia prodded, "So how do you define ghosts?"

Dimitri took a deep breath. "I confess I don't really know." He grinned at them. "Sorry. I'm not a theologian. But I do believe there is more and we don't cease to be. And I am angry." He stopped and tested the word. "Angry? Yes, angry at how our experiences are ridiculed or reduced by others. My mother, a few hours before she died talked to her dead mother and was surprised we couldn't see her *Mana* by the bed. People ridicule me for repeating that story. I have been told it is nonsense because my mother was dying and therefore she did not have clarity of thought. I was there. My mother was very clear in her conversation with us. The massive heart attack that killed her came a few hours later." He paused and ruefully laughed. "OK so my thoughts are affected by my anger. The point is she saw a presence. A benevolent presence of someone she loved who had died. A ghost."

Genia responded, "I've heard similar stories. Often dismissed as delusional. We live in a post-theist world; God does not exist for many people. Therefore, anything supernatural is fantasy. Often horror. Entertainment. The scientific materialism of our time interchanges the words wonder and curiosity. I believe wonder is our mystical eyesight."

Dimitri turned back to Daniel. "I have heard of something called residual energy. It is believed to be a powerful emotion which becomes imprinted into a space and a time. The intensity of the pain and suffering caused by the Famine could have left scars in time; within the universe. I wonder if what you saw was something like that since there wasn't a response. Was there movement?"

Daniel was thoughtful, clearly searching a recording in his mind's eye. "I don't remember movement."

"Were there emotions?"

"I don't remember emotions. I sensed distress. I really did think it was people who needed help."

"How was that communicated?"

"Time of night. Drooped shoulders. Lack of response. I thought of desperation when I saw them because of the posture of the tall figure."

Genia came back into the conversation. "Your father said the house had a history. Doesn't always mean happy."

Dimitri asked, "Then maybe an imprint from an unhappy moment. A moment frozen in time."

"Yes, possibly," she answered. "A previous accident? Why the back door? Could you distinguish clothing?"

Daniel answered her, "The female figure had a long dress or cloak. I thought of it as a female because of the long dress. The children seemed to be in shorts. But wait, wait. I think I am dressing it up now. I no longer know what I saw and we're assuming it was human forms. Yet, I, we, have to resist those assumptions becoming facts. There were shapes that looked like a woman and two children. Looked like! Not actually."

"Warning! A Supernatural Rabbit hole ahead," chimed in Dimitri. "We could always sit outside for a while and test the assumption. If it is a residual energy it could appear again."

"Not me," Daniel responded. "I am lacking sleep because my assumptions kept me awake in the wee hours. Bed is in my immediate future. To be continued, as Fel says?"

Genia laughed. "I'm glad she's here. I think Fel would not have allowed us to have continued this conversation without throwing her critical thinking into the mix."

"Probably a good thing to keep us from the edge of that rabbit hole. I might do some digging in the library tomorrow. Look for that information about the history of the house," Daniel said.

Dimitri asked, "Does anyone want to walk me back to my cottage? Keep me safe from the ghoulies?"

Genia laughed at him. "No."

Daniel responded as well, "No. On your own mate. We can watch out the window."

Dimitri said, "With that comforting promise I will depart, alone, to my solitary cottage. Alone. By myself. Alone."

"Call us if anyone transparent shows up," Daniel offered.

~~~~~~~~~~~~~~~

As soon as he entered the kitchen the next morning, before he could pour coffee into his mug or speculate on breakfast possibilities, Fel, who was sitting at the table, spoke, "Daniel, we both know Genia is a susceptible person. She finds supernatural nuance in a butterfly. I think it comes with her career. A breeze blows her hair and she thinks an angel is touching her. A light shining in a dark room couldn't possibly be explained away as moonlight reflecting in a mirror for her. No, it has to be ghosts and spirits. She thinks this old house has dark energy. Frankly it just needs some more lamps. If she dumped most of those old books in the library and brought in some modern titles with bright covers there would be a difference as well in that room. I am sure when she is in that garden of hers she talks to the wood spirits and elves. This country attracts that kind of nutty thinking. But she is a fragile woman and we must protect her from her wilder imaginings. Don't
~~~~~~~~~~~~~~~

encourage her like Dimitri does. He gets a few drinks and raves on about "Madame", a ghost he has created out of creaky floors, bad lighting and draughty windows. Help me please Daniel, to keep some sanity within this house."

Daniel stared at her in silence as the narrative continued, recognizing her usual tactic of driving wedges into relationships. Genia and his father had shared the marvel of life, the excitement of new possibilities and opportunities, always ready to free fall into the next adventure. Fel was the beautiful youngest child, cosseted and petted by her parents and grandparents. As the younger sister she had limited her wonder with words like 'safe', 'responsibility' and 'sanity'. His father and Genia, much older, had had each other to secretly share the marvels of their discoveries. Fel had been left out and left behind.

Today Fel was placing him in the role of his father as her stream of loving concern for Genia's sanity washed over him. He wished fervently for his dad's humour. Right now, his dad would have interrupted with a joke or a comment that would metaphorically have built a protection against the flow.

"Fel," he began sharply. Then he hesitated. He could hear frustration in his voice. What words? What words to use? Softer now, with affection he spoke again, "Fel, I miss my dad and my mom deeply right now. Just being together as a family brings out so many memories. My dad would have loved this conversation with you. In fact, he is possibly the only person who could have found the middle ground. He would have rushed to Genia and asked about the spooky moments. He would have invited spook investigators and put up cameras and had a blast with an idea of ghosts among us. Mom would have been teasing him about his enthusiasm while coaxing him to greater adventures."

Fel stood up.

Before she could speak he continued, asserting his own personality into the mix, his voice losing its gentleness. “I don’t know what Genia saw or heard. I don’t know about ghosts and elves. I do know Genia and I know she is not fragile. She is not insane. She is not a lightweight. So let’s begin this conversation again with that context in mind. Instead of questioning her sanity let’s deal with what she has said and take it from there.” His words had gained in volume as they followed her out of the kitchen.

“Well shite,” he said to her back.

Chapter 9

He had stalled long enough. These last few days had been peaceful with solitary runs on the beach, explorations into the Irish countryside and naps in the garden. The peace had helped ease his tension. The disturbing dreams had ceased and his sleep was now relaxed. The notion of ghosts and residual energy had faded from his thoughts.

Today a misty dampness, that seemed particular to Irish weather, was seeping into the ground. A thick fog had descended. The idea of a walk in the fresh wet was appealing but it was time to open his dad's files and explore the family history. His dad had said the 170-year-old letters from his great, great, great, great grandmother, whose name they still didn't know, to her son, Daniel Irial O'Donovan, in Canada, held some surprises. They never got to discuss those surprises.

Daniel opened the file folder with the photocopies of the Gaelic letters and pinned the copies on the bulletin board he had placed above the desk. He opened the folder with the translations and saw his dad's comments on the inside cover of the file and his messy notes within the printed translations. Always in pencil. His dad liked a sharp pencil when he was translating. He had been delighted to learn that Michael Collins, the Irish rebel whose intelligence he admired, had insisted on using pencil as well. He said he felt connected to Irish history by this small similarity.

He rubbed his fingers over the pencil strokes thinking about his dad with his thick reading glasses pondering over every word as he translated; probably stopping often to sip from endless cups of tea.

His dad had written:

'Some initial thoughts before I translate. There are 4 letters. Considering the handwriting they're not all written by the same person. One short 1 I think is written by a priest; Doyle. I will leave that translation to the last. To start I will work on the 3 with the same handwriting: 2 long and 1 shorter letter. A cursory look shows these 3 letters are from mother to son. 2 envelopes have a wax seal. Broken of course. The seal pressed into the wax looks official. Maybe she got the church to put their stamp on it. It is smeared and hard to tell what it was originally. The envelopes are yellowed and the notepaper is yellowed and creased. Some of the writing has faded. Miriam plans to research what type of ink would have been used. 2 letters are addressed to St. Mary and Joseph Cathedral, Montreal with Daniel Irial O'Donovan written below the address. The Gaelic is from 170 years ago which may pose a challenge translating it. It seems to be excellent Gaelic. My 'humble' amateur observation. I have had little exposure to the Gaelic of earlier decades but I will do some drafts and then get some experts to look at them. The cursive is beautiful. A well-trained hand. Maybe the priest or an acolyte wrote them for her? Curious if she was Catholic or Protestant. I don't think our family ever specified.

I can only guess at the other side of the conversation that takes place in these letters. There must have been months between them. No dates. I'm curious about how long it took to travel across the ocean. Miriam plans to add that question to her list of research notes.'

First trans Draft (May 2015)

'After a cursory look I think this is the earliest letter. There isn't an address on the envelope just his name. I have put my comments and questions in brackets.'

My dearest son (*A ṁic mo ċroiḋe*)

How I miss you. I hope this letter finds you somewhere on your long journey. I am sending it with the Kennedys who are leaving on the same ship you sailed on last year. They will be following your journey and docking in Montreal as well. Will they see you? Tuama says they will hold my letter to you forever if need be. I gave them some coins hoping they could buy some food for their journey. They are so frail. I pray you were able to get a good sum for the brooch I gave you. It should have gained you a fair bit of coins. I pray you can help them. Your new country is so far away. I can't imagine the size of that land. How long was the journey for you? I just pray this letter reaches your hand.

Ireland is a deserted country. So many people have died for want of food or they have entered the work houses or jails. This is the second time the potato crops have failed. (fall, 1848?) The priest said thousands of our people have left on ships. The lanes are empty. The village is empty. Entire families have disappeared. People have eaten the grass, the worms in the ground and anything they can find on the beach. They eat the seaweed. Many landlords have expelled the destitute from their homes. The elderly Ma of the Grant family was lifted out of her sick bed and dumped into the ditch. The sheriff helped carry the poor old soul. Now the people sleep under any tree or shelter they can find. Some sleep on the beaches, covering themselves with sand. It will be getting cold soon. Already it rains too often.

Last week your aunt had a family arrested for trying to catch fish in the sea on the beach. You remember the Byrne family, the tenants your father evicted from the land? They were so frail. The littlest boy was clinging to his brother. May God forgive her cruelty for leaving them hungry and sending them to the gaol the night they came for food. May God give hope to his people. God must weep at the cruel indifference of the people. We have abundance and there are so many exhausted whimpers for food. I hear them in my sleep. I wake in the night crying with grief and frustration. What can be done? Last week, some of the local landowners, who have been supporting the workhouses with food and blankets, came to ask for help. I said yes, praising them for their faithfulness but your aunt refused to honour my promise. The second time they came I gave them the earrings your father gave me when we were married. Your Aunt Alice doesn't know yet. She roams the land looking for ways to expand her power and increase the land she owns. She berates and abuses the servants demanding extreme obedience for a piece of bread as their wage. Dear Tomas took some extra pieces for his children last week and she had him arrested.

I hang my head as I walk to the village. I hide my morning biscuits and bits of meat in my clothes and take it to the priest. The church makes some soup once a week but there is little nourishment in the soup. I dare not hand out food on the street because I would be surrounded by many beggars. The thin, quiet children break my heart. They no longer cry.

> (She isn't hungry. She had money? Food? Earrings? A mystery here)

It has become a very dark place without your smile and your bonny (happy?) presence. Thinking of you safe gives me peace. I think of you every moment of my days. It has been so long since you escaped and left Ireland. I have so many precious memories of your handsome (? *ᴅaċúıl*) face to give me comfort.

The roses are beautiful in their seasonal change: peacefully they fell asleep in the fall and then awoke again in the spring bringing beauty forth and a sweet perfume. The roses are almost out of control around the little chapel this year. They climb over the stones. I am glad you chose to plant yellow roses for me. Yellow is a happy colour. A colour of hope and possibility. My first look is to them when I step outside in the morning. I say a prayer for you, for our country. Your last gift has given me bliss. (or does the word mean delight? *aoibneas* I notice it's a word used in the name of a Woman's shelter in Dublin. So maybe it means refuge.)

(Note: Did she live in a village with a view to the village church?)

My letter carries tragic news. Your friend, Cian O'Brien died in Wicklow Gaol last month. He had become involved with a group of free thinkers (not sure of the meaning here but 'thinkers' seems to work). No one knows the exact circumstances (or is it facts?). They were overheard talking about a plan to go to Dublin Castle to demand help from the Queen. Cian was the only one arrested and he wouldn't give up the names of the others.

Devlin and George were caught stealing fruit from the orchard that belongs to the Duke of Welaff. Just a few fallen fruits. Devlin's oldest son had died working alongside him doing the Relief work. The government of England is paying people pennies to build roads. It is the English solution for famine, a famine they deny is still taking place. The hard labour and the long days are too much for many. Devlin and his son were so starved and beyond able to do the work. Very little food is provided to sustain them. George's wife, you remember Abbie, had died in childbirth and he needed some food for the babe that survived her. His Ma was looking after the babe. It was Fial and Peter who caught them taking the fruit off the ground. Fial and Peter had been hired by the estate to protect the crops from thieves. Their pay is simply a meal a day but they can share it with their family and stay in the sheds out of the rain. I was told Fial and Peter wept as they chased their friends. They would have let them get away, I'm sure, but the estate had sent tough (?) men and huge dogs from the Duke's English estate to enforce the law. The dogs chased them down. I don't know what will happen to the babe or George's Ma, with them both in the gaol. Father at the cathedral said he would look in on them. He has so many to bury. I wish I could bring them here.

(Note to self: I couldn't find any facts to back this up. I'll look into Wicklow history around those years. There might be some jail records.)

The priests tell me the gaol is filled with many desperate people. Many stole something so they could get into the gaol to get some food. Children of all ages are there. Worse than when you were there.

(What? When was GG Grandpa in jail? Maybe find out more in subsequent letters. Our great, great was a jailbird? Our family gets more interesting as we research.)

There is no room for them to sleep. They are standing in the walkways and the outside courtyard. The windows are not covered so the night cold seeps into them. Disease from the filth has caused many deaths.

The English have said the Irish deserve this because they are lazy and God is punishing them. How dare they justify their sin against God by blaming those who suffer. It is what your father and grandfather said as well. You heard those horrible justifications from your father before he died. The new order of government punishes the poor. They justify greed and their lack of humanity with these foul thoughts. It is worse now than when your father caught you giving food away.

My darling. I wish I had happy news to share but it is impossible to find joy in Ireland. I am praying for you with my whole heart.

Be well my love.

Mother

1848

My dearest son, (*a ṁic mo ċroiḋe*)

Your letter reached me. I am filled with joy. I haven't stopped weeping since it arrived. I have worn the edges already, reading every word. You were smart to send it through the Church Fathers. Father Doyle slipped it to me during Mass this morning. Your aunt must never know about your letters. I will hide them in the chapel under a stone near the altar.

I cherish your news. Your trip over sounds peaceful. You played the flute for them? The Irish dancing sounds delightful. Lots of food. Grosse Isle seems like a paradise. But alas, I know you are trying to spare me, my son. The reports from Montreal have been in the papers here. I know about the hundreds of people dying of cholera. I know the fever struck many down. I thought we had agreed to keep truth between us. But I love you for trying to ease my worry.

Father Doyle told me you have been working with the priests to help find order amid the chaos and suffering. I know you will bring sunshine into the midst of so much misery. Father also shared the news that Tuama and her smallest daughter didn't survive the journey. He has told their family.

I walked to the village today. There are two dead people on the side of the road, at the village intersection. I think they have been there for a day at least. A young mom and a baby. It looks like she just couldn't walk any further. Her mouth was green from eating the grass. I checked the babe but it was dead. It was so frail with dried tears on its emaciated little face. Not far from our estate. I didn't recognize the mom. The cart that picks up the dead will take them away for burial. A mass burial which won't record the names. Father Doyle is trying to keep the names and I help by making lists for him. Many of the people who lived on the plots of land around us are gone; dead or emigrated. My heart weeps. I miss those dear, dear faces. I'll never know whether little Sean grew to be a strong man. He wanted to be a farmer like his dad. Or did he die from hunger or disease. Will the sweet child Sylvia who was baptized by the father last year live? Will her parents die and leave her and her brothers orphans?

While we continue to send our wheat and fruit to England, babes die at our doorstep. Your aunt caught me feeding people at the back door last week. She locked me in the cellar again. Don't worry. I do not fear her. I was prepared for her cruelty. I had hidden a blanket and some notepaper to write to you while in the cell.

(Ah so she does write)

I saw your carvings on the wall and traced them with my fingers over and over. I added a few scratches. Your scratches in the stone gave me an idea. The next opportunity I had, I sneaked to the fairy stone to carve a warning to people who would come seeking refuge. Someone had been ahead of me and had carved a curse and a warning into the stone.

I have started planning a way to break her control. I have no money to bribe those loyal to her. I could offer the rest of my jewellery but she took it when she found I had given some away. But it has little value when people are starving. Food is the currency now. That is also locked away in the kitchen and in the cellars. The orchards have been emptied of their fruit and sent to England.

I have contacted my family in Cork. They are suffering but they still have the farm and they have not evicted anyone. My father planted large crops of beans and turnips as well as potatoes this past summer. He has been giving food to people but says the need is so great he won't be able to offer much more succour to others. He and my sister cook a huge pot of soup with some meat every three days. Barely enough to keep anyone alive. Why did they put so much trust in the potatoes again this past summer? People still try to eat the rotted potatoes

The news from the west side of the country is devastating. They say more estate owners are pushing people out of their homes. They say the people with even small plots of land are selling them for a few bags of food. The government insists people cannot enter a workhouse if they still have land. What use is the land if the crops are rotten? I have seen great compassion and I have seen violent greed. I beg God for answers.

I pray every day for you as I sit in my lovely chapel surrounded by the roses you planted for me. Their fragrance surrounds me like a peaceful blessing. With God's Grace I send this letter to you praying it will reach you. I pray God's angels will carry it to you.

My strong son.
My love.
My prayers always,
Your loving and proud Mother
1848

Third letter:

My dearest son, (*A ṁic mo ċroiḋe*)

I am answering your last letter immediately with this short missive. I am hiding in a confessional at the village church, writing to you, while Father Doyle waits to send this letter back with those who delivered it. I beg you, please do not return to Ireland. I need to know you are safe. It gives me peace and strength. If you return you will be jailed and executed for your father's murder. Do not worry about me.

(What? GG Grandpa murdered his father?)

Your aunt has given false witness against you. She told the local authorities she saw you beating your father by the fairy stone. She had the servant who helped beat you give the same testimony. She gave them the bloody cane he had used on your back that morning. She didn't say he had beaten you. She didn't mention that your father had ordered the servants to hold you while he beat you.

(Servants? GG Grandpa had servants?)

She just showed the blood and said it was your father's. She has given false witness. I think she knows who killed him. I am trying to find out. Your friend Liam had been helping me. I told the local council (authorities?) you were innocent but they believe her since her father is a Marquis and he owns the land.

(what???)

Don' worry about me, my son. I am well. I play the submissive sister-in-law, timid and obedient. She taunts and she insults but I do not respond. I listen well to her words and wait for her to betray herself. I can escape to the peacefulness of my little chapel and be in prayer. If only I could find a way to feed the people. My heart burns for them.

I have written to your grandfather, the Marquis

(Obviously our family had a few secrets. Can't wait to tell Genia)

in London and asked for his help. Will he challenge his daughter? Will he free the food for the poor and dying? I hope he will find a way for justice.
(Awkward sentence. Not sure of her meaning here. I think by justice she means to clear his name? Feed the people?)

I think he accepted you when you attended Oxford even though he hates your Irish side.

(Again. What?? our GG Grandpa an Oxford grad?)

Do not come to Ireland. I will let you know if it is safe for you to return. If you cannot return I will come to you. Or I will go to my father's in Cork.

My strong son.
My love.
My prayers always,
Your proud Mother

Daniel was feeling gob-smacked. Bemused. Stunned. Whose life is this? This can't be his ancestor. His parents had not told them much about the letters although remembering their last video call, there had been giggles and smirks, about a surprise they had to share. Daniel reread the letters making his own notes on a separate piece of paper.

Chapter 10

Several hours later Daniel entered the kitchen through the back door. He had been to Wicklow to photocopy the translations and buy dinner. He carried three boxes of pizza, two bags with beer, salad, dessert as well as cheese and crackers. A file folder was sliding about on top of the boxes of pizza. He set it all down and went to move the car to the garage. Returning to the kitchen he found an unknown person sitting at the table drinking coffee and writing in a notebook. She was petite, brunette and roughly the same age as his Aunt Fel.

"Oh hello," he said with some surprise. "I think you must be Dr. Brandy Bothwith in charge of restoring the chapel?"

"Yes, call me Brandy, please."

Brandy had a lovely Australian accent, "I'm Daniel O'Donovan, Genia's nephew. How is your work coming along? Genia is excited to see the finished product. Well almost finished product."

"Yes, me as well. The exterior is solid now. Sorry about the noise this week from the heavy machinery. We needed both machines to get the top stones back in place and the roof on top of it all. Your aunt probably told you we had it built at a local warehouse to exact measurements and specifications and this week we just popped it on."

When she stopped to make a face to show her relief, Daniel began to ask, "Was the ...", but she didn't let him finish.

"We had lots of good fortune. Fortunately, it fit. Fortunately, the rain held off or we would have created deep tracks in the mud. And fortunately, we were working with some first-class mates with good will and patience. The experience was painstakingly slow because of the need to be precise in every detail. I am just making my notes about the interior."

Daniel tried again, "Was the ....?".

"Genia and I walked through it this afternoon. There are most definitely signs of a past fire and we found some interesting carvings in the floor behind the altar and a rusty plaque on the entry wall. Some of the words are faded from the weather and scorched from the fire. I don't know how it caught fire. The stone itself would not have generated enough fuel to feed a fire and create that much damage. The chapel will have to be cleaned and the stone polished. The roses took a bit of a beating these past few days but Niall says they will revive. I think......"

Genia entered the kitchen at that moment and interrupted, "Daniel I was looking for you. Do you want to look through the chapel now that we have access?"

"Can't. I'm in charge of dinner so I am chained to the kitchen. Oops. I need to cool the beer."

Genia looked at the items on the counter, "Yummy, pizza. Again."

Daniel laughed at the sarcasm in her voice, "And a salad this time."

Genia responded with the same tone, "Who said the weaker sex couldn't evolve?"

"Oh *Ainteen*, that wounds."

Genia turned to Brandy saying, "I heard you telling Daniel about the chapel."

Brandy looked at her watch and stood. "Hmm, yes. I need to be off now. Can we meet in the morning and you can tell me your thoughts on finishing the interior? We need to consider windows and doors. Will you be using it as a worship place, a cottage for someone to stay or would you prefer to design it as empty space? Heating and furniture will need to be considered. Also, I made some progress with the local authority to get permission to do some initial cleaning of the gravestones. I was told we can't clear vegetation until some inspectors come to survey it."

Genia said, "Niall...."

"I'll know more tomorrow. And the roses need attention as well. The machinery may have trampled some of the patch. But Niall kept a sharp eye on the work."

Genia jumped in, "OK. Ten o'clock in the dining room? Niall will be around tomorrow. He has some ideas about the roses."

"That's a plan. See you Daniel."

After Brandy left, Genia said, "I think I will go to my room and shower off some of this mud and rain. What time will the pizza be reheated?"

"Hilarious Genia. You have thirty minutes. And I have a huge surprise for you!"

Genia paused, raised her eyebrows at him and left the kitchen.

~~~~~~~~~~~~~~~~

Thirty minutes later all activity was taking place in the dining room. Daniel had set the table simply; without tablecloth or place mats. The candles in the fancy candle holders weren't lit. Some take-out paper napkins were in a pile near the stack of plates and cutlery. The cheese and the crackers were still in their packages. Daniel was not creating a fine dining experience. Dimitri was tossing the pre-washed salad ingredients he had dumped out of the plastic packaging into a large bowl while Daniel opened the beer.

Fel was speaking, "Where's the wine, Daniel? I don't like beer. It has a foul taste. Did you buy the pizza at that local joint by the beach? Their pizza is often tasteless. I went there once and the staff were colder than their pizza. Where are the manners of the young people today?"
~~~~~~~~~~~~~~~~

Daniel was thinking, as Fel continued speaking, people seldom paid attention to her. Fel's accusatory tone of voice caused people to tune her out. A shame, he often thought. Fel was the beauty of the family. She had high cheekbones, generous red lips, a mane of rust-brown hair and a tiny nose. It all added up to a beautiful face. Yet, at this moment, with her face radiating disapproval, she looked ugly. Dull.

She was still talking, "Young people are consumed with their cell phones. They never look up from them. And they mumble. They are forever mumbling."

"Good evening all," Genia said cheerily when she entered the dining room.

Fel claimed her attention immediately, "Genia, the noise from the machinery has been giving me headaches. Are they finished yet? They have been slow as usual. I talked to them and told them to hurry up. You keep hiring the same crew and they take advantage of you."

Genia was smiling, "All done now and the work was completed to perfection. The interior is safe and you can walk inside if anyone wants to explore it. No windows or doors yet but still safe. It will be steamed clean tomorrow and I'll get some lanterns and candles in there."

She turned to Daniel, "Daniel, pizza! How wonderful. I'll have a cold beer please."

Daniel grinned at her false enthusiasm, "Only the best for my family. If everyone can be settled in their chairs I have something special to tell you. Dimitri, I think the salad is thoroughly tossed now."

Dimitri handed him the bowl and the spoons, "I put in an Italian dressing instead of the small dreary package provided. I added a few tomatoes and herbs. I took out some of the lettuce. Most of the bag was lettuce." He took his seat.

Daniel said, as he passed the salad to Genia, who began filling her plate. "We are eating in the dining room tonight because I'm going to put you to work and we need the larger table space. Don't drink too much. I need clear heads."

He left them to get the reheated pizza. When he returned he set the boxes on the sideboard and settled into his own chair. "It's self-serve this evening. I got a better variety of pizza than last time. There are no onions or peppers or pepperoni, Fel!"

After they had settled again Dimitri lifted his glass and said, "May She be pleased with our gratitude."

They all lifted their glasses in response.

Daniel took a sip of his beer. He said with a hint of repressed excitement, "I opened my parent's files today and started reading their research. Dad had translated three of the letters. A rough draft. I'm not going to tell you what's in the letters but they're fascinating. Surprising really. I have copied them. One copy for each of you. I'm hoping after you have eaten you'll read the letters and write down your impressions. There are some amazing revelations. Then we can share our impressions."

He looked for agreement.

Dimitri spoke first as he stood to get more pizza from the sideboard, "That sounds intriguing. If I remember these are letters your father found that belonged to your ancestor who received them from a relative in Ireland?"

Fel spoke up, "I found them in an old trunk in the attic of the farmhouse when I was packing up. Which I did by myself I might add."

Genia didn't let this complaint fester, "If I remember a few of the neighbours were hired to help you pack up the farm. A local cleaning company finished the job."

"Unreliable people. They were looking for some freebies. One neighbour wanted to know which bedroom you had slept in so she could take pictures." Her voice became sarcastic, "Genia O'Donovan's childhood home. Genia O'Donovan's childhood bedroom. Genia O'Donovan peed here." Fel rolled her eyes. "Give me a break."

Dimitri was making choking noises. Daniel reached over to thump him on the back but retracted his arm when Dimitri waved him away. Reaching for a drink of beer, he took a sip to clear his throat and spoke, "You're killing me Fel. I can see the headlines in bold script. 'Genia O'Donovan slept here. This is the window she looked out as a young girl dreaming of an escape to a golden world of stardom. These are the cows she milked or at least they might be related to her childhood cows. Our top news research team will have that important information for you shortly.' The article would have quotes by neighbours who had never met Genia giving detailed and intimate information of a close relationship."

Genia started giggling. Then they were all laughing at the crazy images.

Fel less so.

Genia spoke to her sister when the mirth decreased, "Fel, I am sorry. I wasn't thinking. It must have been a struggle to pack up childhood memories all alone, sell off family remnants and say good-bye to a place we all loved."

Fel looked at her coldly. She did not respond with grace. "If you loved it so much why didn't you visit more often? They missed you. Both you and John felt if you sent some money that would be enough. They didn't want your money. They wanted you. And when you did come, it was like a big sparkle in their lives: sparkle, glitz and light. Then you were gone and they missed you. All they had was me."

Genia said, "They all loved you deeply. They talked about you whenever I spoke to them. They adored you."

Quietly Daniel changed the subject, "Aunt Fel, I'm curious. When you found the letters, were there other objects nearby or in the trunk?"

Fel reluctantly looked away from Genia towards Daniel. She wasn't happy to break the connection with her sister's eyes. Her voice was churlish when she responded to her nephew, "It was just an old trunk. The letters were wrapped in a cloth. There were some old newspapers and some ticket stubs. I gave it all to John."

"Which set my parents off on a happy adventure. Has everyone finished eating? We can clear the table and begin to look at the translations."

Dimitri asked, "I presume there is dessert, Daniel?"

Daniel jumped up and headed to the kitchen saying over his shoulder, "How could I forget?" He returned with a box repeating, "How could I forget the dessert? I spent hours of my day making this and then I found this nice bakery box which makes it look professional. It's an Irish cream cake. An old family recipe." He winked at their disbelief. "You don't believe me? OK, I might be exaggerating the time I spent making it." He cut the cake in generous portions. "Now eat fast so we can get to work."

They ate slowly, giving each bite their full appreciation. Dimitri was grinning at him as he savoured the bites.

Chapter 11

In his impatience it seemed like that one piece of cake took them an hour to eat. Yet five minutes later he was able to pass out the photocopies and pencils. "Dimitri, these letters are from a mother in Ireland to her son in Canada, circa 1847. We know he was nineteen years old." He looked at all of them. "These letters challenge our assumptions about him. We grew up believing our ancestor left Ireland in 1847 on a ship to Montreal because of the Famine. I think he was from the Wicklow area. These letters from his mother give us more information. I need to test my assumptions through you. So please just write down your thoughts. A second piece of cake for you when you have completed your assignment." He smiled at them and wiggled his eyebrows. "I might add ice cream."

A minute later Genia gasped and looked at Daniel. Then she returned her gaze to her pages. A long silence followed. Daniel was trying not to drum his fingers impatiently. He had to move as he waited for their responses. He packed the leftover pizza into one box and took the empty boxes to the kitchen for recycling. He returned for the dirty dishes and took them to the kitchen. He filled the dishwasher. The salad was transferred into a smaller bowl and set in the fridge. The larger bowl to the dishwasher. He brought back a cloth to wipe the sideboard. He took the crumbs to the kitchen. The cheese and crackers came out of their packages and were transferred to a cheese board. He added some grapes and pears. He brought back fresh plates and cutlery into the dining room. He gathered the empty beer bottles and brought back some cold ones. He tried to look over Dimitri's shoulder but Dimitri blocked him saying, "Patience young man." Daniel went back to the kitchen. He wiped the counter tops. He took out the garbage. He had just grabbed the broom when he heard voices from the dining room. He dropped the broom.

Dimitri was asking, "What do you call the fourth-generation descendants of a third son of a marquis?"

Daniel didn't respond. He sat down and looked to his aunts for their initial reactions. Fel's head was still down and she was making notes. Genia was staring into space. Slowly she looked over at Daniel and said, "I will never understand how anyone can be indifferent to the suffering of others. How absolutely tragic. A baby starves to death on the side of the road? On the mother's corpse? In the mother's dead arms?"

Daniel nodded, "Our ancestor must have suffered terribly knowing she had the means to help and was prevented. Bullied by her sister-in-law. I think she had great courage. Great strength of character. I have had the same impression of her son. I wish I had known him."

Genia said, "I know little about him. He started the farm we grew up in when he was thirty-seven. We don't know what he did between Montreal and the farm. We know he had just been married when he claimed the farm land. Their only child was born the next year. That would be 1866. Maybe he did come back to Ireland and that's why there are only three letters. He died at age eighty-nine, a year after his wife. That would have been 1917. My grandmother told me he was a quiet man. He seldom shared his thoughts. He showed a simple love for others. He was encouraging. He respected their space and had insisted on building another house for them on the farm, when she married his son, my grandfather. I never heard a hint of the ancestral history revealed in these letters."

"I know he died peacefully on his farm. A farm he loved. But what about his mother? I have an urgent need to find out what happened to her," Daniel said. "I can research the name O'Donovan when I get back from Dublin in a few days."

Genia said, "I know so little about the Famine except that a million and a half people starved to death and another million left Ireland, some dying in the ships along the way. I have never looked beyond the numbers. Babies too weak to cry for food; whimpers she says. People who already lived daily in poverty pushed down that much further. A potato crop on a quarter acre plot of land is the difference between life and the slow starvation of a family. I know some landlords tried to help. But some had malignant hearts. She is right to call them foul. The same cold culture of *laissez faire* is in evidence today. Just look at some of our world politics."

Dimitri reminded them of his question, "I am curious about your lineage. You are not the descendants of a starving peasant farmer as I had imagined."

Daniel said, "Yes, indeed, we made some assumptions about him. Famine, famine ship, Montreal, all added up to poverty not escape. Never did I suspect he was a grandson of a marquis. We will need to find out which British marquises had an estate anywhere near where a Father Doyle lived. I am interested in finding more about them. Or him? Yet the name O'Donovan is Irish, isn't it? Maybe Irish aristocracy?"

Fel spoke up, "I'm stuck on his education. Oxford? He went to Oxford? That is more than a surprise. It is shocking. It raises so many questions. First you have to reconcile the man with the education. The farmer who broke ground with his wife on barren prairie land through sweat and sacrifice was an Oxford student. We never knew. No hints. Obviously, he knew about farming and weather conditions since he was so successful. And I have to ask why not an Irish college. Why not Trinity? Was it usual? What subjects would he have studied? He certainly understood Gaelic. Also, English."

"Maybe they were trying to anglicize him though an English college," Dimitri suggested. "Trinity is a Protestant college. I think that mattered. Being Irish she might have been Catholic and being English his father was possibly Protestant. So, he could have gone there."

Daniel looked at each of them pointedly and impatiently asking, "Where do you think they lived?"

Dimitri answered, "I can't tell. I see lots of research in our future."

Genia put down her pages and spoke haltingly, "I know what you are implying Daniel. There are similarities to this estate. Did anyone else notice them? The chapel with the flowing roses, the beach, the fairy stone which could be our large stone at the beach pathway. I guess the cellars as well. But then again, many old homes have roses, small chapels, large stones and cellars. Is that a leap too far? A coincidence too great? The proximity to Wicklow is a clue. It is an excellent thought and maybe why your father, having translated these letters, was insistent I purchase the property."

Daniel responded, "I made the leap and then stepped back from it. The stones over the fireplaces have the name Loth and a Coat of Arms. And the symbols on the Coat of Arms are English. So not O'Donovan. Although the name could be later, a land grab by those with wealth. I wonder when it was carved into the fireplace stone? As Dimitri says there is some interesting research ahead of us, especially regarding the history of this place. There are newspaper articles in one of the file folders which might give us more clues. Some are in English, some French. There is a letter in Gaelic which my father didn't translate. It has a different handwriting than the others. The script looks impossible. The English papers are from before Canada was Canada, twenty years before. I didn't read them all but it looks like some news about Irish arrivals, the illnesses. My French is rudimentary so I don't know what information the French paper contains. I can take the Gaelic letter with me to Dublin tomorrow and seek out a translator. I might as well take the rubbing from the stone by the beach and see what I can find. And a reminder I won't be back tomorrow night or maybe the night after." He looked at Genia with a grin, "The leftover pizza is for your enjoyment."

Dimitri was intent on the letters and ignored Genia's snorted response. He said, "I will take a look at the French news clippings. My French gets me through airports and ordering delicacies in Paris. Maybe I can piece together some idea of the contents. Can you get them now so I can look at them over the next two days?"

Daniel got up from his chair saying, "I'll get the photocopies dad made from the originals. Just a minute."

When he came back Genia was handing out the promised second piece of cake to Dimitri and Fel. "Where's the ice cream you promised Daniel?"

"Isn't there some in the freezer?"

"No," Genia answered.

"Oops." Daniel grinned. "It never occurred to me that a well-stocked pantry like yours wouldn't have ice cream. I'm shocked Genia."

He went to the kitchen and came back with a bottle. "Let me make up for my sin by offering everyone a taste of Irish cream." He held up the liqueur temptingly. As he started filling the glasses he had brought from the kitchen he said, "I think better than the ice cream, eh?".

Fel protested his language, "Don't say 'eh'. It supports the vulgar stereotype that states every Canadian says 'Eh'."

"Like the Greek stereotypes that suggest all men from my home land are loud, hairy, momma's boys who pass their time in gossip and smoking too much?" queried Dimitri.

"Or," Genia added after taking a smooth sip of the cream, "that all Irish are lazy drunks. I believe that was the story fostered by the English even before the Famine, to justify their domination.

Otherwise known as oppression and exploitation of their land as well as the attempt to eradicate their culture, their language and their religion. By telling the rest of the world that the Irish needed to be dominated because of their laziness and their drunkenness they justified taking what they wanted. The stereotype still sticks today. When you say Irish, the perception people have of Ireland is a land of drinkers. Not true. Like any other country, Irish people gather over a beer. My impression of Ireland is a land of poets and saints: James Joyce, Beckett, Seamus Heaney, Wilde, Yeats, St. Patrick, St. Bridget, St. Kevin." She stopped to take another sip of her drink.

When Fel tried to interrupt she said, "No, let me finish. People should think vibrant art, poetry, music and spirituality when they think of Ireland. I often find the Irish people more educated about their history than people in most countries. I find them lyrical. Often some of my deepest conversations have taken place over a pint with an Irish person." She looked at everyone, aware she had stopped the momentum of the conversation. "Well, it pisses me off."

"Oh great," said Fel, "my sister is drunkenly defending a nation of drunks and slurring her words as she airs her opinions."

"Unfair dearest Felicity," said Dimitri pouring more liquid into Genia's glass. "Genia isn't singing yet so you can't diagnose her as drunk. When she sings she is half way there. When she begins to dance we know she is drunk." He winked at her. "She isn't even tapping her toes yet. Why I remember a time in Venice......". He wiggled his eyebrows at her.

Genia laughed at him. "A questionable defence of my character, my friend." She took another sip and looked at Fel. "My beautiful sister, you have yet to see drunk. Here, have some more lovely Irish cream. I miss your giggles and you only giggle when you have been drinking."

Fel stood up and with a glare at her sister said, "Piss off Genia."

Genia giggled.

Daniel poured another drink for himself saying, "I might regret this in the morning. The sugar alone from this stuff will give you a headache."

Fel turned her back on them and left them.

Chapter 12

After Fel left them, they moved to the sitting room.

Genia picked up a throw off one of the sofas to wrap around her shoulders. "The air is cold again," she said.

Dimitri responded, "I don't think it's Madame. She must be on vacation. The energy in the manor has been peaceful. I assume ghosts get breaks once in a while from scaremongering. I wonder if they have to take some courses on how to improve their technique?" He set down his empty glass and started laughing. His laugh encouraged Genia and she started laughing. Daniel watched two old friends sharing a merry moment. Probably a release Genia needed.

When the laughter lost its energy, Daniel offered some more drink. Dimitri refused. Genia didn't.

"Maybe Fel has been right all along and it has been my imagination," Genia said.

"Did you imagine your fear?" Dimitri asked.

"No, but maybe I imagined the reasons for it."

"Let me say, Genia, I felt an oppressive sense of darkness the first day I walked into this place. I wasn't forewarned. You had never mentioned any concerns to me before I arrived and yet it was my first impression. I felt fear. Daniel how did you feel?"

"Nothing like you and Genia describe but I have never claimed to have any spiritual sensitivity. When I saw the shadows outside I felt curiosity rather than fear. I never think about the possibility and therefore I don't look for it. A ghost would have to pop up in front of me and say, 'Boo' to get my attention."

"I don't think I look for it either but spiritual sensitivity is a part of who I am and in a few cases I have seen beyond the thin veil," said Dimitri.

"When have you seen a ghost?" asked Daniel.

"A few times in old theatres. It seems many actors never want to leave the stage even after death. A few times I have seen orbs float over the heads of an audience, usually in some of the old theatres."

"What is an orb?" Daniel again.

"It's a small semi-transparent pearlescent ball that is often seen in photographs. Some people think it is a drop of moisture in the air and some think it is a ball of spiritual energy; souls of people. Often, they are named as angels. Who knows, but it is a rare sight to actually see one. I once visited the parliament buildings in London and took lots of photos. The photographs showed hundreds of the little balls of light, particularly in one area of Westminster Hall. Either it was a damp space and I caught the moisture in my camera or it was the souls of many who linger there. That building is the oldest and has a long history. Some of it quite horrible."

Dimitri paused, remembering. "But a ghost, that is different."

Genia said, "Tell Daniel about your experience in Scotland. It is really delightful."

Dimitri resettled in his chair, "Genia's talking about a particular experience I had in an old theatre in Scotland. It was many years ago. I was standing behind the curtains, stage right, waiting for my cue to go on stage. As I watched my fellow actors this transparent man, dressed in Elizabethan costume, totally out of sync with the 21st century play, entered stage left. No one reacted to him. The other actors in the play were following their lines leading up to my cue to enter the scene. He, the ghost, was enacting a scene of his own and even drew a sword to make his point. I don't know whether he noticed the actors even. My cue came while he was still on the stage. I didn't know whether to go on or cry ghost." Dimitri laughed at his strange predicament.

Daniel prodded, "And you did what?"

"I figured I would look like a fantastic idiot, stopping a play and yelling ghost so I kept silent, entered the scene and tried to stay away from the sword. I had a suitcase as a prop so I used it as a shield between us. I don't know what I thought I would do if he suddenly turned his attention my way. Hit it with my suitcase? Fortunately for me, the spectral argument ended suddenly with a downward plunge of the sword. Then my transparent friend just faded away."

"No one else saw it?" asked Daniel.

"No. Maybe they did but, like me, felt it best to stay quiet. I have thought of it often. Was it residual memory forever imprinted into one emotional scene? Or maybe it wasn't a play but the re-enactment of an actual murder; the murderer's fate is to re-enact the violent deed over and over again, never finding peace; never knowing closure or forgiveness."

Genia spoke, "A horrible thought that our deeds would haunt us for eternity."

Dimitri turned to address Daniel, "You know, I didn't feel fear. Like you, I felt curiosity. And some anxiety trying to stay in my character, say the right lines and keep the figure in my sight. There was something pathetic about the apparition. Now if it had been just he and I in an empty theatre one night that might be a different story. I would have been fearful."

Daniel turned to Genia. "Have you ever experienced a ghost?"

"No, but I have an awareness of presence." She stopped, pondering. "OK, that doesn't make sense to be aware of something you can't see. Perhaps I should say I am tuned into energy; negative and positive. Much like the difference in the energy of the chapel and the manor. The chapel is peaceful, beautiful energy. Like most places where people pray those prayers seem to soak into the walls, saturating the space with goodness and grace. The manor is different, oppressive. As though horrible events have taken place and that sadness and ugliness have permeated these walls. A thick energy. All the time I was painting and scrubbing, trying to claim ownership of my new home I often felt it difficult to breathe. My limbs were heavy like I was walking through water. Some days I felt like I needed to just shout happy thoughts into a room before I entered it; like an exorcism of hate and negativity. If Fel had caught me she would have had doubts about my sanity. It was and is mostly in the downstairs rooms that I feel dread. I don't know if that is fanciful thinking but I do feel fear …."

Just then Fel walked into the room, obviously with something important on her mind and rudely interrupted Genia. "Wait a minute. Our ancestor was accused of murdering his father? That was never mentioned in the family history. A father from a prominent family! An aristocratic family. There must be records somewhere. Genia, I'm taking your car into Wicklow tomorrow to do some research at the library. I'll see if the Gaol is open for visitors. Oh, and I'll check out the historical society. There must be some dinky little hole that keeps old records for research. Possibly the library."

Dimitri said, "If you need some help, I'm available."

She left without responding or acknowledging him.

Chapter 13

Daniel woke up slowly, aware of being nudged, prodded. His bed was shaking. He mumbled a response to the nudging. "Yes? Hmmmm, who is, what?" He moved his head back and forth against the pillow seeking awareness. His eyelids came unstuck: unwillingly. Ugh he felt thick. He looked for who or what was disturbing his sleep. The nudging had stopped. The room was freezing, damp. And empty. He sought reason. He rolled over searching the door to see if it was open. Did someone's cat get in the house and walk on his bed? Did an earthquake happen and shake the house, moving his bed? Did I just have another whacko dream and cause the bed to move myself? His head was foggy from the late night. Good grief they had talked past midnight. He must have been having a restless sleep. But, just then, he realized he was staring at an open bedroom door. His door was moving silently back and forth as though someone was controlling it. OK, maybe not a dream. Earthquake? Seismic shifting? Weather anomalies?

His watch pointed to three o'clock. In passing he thought of some dialogue from a horror film that named three o'clock as the hour when the horrors come out to play. Dreadful organ music began to play in his head. He shook it. Have a sense of humour about this and channel the absurd wit of Abbot and Costello. Change the emotion. Purpose overcomes fear. Purpose overcomes fear. Purpose overcomes fear. Put on a light. Wake up. Stand up. The air was cold. Close the windows. Walk to the door. See if anyone else is up and about. He stalled by putting on socks and a sweater. By then his bedroom door had stopped moving. By closing the window, had he stopped a breeze? That thought gave him courage and the organ music in his head was silenced.

The house was quiet. And, of course, dark as usual. He walked along the hallway, guided by the bedroom light behind him and his left hand on the banister. He headed towards the central staircase. He peered down into the foyer where the night light was usually lit for midnight trips to the kitchen. It was out but he could see light at the bottom of the staircase coming from the right, from the library.

There was a draft of air swirling up the stairs. And the sound of creaking. The front doors were open and a breeze was blowing billows of fog into the foyer. He started down the stairs to close the doors. Odd. He stopped. A light from the library was distorting the fog. The fog gathering in the foyer seemed to have substance, a figure with design. The substance seemed to have purpose. It was his height with arms and graceful movement. No legs. It resembled a flowing diaphanous, blue-white dress. A full dress. No face. No face yet. Good grief he was anthropomorphizing vapour. Still he began to envision a course of action in case a face appeared. Scream? Run?

He had stopped walking down the stairs. He stood, one foot hanging above the next step down, uncommitted. He was maybe six steps above the ghost. Fog not a ghost! Yeah, all the spook talk less than three hours ago was crowding out his reason right now. Maybe the drink played a part as well; confusing his reason. There were no sounds in the house. No sounds from the fog. Move forward his brain said. His foot twitched downward. No, his emotions shouted back, 'Don't do it'. Courage said, 'Remember, purpose overcomes fear'. Yes, he needed the steadiness of purpose. Close the doors. Find out who is in the library or at least why the lights are on in there. Forget that it is three o'clock in the morning. The haunting hour. The tenacious doleful notes of an organ played again in his head to mock his fear. Big brave guy that he was, he stepped forward, towards the fog.

A face appeared. Dimitri's face. Dimitri had come to stand in the library doorway. He was muttering to himself.

"No wonder it's so damn cold. The doors are open." Then he screamed and stepped back into the library. He peered slowly back into the foyer. "Sweet Mother of God! Fuck! Daniel? Is that you? What the hell are you doing?"

So that's how you react to fear Daniel thought as he answered Dimitri. "Yes, it is me. I was coming to close the doors. Did you leave them open for air? Or were they not latched tightly? Maybe the wind popped them open."

Dimitri headed to the doors to close them. The fog dispersed as he walked through it. "Possibly. Probably. I thought I closed them tightly when I came back. It may have been Madame. The doors often 'pop' open in the night. I had fallen asleep over my research. Come into the library. The fire has died down but there are some embers we can encourage."

Daniel was guessing Dimitri had not seen any form in the fog.

"What are you researching?" Daniel asked as he released the fear in his knees and headed into the library.

"I was looking at the letters and the newspaper articles, seeking some clues about the ancestry of the house. The dusty, and in some cases musty, books should have some interesting pointings. Your father's translation of the letters fascinated me and I couldn't meekly go to bed knowing the answers might be right here. So I came back."

Dimitri had returned to the stack of books on the desk in the corner of the room. "I haven't found much. I had hoped for a deed or a list of owners. Or a document that says, 'Here are the answers you have been looking for'."

"Yeah, good luck with that." Daniel picked up a heavy ledger. "This looks interesting. There could be some info here."

"No, I've flipped through it. It's mostly from the years 1910 to 1920. It's a list of cows and sheep and pigs and chickens and the sale price of each beast. The prices are interesting. Otherwise not helpful because it doesn't give any names of the people who owned the beasts. I think there must have been much more land at one time to support the large farming project indicated by those inventories. Possibly gained during the Famine. There were huge land grabs by the wealthy."

Daniel looked through a few pages and then set it down. "I see what you mean." He looked around the library. It was a dark room. Allowing for windows, doors and a fireplace, all the remaining wall space had floor to ceiling glassed bookshelves. All built in oak. "How many of these books are related to the estate? How many historical books?"

"I don't know. Most of the books are old as you can tell by the dark spines and covers. Fel complains about a lack of modern titles. I found these books here, above this desk." Dimitri waved his hand towards the books. "I read the French newspaper clippings. The Montreal clippings name people who died on the ships and in the hospitals. So many. There was some government intervention to ease the problems but there were some jobs available. Only a few. Some in an Irish project in New Brunswick; an attempt by a local Wicklow landowner to help people emigrate and have a job when they arrived. Probably most of them died on the coffin ships. The clippings mention tension with the people already living in the areas who needed work but watched the jobs being given to the new Irish. There is an undertone of bias against the Irish.

The newspaper clippings from France have references to the loss of life in France and the rest of Europe due to the failure of the potato. Nothing like Ireland. Or Scotland which was heavily hit as well. Two of the clippings report the revolutions in Europe in 1848. There were some violent mobs protesting the mechanized factories and the loss of jobs. The industrial age was causing an upheaval of who had wealth and who did not. There were major land grabs there as well. I think more lives were lost in the revolutions in Europe than from the failure of the potato. Each country handled the crisis differently and the demands were unique to the country's social and economic situation.

Ireland had a brief revolt in a village called Ballingarry in 1848; a minor skirmish that lasted a day. It might relate to what is mentioned in the mother's letter about a friend that died in jail. An O'Brien was involved. That will be some interesting research. I'll mention it to Fel. She seems to like researching."

Dimitri moved some papers around and placed the photocopied English clippings on top. "These are not from early Canada. Well one is but the rest are clippings from papers in England. Mostly political opinions on the British government. One clipping is an article about the Communist Manifesto by Marx. Which is possibly why your ancestor kept it. With an Oxford education he probably knew the situation was more profound than some failed potato crops. And it was an age of new thinking for him, especially in his new country; a freedom from old confines of thinking. Democracy was an evolving concept as well as liberalism and republicanism. Maybe he saw hope."

Dimitri finally noticed Daniel's body language was yelling tiredness. "My apologies Daniel. This is fascinating stuff but at another time. I will be here for another hour or so and then I'll lock up before I head to the cottage. The trials of a night person: seldom able to sleep before 3 o'clock."

"It's past three o'clock now Dimitri."

"Oh? Well I will just take these documents to the cottage and read them there. Set the fireplace screen in place, please."

Dimitri gathered his papers and headed for the front door. "I have not been able to go out the kitchen door at night since your spectral encounter. I'm afraid of walking through a ghost." He laughed, opened one of the front doors and disappeared into the clear night.

Daniel closed the doors. Tight. Locked.

Chapter 14

Daniel returned from Dublin three days later. So much had changed in Dublin since his first visit alone post high school. His parents had encouraged him to take a gap year to travel wherever his spirit called him before putting his head down to tackle several years of film school. 'Start in Ireland,' his father had suggested; describing it as an inspiring place for his proposed profession.

His mom had said go find adventure; 'Find your joy'.

His dad had added that he should find jobs along the way to pay for the experience.

He remembered his mom putting her hand over his dad's mouth and speaking loudly, 'Find your bliss'.

Daniel smiled sadly as he remembered the glee in his dad's eyes as he slipped away from the reach of his wife's hand, saying, 'But, my dear, it's called a rite of passage. Bliss can only be found when you dig down through the layers of your own psyche to see the beauty the universe has planted there. Often uncertainty and strife are the tools used to dig.' He then laughed and added, 'Hunger works as well.'

Daniel had spent the summer before his trip on his paternal grandparents' prairie farm earning money to fund his gap year. His maternal grandparents, who had emigrated from Ireland to Vancouver to be close to their only daughter, had been delighted he was starting his gap year in their native land. They had given him maps indicating where all the relatives lived. Basically, a map of anyone with a faint connection to his mother's side of the Irish family. They slipped him some money as well. His parents gave him a plane ticket and lots of advice.

He remembered that first day; the anticipatory delight he had felt as the plane circled Dublin. No parents, no schedules and nothing to prevent him from following his bliss. Money in his pocket. Freedom!! He headed to a pub and in the first few weeks spent far too much time experiencing the Irish pub culture. When he woke one morning in an alleyway with a feral cat licking puke from his face he ruefully accepted he had mistaken his bliss. That conversation with his parents about a rite of passage guided his next choices. He learned to cope on his own and as he learned to cope on his own, he learned the skills and talents embedded within his soul. He found courage through compassion. He found strength through hard learned experiences and mistakes. He found some of his youthful beliefs challenged by world truths outside his safe childhood bubble. He met and accepted his shadow side. He eventually began to see the world and the cosmos as essentially friendly and good. He accepted the invitation of that friendly and good cosmos to just 'Be'. Not to be someone else but to live out his own creative self. The most important seed he found planted within the depth of his soul was a universal truth: courage in love.

So now he had seen Dublin again. Eighteen years later. The Celtic Tiger, the prosperous foreign investment upturn that had brought such wealth to Ireland had slowed. The Tiger had changed the country and the culture. Before the explosion of money, the country had been fairly isolated from the influences of other cultures. Now some of what made Ireland unique had been submerged under the influx of the new influences. The same food and clothing franchises that can be found in any major city in the world had taken over the main streets. A caricature of the deep and rich Irish culture was promoted for the tourists. The youth now lined up to experience the glitzy nightclub culture. Unfortunately, playing to this superficial dynamic had become an important aspect of the tourism economy. In the city more so than in the country. The country village pubs kept the real Irish cultural rhythm alive.

And yet, he mused, how amazing it was to sit at a pub and hear the accents of people from all corners of the world, sharing a bit of the *craic*. He had been charmed when he registered at his hotel for his stay and was greeted by a young Asian face speaking with a strong Dublin accent. There were disadvantages and advantages to any change.

It was about seven in the evening when he turned into Genia's driveway. He had left the city before the work day ended and the streets began to fill with people heading home to their dinner. He was hoping there would still be some dinner left at Genia's. If he remembered the dinner schedule on the fridge, Dimitri was cooking.

The kitchen and dining room were empty. He found them in the garden gazebo overlooking the sea, with a picnic of cold cuts and salads. He was already picking up a plate as he greeted them. "Hello all. What a brilliant idea to eat out here."

Dimitri responded as he reached for Daniel's plate to begin spooning food onto it, "I was craving sunlight. I've spent too much time inside looking at the books and papers in the library."

"How's that going?" Daniel asked as he bent over Genia to kiss her cheek. He looked to Fel and nodded. He had learnt some time before that his Aunt Fel did not like affectionate gestures. She nodded back at him. She was frowning.

"Where is the translation of the letter?" she asked.

He sat down as he was answering her, "I had to leave it with Patrick's secretary. He won't be back from his trip for another week. His secretary glanced at it and told me it looked like it was from a priest called Father Doyle. He couldn't elaborate because he said he had only just begun his Gaelic studies. So sorry dear friends. My trip was not very successful although I was able to catch up with some old friends. How about everyone else?"

Genia spoke, "Dimitri and I searched the attic rooms looking for anything stored there. We found a few portraits in one room. I'll get a curator to come out from Dublin to look at them before I move them downstairs. At first sight they look typical for the period. No smiles, no personality really. They look dour. Except one that looked friendly. Lots of dust on them. We brought down some books and Dimitri has been working through them. We were just beginning to discuss his research." She passed Daniel the rolls. "Dimitri can you repeat what you were just starting to say and finish the thought?"

"OK. As I was saying," he stopped. "Daniel did you want a beer? Or a cola? Oh, and some gorgeous homemade lemonade is available."

As he passed Daniel the lemonade Fel said impatiently, "Dimitri, it takes you forever to tell anything. Daniel, I'll begin. At least I made some progress." Dimitri just smiled with forbearance and nodded.

Fel continued, "I went to the Wicklow Gaol. The records are all online but it's being updated for the next week. I spoke with a staff person. She was less than helpful and her accent was so thick I had to get her to repeat everything but she was able to give me some websites to browse. She also invited me to join the ghost tour. Really!! The Wicklow Gaol was crowded with tourists. A lot of well-fed whiners. A bunch of loser tourists. They were looking at the misery of a people over two centuries of history and taking pictures like they were at a Hollywood theme park. Everyone had a cell phone with one of those long sticks they hold in front of them. I was hit three times by people oblivious to anyone but themselves. And I heard someone complaining it was a dull scene because there weren't enough torture chambers or descriptions of the tortures.

Foul people. No dignity or respect." Her voice was rising, reflecting anger, "No wonder the world is going to hell."

Dimitri, Genia and Daniel stared at her, unused to a spirited speech from her.

Dimitri broke the silence with a single sharp clap of his hands. In a fast-clipped director's voice he said, "Scene! The curtain comes down. The audience stands applauding wildly. As a bonus, a few whistles are heard from the back of the theatre. Well-spoken Mistress Felicity."

"Fuck off Dimitri. So, I show a little passion about how fucked our world has become. There is no need to mock me."

"On the contrary I was appreciating your compassion and spirit."

"I don't feel compassion for a screwed-up world. People have a voice, they have power and they have opportunity. If your personal world is screwed then it is your own fault. You are lazy and expecting people like me to pay your bills and fix your problems. We live in a world of victims."

"Now you have lost my appreciation. You might be channelling the heartlessness of Madame."

She stared back at him with a look which suggested doubt about his intelligence, "Dim you are an ass. You have given your imaginary friend a personality. It's probably your shadow side haunting you."

Daniel interrupted, "Dimitri, I have been meaning to ask why you think there is a ghost in the house and why you think it's feminine."

"A great question. I've wondered about it myself. I have never seen it but I have felt some kind of ugly looking over my shoulder when I'm in the kitchen. That's why I sing to keep the ugly out of my head. I have no idea why I think of it as feminine. It's a thought that entered my head one day when I felt the negative energy near me. But not just negative energy but something thicker, more substantial. I was cooking dinner and I felt like someone looking over my shoulder. About to touch me." He shuddered. "It was cold and the kitchen smelled like garbage."

Fel interrupted, "Anyway, back to reality. I focused first on Father Doyle. I found out there was a Father Doyle during the Famine; a Catholic priest, who lived in Wicklow. He was buried in the churchyard of the Catholic Church in Wicklow. I walked among the rest of the gravestones looking for the name O'Donovan but I didn't find it. I am assuming she was Catholic since she consulted with a Catholic priest. Is that one piece of information we can take as valid? So probably Irish as well since the English were mostly Protestant. He was in Wicklow so she lived near Wicklow. Too far to have lived here if she was walking to see him. I don't think this was her home." She looked at them all for confirmation.

Daniel held up his plate for a refill as he mused over Fel's assumptions. "Thanks, Aunt Fel. Your first point: we know she was a great friend of a Catholic priest. She trusted him. Her family was from Cork, therefore Irish. She wrote her letters in Gaelic so I vote she was Irish born. If Irish probably Catholic or a hidden Catholic."

He stopped to nibble on a carrot and muse further on her words. "I don't know if we can assume the second point about where she lived. As you said, she wrote of walking to a village. Was Wicklow the village? That is a long walk from here. Maybe there was a local village church near here where the Father visited. We have two mysteries to explore: Where was our ancestral home? The second mystery is the history of this house. They might converge. Or not."

Fel was nodding, "OK, good clarifying points. I will focus on the first mystery and prove this isn't our ancestral home. I will look for the ancestral home within a limited radius around Wicklow. Obviously, there was some money involved so I will look for a larger estate. Dimitri and Genia can search out information about this house and prove it is the ancestral home. I will do you a favour and add a local village to my search. But if I can't find one is that enough to disqualify this house as our ancestral home?"

Daniel said, "No, I don't think so. We go back to the clues in the letters and reassess."

Fel nodded. "Ok, so moving on. I did find the name O'Brien on several headstones in Wicklow. Though not the Cian O'Brien from her letter. Dimitri found something about an Irish revolution during the Famine in the newspaper clippings. I looked for a connection to Cian O'Brien. I haven't found it yet. There was a William Smith O'Brien who was part of a brief rebellion in 1848, the same year our O'Brien was sent to the Gaol. William O'Brien was part of the Young Irelander Rebellion that took place in Ballingarry. He was shipped to Australia rather than killed. I read an article saying all the perpetrators were to be hung, drawn and quartered but it hurt Queen Victoria's sensibilities so they were shipped to Australia. I think they were referring to it as mercy. Where was her mercy for the starving thousands?"

Genia responded, "The two O'Briens could have been related. When will the Gaol records be available again?"

Fel said, "Next week. Our O'Brien could be Protestant. I will look for more graveyards. Protestant graveyards. Did you get anywhere with the graveyard here?"

"Yes, Brandy, Niall and I walked through the grass yesterday. There is a fair bit of backbreaking work to be done to clear it. We mapped the perimeters and set up some ropes to designate those perimeters. I counted at least ten graves. Two are very small so I assume children. Some stones are covered in moss and most of the letters are faded. The weight of the larger tombstones has caused them to sink into the ground. It will be a few more days before we can examine them more closely. There are also some legalities to observe which Brandy is researching."

Dimitri said, "So this is where my news is relevant. I found in the library," he paused for effect, "a book about Wicklow with a chapter about the murder of the third son of the Marquis of Loth by his own son in 1847. The book says the father and son had argued about the son's wasteful ways. The son was spoiled and disappointing. He squandered his father's money on gambling and sport. It also refers to a rumour of an improper dalliance. His father denied him further funds and intended to send him to London to be with his grandfather, the marquis. Witnesses say the son hit his father viciously with a club. A few times. He was confined by servants and held until the local authorities arrived. He was taken to the local gaol and escaped a few days later. The family were offering a reward. He was never seen again."

He let them absorb the ramifications of that bit of research. "I am assuming it took place here in this estate. The name Loth is carved into the two fireplaces. It could explain the negative energy."

Genia asked, with amazement in her voice, "A murder in my home? I'm having trouble absorbing this information." She was looking back at the house, "Where I wonder?"

Dimitri answered, "It was outside by the stone."

They all turned to look in the direction of the stone.

Genia said, "So there is blood in the dirt around the stone."

Fel spoke up, "Blood that has been rained on for two centuries. Before the actress gets too fanciful let's explore the connections to our story."

Daniel said slowly, "It is a similar story to our ancestor's. A son is accused of murdering his father. A beating. 1847. The name is Loth so you're right Dimitri it probably isn't much of a jump to place it here in this house since that name is carved into the fireplaces. It does establish the circa date of the names engraved in the fireplaces. Different story from ours because the son is depicted as vicious and wasteful. Not my impression of my ancestor. The name is wrong as well."

Genia spoke up, "She wrote in the letter that the aunt had gathered false witnesses. That story could have been the result. To discredit the nephew. Did the book give the age of the son?"

"No, just an impression of youth," Dimitri said.

"How does someone escape from a gaol? There would have to have been bribes. Someone with money? Who? Relative?" asked Fel.

"Probably a relative. In the midst of the Famine no one had money except the landowners, and many were distant landowners, often aristocrats from overseas," said Dimitri.

Genia said, "I am still gobsmacked." She laughed, "I have been wanting to use that word. It expresses so very well what I am feeling. I am still gobsmacked about the similarities and I am trying not to jump to conclusions. Fel, you are searching the name O'Donovan?"

Dimitri interposed with his thought, "I have been pondering the name O'Donovan. It is an Irish name. How is it that an Irish marquis with land in Ireland is living in London?"

"Maybe he held office. Parnell did and he lived fairly close to here," said Genia. "Yet, it was later. He had just been born during the Famine."

Daniel spoke, "So Fel will search the county for a graveyard with O'Donovan and O'Brien. If there is as much wealth as we think then Grannie O'Donovan might be buried on a private estate. If we find the estate we find the graves. Also, Fel, look for the same names in the gaol. Church records and County records as well as a local village? OK?" Fel nodded.

He continued, "Dimitri you will continue going through the old records, books in the house? OK?" Dimitri smiled and nodded.

"Genia," he said, "the portraits upstairs might have the clues you need to prove this is our ancestral home. Have you contacted an art curator?"

"Yes, she will be here next week."

"You will also continue with the graveyard here? Look for the name O'Donovan. Any clues in the chapel?"

Genia nodded slowly, "No but I will definitely look again since it was getting dark when I looked yesterday. I had looked at the carvings in the floor near the altar which she mentioned in her letter, but I didn't find any or any loose stones. I can tell you I really wanted to have that wow moment and read the carvings, discover the loose stones and his letters to her. That would have been beyond amazing to find his letters to her."

Daniel said, "I will look for the name Loth in London and search Oxford historical sites for records of our ancestor. I also want to look at the cellars. She mentioned marks in the cellar walls. I will look to see if there are some here. How does that sound as a plan? Will we have explored every clue in her letters?"

Fel said, "I can't look at Cork records for her. We don't have a maiden name. Dimitri, let me know when you find it."

Daniel said, "Sounds good. I am heading for a shower and a read. Genia when are our friends arriving?"

"Tomorrow. Some of our sleuthing will be interrupted."

"Not mine," said Fel. "They're not my friends." She picked up some dishes off the table and left them. They all followed.

Chapter 15

The banging on the front doors began at five minutes past four. Daniel's body jerked awake. His mind followed slowly. He looked around confused. The light beside his bed was still lit. He had been reading a book about Wicklow history when he had fallen asleep. It fell off his chest as he sat up seeking the reason for the noise. Silence. Then he heard a steady and forceful bang, bang, bang on the front doors. Dressed in a t-shirt and sweat pants he left his bed and headed into the hallway. He stood at the top of the stairs listening. Silence again. Genia's bedroom door opened and she came into the hallway. She had the muddled look of someone still exiting a deep sleep. The banging started again. She followed him down the stairs. With this round of banging came shouting. And was that someone singing?

"It's Cordelia. Cordelia Cambridge," Genia said. "It's hard to mistake that voice. Of course, they're early."

Daniel hurried down the stairs and reached for the switch to add some light to the dim foyer night-light. Cordelia had now broken into a show tune about rainbows. Genia looked at Daniel and shrugged her shoulders.

They heard someone say, "I hope we have the right house. This will be incredibly awful if we've screwed up."

There was giggling.

Someone else said, "But it looks like the pictures Genia emailed."

Another voice said, "Yes but there are a lot of big houses in Ireland with large windows. And it is dark and ...." At that moment Daniel opened the front doors to greet their house guests.

Exclamations of joy and relief filled the foyer as five close theatre friends of Genia's flowed into her home.

Cordelia's husband Gerald spoke above the sounds of friends greeting each other, "So sorry we have arrived hours early. Our flight from New York was early. Dave, Petra and Diane had already arrived from their corners of the globe so we thought why not get started. We thought the drive was longer. We would have called but we aren't that considerate."

"Don't listen to him. We were considerate. We 'considered' calling but by the time this crew decided to call we were turning in the driveway." Diane Tracy, long-time friend of Genia had taken over the narrative, "I guess we would have awakened you either way."

Dave reached over and kissed Genia on both cheeks, "*Bonjour mon coeur*." He gave her a squeeze. "Our producer/director was in charge." They both looked at Gerald. "We were being obedient to his directions." Laughing he moved over to greet Daniel.

Petra replaced Dave and grabbed Genia, also squeezing her. "I have missed you so much and I have so much to tell you." She whispered, "I have a new man in my life." Petra had adopted Genia as an older mentor/confidante when they met a few years ago. Like Daniel, Petra was a generation younger than the rest of the group.

This gathering was a reunion of a few colleagues who had become close during a London play around the time of Daniel's parents' deaths. Petra Shore had been one of the playwrights, Gerald Hebbo had produced, Dave Devenney, a distinguished actor, had starred with Genia as lost loves and Cordelia Cambridge and Diane Tracy, well known character actors, had co-starred as their supportive friends. They had stayed as strong friends but it had taken two years to arrange schedules for this reunion.

Genia gave Petra a return squeeze. "Obviously we are due a long chat. Tomorrow." Then she laughed looking around at everyone and back at Petra. "Today." Genia held her arms up, getting the attention of her dear friends, "I am going to hustle you into the kitchen. Follow Daniel and we can sit down for a few moments as you get your bearings."

Daniel led them down the hallway, turning on lights. He made the coffee pot his first destination. "I'll make some coffee if someone could grab two chairs from the dining room. It's just through that door." He pointed to the door at the other end of the kitchen. As Diane and Gerald moved where his finger pointed, he said, "Light switch on your left as you enter the room."

Genia pulled out some muffins and jam and pointed Petra and Dave towards the drawers and cupboards for napkins, knives, spoons and plates.

Cordelia sat at the table and talked while they completed their tasks. She filled the space with thoughts of the long flight from New York and what they left behind. Eventually the others joined her at the table and began to share some of their flight experiences and their recent news. The kitchen was filled with the bright sounds of people, dramatic people, comfortable with each other.

Petra Shore, a petite, curvy brunette, was working on a new play and welcomed the space of the visit to revise her manuscript. She told them she wanted their feedback. Who knew theatre better than this crowd?

Gerald and Cordelia were celebrating their new status as grandparents. They lived in New York near their daughter and her child. Cordelia promised to show off a thousand photos of their grandson once she was unpacked. She had just completed a play on Broadway and looked forward to this diversion as she let go of the character she had portrayed for a year.

Gerald was in consultations to produce a new film and he intended to explore the Irish countryside and the studios in Bray as possible film sites. They wouldn't see much of him this visit, Daniel assumed.

Daniel especially liked Dave. Dave Devenney was a charming, kind man. Uncomplicated. Handsome. He and Genia had been lovers for many years but their work had caused too many separations. They had stayed loving friends. At the moment Dave was between films. He lived in Paris, his birthplace, when he wasn't working. The sophisticated, elegant ambience of Paris characterized him.

Diane was preparing for a new film and had brought her script. She wouldn't be able to stay for the full visit because the production date had been moved ahead by a week. Daniel hoped she would tell them the plot and share her personal strategy as she developed the character. He was fascinated by an actor's process to develop a new character, especially someone with Diane's talent. An actor took a page of words, basically black marks on paper and crafted a personality through poise, accent, facial expression and a deep imagination. Spencer Tracy had been quoted often as saying all you needed to be an actor was to know your lines and not bump into the furniture. Daniel knew that an innate ability to sink into another reality and carry it through several weeks while the story developed on film was essential. It wasn't as easy as Tracy had made it look.

"Genia, your Irish mansion seems very grand," Dave said.

"Hmmm, my intent has been to make the space cosy and bright. While you are all here I hope you'll feel at home. My style as hostess is not to fuss. Feel free to sit in the library with your feet up, fall asleep in the garden, play the piano, or borrow one of the cars. Ireland is beyond beautiful. Breakfast and lunch are your own responsibility. The pantry is full. We take turns planning the evening meal. Our list is on the fridge."

She looked at her theatrical family with intent, "Which means your name is on the list." Then she laughed, "But Dimitri, Dimitri Constantinides is here, staying in his cottage out back. He can usually be charmed, bribed, coerced into taking your turn at the stove. My sister Fel is also here. I guess your arrival didn't wake her. I'll let you explore the rest of the house, the gardens, and the Irish Sea at your leisure. In fact, there is probably a gorgeous sunrise happening over the sea right now." She looked at everyone and asked, "Is it time to get you settled into your rooms?"

Everyone nodded. Genia stood up.

"OK. Everyone is upstairs. The upstairs layout is a simple square shape. Dave your room is between mine and Fel's. That means you head to the top of the stairs and turn left. Middle door. Petra your room is at the top of the stairs. First door in front of you. You have a view of the sea. Daniel's bedroom and study are the next two doors along the hall heading south. Cordelia and Gerald, you will turn right at the top of the stairs past Daniel's rooms to the end of the hall. Your door is straight ahead. I have given you a second bedroom to use as a sitting room. Gerald, I know you have some work to do while you are here. Use the extra space. Diane, you will walk past their doors to the last door. Your room looks over the driveway and the front gardens. All the rooms are en-suite." She looked at the clock. "The maid Fiona will be here in less than two hours. Dishes in the sink." She looked at everyone, "OK?"

Nods again.

"Good," she said. "I'm going to see if I can sleep another two hours."

They dispersed.

Chapter 16

Several nights later, Genia entered the library and set the coffee tray on the sideboard by the wide fireplace. They had lit the fire because it was cool and cloudy this evening; early summer temperatures. She stood looking at her dear friends. These last days had been marvellous. There had been long comfortable walks along the beach, some local touring, day trips to Dublin and of course garden naps in the sun. Each day had ended with meals spiced with laughter and stage stories. Sometimes music and games followed. Gerald had treated them last night to a meal at a Wicklow pub. Even before the first beer had been poured the singing had begun. The locals had ignored their celebrity and invited them, with enthusiasm, into their community. Petra and Dave had attempted some Gaelic dancing but their feet couldn't find the rhythm. Dimitri had tried to introduce some Greek steps but it was late in the evening and all feet were stumbling and faltering.

Gerald interrupted her thoughts when he walked over to her and set down two bottles of whiskey and two bottles of wine. He had been to Bray investigating the studios and had obviously done some shopping. He said, "This is my contribution to your cellars."

Diane joined them and picked up a wine bottle to examine the label, "An Irish wine. I tried this wine recently. It's very fine. During my trip to Wicklow today with Dave and Daniel, I ambled around the neighbourhood and found a shop with a good stock of Irish food and art. I spent a few Euros there. I wanted to go to the Wicklow Gaol but ran out of time. I understand it's haunted." Her words were drowned out by Cordelia, their self-appointed entertainment director, who had jumped up from the sofa, clapping her hands for attention.

"Gerald honey, Diane, sit down over here but don't get too comfortable. It's game time." She said it like a profound announcement and Daniel felt an inkling of fear. Their kind of games were great for actors but as a director he didn't fit in.

As they moved over to the snug grouping of sofas and chairs in front of the fireplace Cordelia bowed towards Dimitri saying, "Thank you my friend for the excellent finger-licking repast. I'm sure no one wanted to taste my cooking."

There were exaggerated groans and nods in response.

Daniel responded in an exaggerated pastoral voice, "You have other gifts Cordelia."

"Ha. Ha. You are all so funny. We are playing Charades," she paused before adding, "the theatrical version."

Fel stood up. "I'm going to my room." She walked out without responding to the encouragement for her to stay.

Cordelia shrugged. They were used to Fel's dismissal of them. "You know the rules. Tonight, the category is 'hands'. Present a moment from film or theatre focusing on the hands. We will guess the moment. Each person tries to win as many points as possible. No teams. You are on your own. We, as your audience, will try to guess as soon as possible. Ready?"

Dimitri asked, "Wait please. Say more. I have never played the theatrical version of Charades."

Dave agreed, "Yes, more instructions please. I think the rules in France are a slight bit different."

Cordelia responded, "OK here are my rules. Which means New York rules. As the presenter, you have thirty seconds to 'present' your action. After thirty seconds the guessers can ask for it to be repeated once or ask for a clue. Guessing the actor within thirty seconds is five points, the play or film, the medium in other words, gives three points and the date is two points. If the guessers, don't get it despite the presenter's very best acting, the presenter gets all ten points. This game relies heavily on your pride as an actor. See the dilemma? Ha! How will you define winning? By confounding everyone and getting the ten points or by someone guessing because you are such a great actor? Love it!"

She looked at her friends settled into the chairs and sofas in front of her.

"Confused? Yes? How about I start as a trial run and we can work out the kinks as we go? Got it? Oh, and remember the presenter is silent."

She moved the coffee table back to get more room and then moved the clock on the fireplace mantle to the side table so she could watch the time.

"Starting now. Thirty seconds."

She stood sideways to them. She looked over at them with a thoughtful look and started walking. Her stance had a slight bend from the waist. She was pacing. But it was a tense, thoughtful pacing. Legs rigid. Her hands were clasped behind her back and her little finger on her left hand was wiggling.

She stopped, "Oh and by the way you can shout out guesses." She turned and paced back again. Same hand motions.

Dave jumped in, "Charlton Heston as Moses, walking in front of the people urging them to follow him by wiggling his little finger."

Everyone laughed.

"No," Cordelia said.

Diane spoke up, "Oddly enough it looks familiar."

"15, 14, 13, tick, tock my friends," said Cordelia.

"Monsieur Hulot's Holiday with Jacques Tati, 1953. He is walking along the beach before it all goes sideways for him," yelled out Dimitri.

"No," said Cordelia, "9, 8, 7."

"Wait a minute," Diane jumped up waving her hands. "I got it. It's a play. Dublin." Her voice was high and fast. "Um, um, um,

Gaiety Theatre or the Abbey. Peter O'Toole, sometime in the 1960's." She yelled, "George B Shaw's, Man and Superman!" She fell back into her seat. Her voice was still high. "Am I right?"

"Yes, exactly right," Cordelia laughed.

Diane said with amazement, "Oh thank you Cordelia for the memory. I was a very young star struck usher, handing out the programs. It was a short run. I remember that famous walk very well. O'Toole could convey a single emotion with the wiggle of his fingers."

Dave said, "That is amazing Diane that you had that opportunity to meet him. I'm assuming you met him. What was he like?"

Diane responded with a loving smile on her face, "O'Toole was an artist. Outrageous. And a generous colleague in terms of sharing the stage."

Genia said, "Not fair. That was obscure."

Daniel spoke up, "Well done Cordelia. Diane gets all the points?"

"Yes, she does." She turned to Diane, "I remembered you talking about that moment in that play. I had been in the audience, with my parents, for one of those very limited performances. I knew you would get this. You don't forget your early exposure to the theatre."

Looking back at the rest of the group she asked, "OK, who's next?"

Petra volunteered, "I'm not an actress but I have one idea." She replaced Cordelia in front of the fireplace.

"Cordelia, are you keeping time?" she asked.

"Yes. Love to." She moved the clock back to the mantle, over Petra's right shoulder.

"Ok I'll begin now." Petra took a few steps back from them. "OK. I am starting now." She ran forward, taking short tiptoe steps and stopped. She placed her feet about a half a meter apart, knees together and then bending over slightly she placed one hand on the top of her thighs. And the other hand cupped her left cheek. Then she wiggled her shoulders and faced them with a huge smile and a breathless sigh!

Daniel and Dave yelled out at the same time, "Marilyn Monroe!"

Everyone laughed. Diane had just taken a sip from her glass of water and she began to laugh, causing her to sputter and spit.

"Wait a minute," Gerald said, "as exciting as your performance was Petra, I am calling foul. That wasn't a film or a play. When Marilyn stood over that air vent it was a publicity stunt."

Petra was laughing. "I thought it was play-ful." She looked to Cordelia, "Close enough?"

"No," said Cordelia. "I side with my husband. A nice commercial break but not within the rules. Who's next? Dave?"

He stood slowly. "Yes, I have something in mind. I need a chair and I'm going to use this table. I need a jacket. Oh, and Gerald your glasses please." He sat down, facing them. He picked up a cloth napkin off the table and created a loose cravat around his neck. His head was cocked sideways. He stuck his chest out, increasing his girth. His chin rested on his chest. With a look of disdain on his face he stared at them silently. Then he stopped. "Oops. I am wrong. No glasses. Here, take them back, Gerald." Dave returned to his pose of disdain. "Starting now," he said. He raised his hands onto his extended chest, interlocked them and started twirling his thumbs. After a few seconds, he rudely yawned.

They all stared at him silently for the full thirty seconds. Then Petra called for a clue. "Can you give us one sentence of dialogue?"

Dave stayed in character still moving his thumbs. In a deep voice, with a bit of a snarl, he said, "I'm not interested in your book."

Diane asked for a repeat.

Thirty more silent seconds passed.

"A year please," Petra again.

"1946."

Daniel spoke up, "I'm thinking it's a film because none of us was around to remember a play. OK gang, we need a group strategy. Name the famous actors of 1946. Cooper, Gable, Power."

Diane objected, "Why are you assuming it's a man. He could be a woman with a big chest. Betty Grable."

Dave was shaking his head no.

Cordelia could be heard repeating '1946' over and over again. She said, "Best picture for the Oscars that year was The Best Years of Our Lives. What other films?"

"Why limit us to Hollywood films?" asked Genia.

"More dialogue please?" asked Petra.

Dave snarled, "All because a few starry-eyed dreamers stir them up and fill them with ideals."

"It's a Wonderful Life," Petra almost screamed it out.

Dave was nodding his head.

Gerald said abruptly, "Lionel Barrymore talking to Jimmy Stewart in that famous confrontation in the boardroom after Stewart's character's father dies and a decision is being made to close the old Bailey Building and Loan offices. Barrymore uses simple body language to covey his contempt for the young George Bailey. I especially remember the simple gesture of showing that contempt by twirling his thumbs. Oh, and the yawn. Brilliant acting."

Dave stood up and bowed to him, "Thank you Gerald. I release all my points to you and Petra. A solid guess. It's one of my favourite scenes of all times. Lionel Barrymore was a master."

Daniel said, "Yes, a brilliant master of his craft. Of course, he had an excellent director. It's all in the direction." Diane threw a pillow at his head which he ducked. "A case in point. Didn't Frank Capra win something for directing that film?" Another pillow was aimed at his head.

Cordelia said, "OK friends, before we deteriorate into a war between actors and directors, playwrights and producers let's keep the party moving. Next? Who's next? Genia? Do you have an act for us?"

Everyone looked to Genia who wasn't responding. She was looking away from them, staring out the window towards the chapel with a look of surprise or shock.

"Genia?" Daniel prompted.

She still didn't respond.

"Genia?" he called louder.

She half turned her head, reluctant to move her eyes away from what had caught her attention in the window, "Can you see her?"

"See who?"

Genia looked at him, "Look. Look out the window."

Daniel stood up and came over to her. "See who, what? Where are you looking?"

Dimitri and Diane followed Daniel to where Genia sat near the window.

"The face in the window. Oh, it's gone now. Did anyone see it?" she asked, looking anxiously at their faces.

All were shaking their heads in the negative.

"Just me?" Genia asked bewildered.

Petra had walked to the window. "Oh, look at the chapel. Do you see that glow? The light? Where is it coming from? What a great lighting effect Genia."

Everyone moved to the windows on either side of the fireplace. The chapel had a bright shimmery fog covering it.

"What is that?" Genia asked. "I have never seen that before and my bedroom overlooks the chapel."

Daniel replied, "I would say it's moonlight reflecting off the crystalline of the stone but it's too cloudy tonight. That's curious. I think I'll take a look outside."

As he headed for the door the others looked at each other startled and then followed.

Cordelia grabbed Genia's hand and said, "A bit of a spooky adventure thrown in to make our holiday even more delightful?"

Genia didn't speak but squeezed Cordelia's hand in response.

Cordelia said, looking at her friends, "I remember a film I was in a few years ago with a ghost as the main character. It was......" She stopped because Daniel had reached the front doors and was having trouble getting them open.

"They seem to be stuck," he said as he pulled on them.

Dave moved to help him. "Sometimes if you just give old double doors like these a solid push and then a quick pull back, it loosens up the obstacle."

Together they tried. Nothing happened. Daniel gave the doorknobs a shake.

"Check the lock," Gerald laughed.

"The lock is off," Daniel replied.

Gerald said, "I'll go through the kitchen door and come around and see if I can help from the outside."

"No!" Genia said forcefully.

Everyone turned to look at her.

Dimitri spoke calmly, looking at Genia. "You're right Genia: we need to be careful. I'll join you Gerald because the path can be tricky at night. There's a flash light in the kitchen. The back-door light is temperamental and often goes out. Let's go."

Daniel looked at Genia and then followed them down the hallway to the kitchen.

Dave, Petra, Diane and Cordelia focused on Genia.

"What's the story here?" Cordelia asked. "Genia, you actually look scared. Are you afraid? Or, are you acting my friend? Taking our game to a new level? You minx!"

Dave reached over and put his arm around Genia asking, "What's wrong?"

Just then the doors blew open knocking Petra, who had been standing with her back to the doors, to the floor.

"Hey guys," she said as Diane helped her stand up, "a little gentleness here please."

But the guys weren't there when they looked out the doorway. The doors slammed closed and then opened just as forcefully a second time. They all moved back towards the stairs behind them. Again the doors crashed open and shut.

"Gawd, what's happening?" Cordelia said with a tremble in her voice. "Genia? This isn't funny anymore. I have moved from amusement to fear."

Daniel, Gerald and Dimitri came down the hallway from the kitchen with Gerald asking, "What's the noise?"

Dimitri asked, "What is that smell? Its foul."

The doors opened and slammed.

"What the hell!?" Dimitri shouted.

Daniel rushed to control the doors. He reached them just as they were opening again with force. He was hit in the shoulder and he fell back. Dave, Gerald and Dimitri moved quickly to help him close the doors by putting their weight against them. Gerald pushed the locks in place.

Nothing happened. No movement.

They were silent looking at each other. Stunned.

Cordelia's voice was subdued as she reached for her husband's hand, "Genia what just happened?"

Genia said, "Are the doors secure now? Locks in place?"

Daniel nodded yes. "Not that the locks make much difference."

Gerald said, "I need some of that whiskey I bought today before I hear what that statement means." He and Cordelia headed back to the library.

Everyone followed him except Genia and Daniel who remained in the foyer. He put his hand on her shoulder asking, "*Ainteen*, how are you? What did you see in the window?"

She was still looking in the direction of the doors.

"*Ainteen*, we should talk about your fears, your experiences. Our experiences. Your friends are the objective voices we need.

She nodded at him silently, still stunned.

As they moved towards the library they heard a loud voice above them.

"What kind of party are you having? Can you keep the noise down?" Fel was leaning over the banister, looking down at them.

Chapter 17

No one was sitting when they entered the library.

No one was speaking.

Gerald was rubbing his wife's shoulders. Dimitri and Dave were looking out the windows on either side of the fireplace. The halo around the chapel had disappeared.

Diane had her arm around Petra's shoulders as they stood in front of the fireplace needing the warmth to decrease the shock. They all looked towards Genia and Daniel as they entered the library.

Genia turned to Daniel and asked, "Could you put some more turf on the fire please? It feels cold in here."

As he headed to complete the task she indicated everyone should sit down. As they settled she offered coffee and tea, wine and whiskey. Daniel knew she was stalling. How do you begin such a difficult conversation?

Dimitri rescued her. In a voice, reminiscent of the Twilight Zone he said, "Into a world of certainty slips an unknown quality, a mystery if you wish." His Greek accent made it sound bizarre, which was his intent.

People laughed tentatively.

Genia began to speak haltingly. Then stopped and stared at them blankly. Her friends were looking at her in surprise. The strong, vibrant woman they knew looked tiny and vulnerable in her chair.

Daniel made an attempt, "OK, so that was strange."

More tentative laughter.

Fel stalked into the library and immediately interrupted the beginning of the discussion, "What the hell was all the banging about? Do you have no consideration for others? Did someone get locked outside? Are you drunk Dim? Trying to insert some excitement into a dull party?"

Dimitri responded gaily, "Dear Felicity, come in and sit down. There's a seat right beside me." She grimaced at him but he continued smiling at her. "That racket you heard was caused by the front doors opening and then slamming on their own. It was pretty violent. And poor Petra was hit by the doors." He turned to Petra. "Are you all right?"

Fel interrupted with sarcasm, "Not this nonsense about ghosts again." She looked at everyone. "Are you all caught in the spooky ghost trap now?"

Cordelia spoke out, "The front doors just banged open and then closed several times without anyone touching them. We all saw it."

Fel said, "And the wind didn't play a part?"

Cordelia responded with uncertainty in her voice, "There wasn't a wind and Daniel and Dave tried to open them just seconds before and couldn't move them. Some of the guys went to the kitchen door to come around and open them from outside." She turned to them asking, "What happened? You came back shortly. Did you go outside?"

Gerald, seated beside her, answered simply, without drama, "We couldn't get the kitchen door opened. It was stuck as well."

Cordelia cried out, "What's happening here? Genia tell us. What is your sister talking about? What ghost trap?" She rubbed her arms against the shock she was still feeling in her body.

Genia sat up straighter in her chair, gaining some control over her own shock. She spoke brightly, "OK my friends. I am so sorry you have experienced this......," she paused wondering about the word to use, "this, this, this 'drama' tonight. I guess that word works. Especially for us. I will give you some background. It seems strange to talk with you about something that is elusive, vague. Although tonight was fairly definitive." She stopped and looked at everyone individually. Daniel put his hand on her shoulder.

She then continued, "I am afraid you are all going to think I am crazy." She looked at her hands splayed on her thighs. They were open as if seeking clemency from her listeners. "I moved into the house about eleven months ago. I had just finished that new play and I was so very tired. My brother," she paused and looked at Fel and Daniel, "our brother and his wife, Daniel's mom and dad, as you know, had been killed about a year before. The purchase of this house, this manor had been a family project, anticipated with joy." She spoke the next words on a sigh, "So when I first entered the house my mood was depressed. I was tired but hopeful. The preliminary work, the necessary updated work on infrastructure, was complete and the house needed paint and elbow grease. The gardens were dreadfully overgrown. It all seemed so overwhelming."

Her voice had become quieter, "I made myself busy. I started first with my bedroom and Fel's bedroom. She had joined me after a few days. I had trouble getting help from the locals. Fiona finally agreed but insisted on leaving early every day. She has extended her hours to at least five, for this week. She said she always feels like she is being watched while she is in some of the downstairs rooms, especially the kitchen. She feels cold breezes on her neck. Sometimes she feels fear for no reason. She wanted me to bring in the local priest for an exorcism. She still mentions it every so often."

She looked at them all and smiled. "Seriously. I told her it's an old house and of course it sometimes feels spooky. But I was starting to feel the same way. I dismissed it as a result of all the components I just mentioned. But sometimes at night I would hear someone crying outside. Wind, right?"

She looked at them and shrugged her shoulders. "The piano would play at night. Musical mice running along the keys?" She laughed at their expressive faces. "Silly I know but really you need a sense of humour in these situations and, trust me, you will look for any explanation other than ghost. There were those 'corner of the eye' moments, when you think you see movement but nothing is there when you look directly. Sometimes it felt like someone was touching my hair. Strange things would happen especially around the front doors. It is impossible to keep them open. I have tried to put a chair or a door stop, a large rock one day at both doors, to let the breeze flow through but it isn't long before the doors slam shut. Cupboard doors close just after you open them in the kitchen. That's creepy but again an old house problem. Right? I feel a sense of gloom or darkness hanging over my new home. Dimitri felt it almost immediately after he arrived. But it is all so elusive and can be explained away easily by wind and imagination and tiredness."

She looked at all their loving faces and the varied emotions revealed in those faces. "Fel didn't have any sense of it and has been feeling quite impatient with Dimitri and me." Genia laughed. "Then Daniel arrived." She looked over at him.

Daniel spoke up, "Genia and I haven't had a chance to really talk about most of this in any detail. I have been experiencing terrible dreams that leave me gasping with grief and in some cases anger. I never remember the dreams. And recently, about two in the morning, as I was coming up from the beach, I saw a mirage, an image by the back door. It looked like a group of people. It disappeared when I approached it."

Cordelia began to speak but he held up his hand saying, "Please, just a moment." He shrugged his shoulders, "I don't know if it was ghosts or the light or a 'middle of the night' imagination." He looked at Genia. "We have discussed my experience thoroughly and feel we could all be affected by circumstances and be lacking in objectivity."

Cordelia tried again, "We did not imagine what we saw tonight!"

Fel jumped in with some frustration in her voice, "OK what did happen tonight? What was all the noise?"

Dave, Cordelia and Petra all spoke up telling their experience. In his excitement Dave was speaking his native tongue.

"Wait a minute," Dimitri said. "How about we each briefly describe to Fel what happened. Fel is our voice of reason. She challenges what we say and tests our assumptions before they get out of control. I'll start. Genia saw a face in the window and when we looked it was gone but we saw a strange light around the chapel. We went to the front doors to go look at it and we couldn't open them. Daniel, Gerald and I went to the back door so we could come around and open the doors from outside. But we couldn't get the kitchen door to open. That's when we heard banging and came back. I saw the doors opening and closing by themselves; quite forcefully."

Each of them had much the same description.

Diane was last and spoke quietly, "I heard a woman laughing."

Chapter 18

"What?" was the collective gasp to what she said.

"Yes, a smirky low throat laugh from behind me. I looked around to see who was there but the hallway to the kitchen was empty. You guys had just walked through there to the kitchen door. There was no one in the sitting room but the lights are not on in there so I couldn't see clearly."

"Stop now," Fel said rudely. "Before you begin conjecturing I want to clarify some statements. Did anyone else hear the laugh? No? Diane, are you sure it was a laugh? Not an echo of the guys in the kitchen distorted by the distance and the hallway?"

Diane shook her head in confusion saying, "I suppose that is possible. Did any of you guys laugh?"

Before they could answer Fel said, "Doesn't mean anything whether they laughed or not. The sound could have been something that resembled a laugh in light of your heightened emotions."

Diane protested faintly, "But it was a definite laugh. I heard a woman laughing."

"A woman?" asked Dimitri. "That's interesting. Madame was here?"

Fel turned on him, "Don't start the Madame nonsense. Stay on topic. Diane since no one else heard the sound we will have to set it aside. Did anyone but Genia see the face in the window? No? Genia you're not saying much about that. Explain more."

Genia looked at her sister for a long moment and then answered quietly, "Dave had just finished his Lionel Barrymore act, which was great, by the way, Dave. As I was looking at him there was a movement, in that window." She pointed to the window to the right of the fireplace. "I looked over and saw a face looking at me."

"How did you know it was a face?" Fel asked.

"It had two eyes and a mouth and hair blowing in the wind."

Fel dismissed it with a condescending smile, "So someone was trespassing."

Genia showed her steel. She looked straight in her sister's face and responded to the dismissal with a clipped voice, "It was white. Foggy, gossamer blue-white. Filmy, but clearly a face."

Fel responded with as much steel, "But Genia we haven't really been able to trust your witness lately. You've already admitted your mental state is not reliable."

"Oh, shut up Fel," Dimitri said as the others protested.

Genia smiled, "No, we need Fel's objectivity." Still looking at her sister she continued, "What we don't need is her personal baggage. Continue your objective interrogation Fel. Maybe we can make some sense of this."

Fel's tight smile showed she recognized that she needed to pull in the spite. And her arrogance. She walked over to the window Genia had named, saying as she walked, "So you are the only one who saw the face in this window. The old glass distorts images and it is night. Clouds. Describe the face."

"It was a lovely face. It was clearly defined. The expression looked sad and desperate. I couldn't tell the colour of the eyes. It was definitely looking at me and then around the room. If it wasn't white I would have thought trespasser as well. That's how clear it was."

"Gosh that's a creepy thought. A ghostly figure was watching us through the window." Diane had spoken.

Fel was standing now in front of the fireplace looking down at them. "Let's take this piece by piece. Does anyone have any opinions to add to the discussion? I need some ideas that are not ghostly."

Silence.

Petra said, "I cannot believe in ghosts. Hell, I don't believe in God, a supreme being, angels, fairies, gnomes, etc. etc. I'm with you Fel. There has to be another explanation."

Fel nodded at her, "OK, that's good. Let's set Genia's foggy face aside since she's the only one who saw it and talk about the group's experience. The chapel. Everyone saw the light? Give me some adjectives, adverbs to describe what you saw."

"Luminous."

"Shiny."

"Shimmery, like a special effect in a film when the director is trying to convey beauty. Like a halo," said Cordelia.

"A fog with sparkles."

"I would say luminous as well."

"Peaceful."

Fel responded, "Obviously there was nothing fearful about the fog since no one hesitated to rush outside."

Everyone was silent considering.

Daniel spoke, "That is a great point Fel. I certainly didn't feel any fear."

The others affirmed his words. Cordelia added, "I wasn't scared. It was kind of exciting because I thought Genia had created a spooky adventure for us." She looked over at Genia. "I don't know if I am convinced that isn't the case."

Genia smiled at her, "No unfortunately, my friend, that isn't the case."

Fel took over, "So you're not scared by the light over the chapel or the fact that Genia had seen a face in the window. You all go to the doors and they're stuck. Then they start banging open and close on their own. Again, any theories besides the supernatural?"

Silence again.

Fel said, "Don't spare Genia's feelings or mine. There could be other explanations. You are all famous and some people must know you're gathered here; especially after your recent pub date. It could be an elaborate stunt to get pictures of you. Paparazzi will go to any lengths to get pictures. And you all know special effects people. Why can't that be an explanation?"

Gerald spoke, "I would want to hire that person for my next film. It was very realistic."

Daniel laughed, "Yes, I agree. It was very well done. Fel, it's a good theory. We can look for any evidence of a set up tomorrow."

Dave said, half joking, half serious, "Does this mean there may be pictures of me in the media rags, standing in the doorway with my mouth wide open in shock?"

His comment grounded them. There was some laughter.

Dimitri spoke up, "Wait a minute. Fel's theory doesn't explain the prior weeks. Someone explain the cold chill on your neck when you stand in the kitchen. Explain the maid's impressions."

"That would be easy to explain. Fiona is young and wants attention. As far as your experiences, remember," said Fel, "I haven't experienced any of these events so maybe you are too sensitive to the cold or you're over dramatizing something that has no meaning. Or someone is targeting Genia and since you are often near her, Dimitri, you have experienced the events as well."

Diane looked at her friend, "But who would do that to you?"

Genia was looking at Fel thoughtfully as she said, "No one I know but our profession attracts nuts. OK that was harsh. Instead I will say our profession attracts overzealous people interested in our personal lives. Fel, any more questions? No? OK, I think that is a theory we should pursue. But how? Contact the police? No. I don't think any of us want that fuss around us. Get security? Maybe. The outside security cameras won't be hooked up for a few weeks yet. I am told the cameras are on order so it can't be done sooner."

She looked at Daniel and Gerald, "You'll look for signs of special effects around the chapel?" They nodded. "Get back to me then? We'll make decisions about what to do if you find evidence."

She then looked at Fel and Dimitri. "I am going to change the subject or maybe deepen it a bit. I think we should share the mysteries we have been pursuing these past days."

Fel said, "OK, that sounds logical."

Dimitri and Daniel nodded.

Cordelia sat forward in her chair, "You mean there is more?"

Genia said, "No more ghosts but maybe some interesting context to share with you. When Fel packed up the family farm to be leased, she found, in the attic, a trunk with letters in Gaelic and some newspaper clippings. The letters were from my great, great, great grandmother, written in 1848, to her son in Montreal. Daniel Irial O'Donovan, was born in Wicklow in 1828. We knew he had left Ireland during the Famine as a young man. We knew little else. We assumed he left Ireland due to poverty and hunger. The letters, roughly translated by my brother before he died, revealed a whole new story. He was accused of murdering his father, who was the third son of a marquis. He was put in the Wicklow gaol but escaped. The family had money. All that is interesting but there are some indications that connect him to this manor. Yet also indications that point elsewhere. It has intrigued us. So we have all been on this kind of treasure hunt to find out more information. Dimitri and I are trying to prove this is the ancestral home and Fel has taken the opposite task of proving it isn't. I hadn't mentioned it before because we are still gathering clues."

Cordelia immediately asked to look at the letters, "How fascinating. And if this is your family home then the spectral events are caused by your ancestors?"

Genia responded, "Heavens I hope not. Maybe later residents."

Daniel offered to have the letters put on the desk in the library by the window for others to explore since they were all expressing interest. "Or I can email the translations to you *sans* dad's scribbles. And feel free to help with the research. Fel, Genia, Dimitri and I are planning to meet here at ten tomorrow morning to share our recent research."

Dimitri said, "Let me report I am still pursuing the estate records." He pointed to a stack of books on the shelves to his left. "The records are there if anyone wants to help. As far as this estate is concerned, we know from a local history book, a son murdered his father in 1847 outside by the stone. We know the son escaped. We also know, although there are similarities in the stories, Genia's ancestor's name is different from the name found in the records. And on the fireplaces. So far we haven't found the name O'Donovan anywhere in the records. That works in Fel's favour since she is trying to prove this isn't the ancestral home."

Petra said, "Wouldn't he have changed his name if he was sought for murder?"

Dimitri said, "It is a consideration which has been in the back of my mind but we have been resisting the urge to jump to any conclusions. Our research falls apart if we name that as more than a possibility. The Famine was a horrible time, beyond horrible and any number of murders could have taken place. We can't base fact on coincidences. Fel is researching those possibilities. Have you had any luck?"

Fel replied, "I decided I would look in Cork for the name O'Donovan thinking it might be her maiden name. She mentions her family in Cork. There were definitively O'Donovans in the Cork area who were land owners. Internet records don't give the back stories so I am searching the Famine books for any land owner who tried to help his neighbours and tenants. She wrote of her father trying to help."

Genia added, "In regards to this manor, whether it is in our history or not, the past owners told my brother John, who was the initial contact, they couldn't get staff because of ghostly occurrences. I basically dismissed it when I heard about it. But now I am curious. Why don't we invite them to dinner and ask them some questions?"

"Great idea," Gerald said.

"Can it be soon?" asked Cordelia. "Diane and Gerald have to leave in a few days,"

"I'll call tomorrow," said Genia. "Meanwhile I am ready to let this rest for the evening. As Daniel says, you are invited tomorrow morning at ten to this very same spot to explore the mystery of our murderous ancestor and/or the murder that took place here. My friends, I wish that I had planned this so we could all sit back and laugh right now. But alas! What do you all need to feel comfortable again?"

"Drink!" Dave said it as a pronouncement, giving the single word energy. "To honour the late great Frank Kelly in the Father Ted TV series I repeat, 'Drink!'. OK I can't quite catch the full body of the word as he did. Someone else want to try?"

Daniel shook his head at them as they all attempted to imitate the tone and emphasis Kelly had put into that single word. Most failing to capture the unique edge he gave to the word 'Drink'. But the attempts lightened the atmosphere. He thought it was a great strategy by Dave.

Fel watched them with disdain. "Is no one afraid of staying in a haunted house?"

Cordelia responded, "Strange but I don't feel afraid. It seems like a happy ghost so I'm not worried." She paused, "Except for Diane's laughing ghost."

"Are you suggesting there are two ghosts? When did that happen? The foggy ghost could also be the laughing, slamming doors ghost," responded Dimitri.

"But I didn't feel any anxiety from the blue-white light over the chapel. The door slamming surely raised the hairs on my neck," said Dave. "Maybe a confused ghost?"

"Drink!" yelled Petra. She laughed at them and said, "Can someone lead me to some warm milk and provide some cookies so I can go to bed with a good novel? A palate cleansing romance is on my bedside table waiting for me."

Genia stood up. "Let's do that. Anyone else?"

They all headed to the kitchen.

Chapter 19

Genia was sitting in the library with her feet up on an ottoman sipping her coffee, talking to Dimitri, when Daniel entered the library the next morning. He greeted them both and dropped into the nearest chair.

Dimitri asked, "You look like you had a late night. Too much 'drink'?"

Daniel grinned at him, "I gave up the drink last week. I was thinking the alcohol was causing the uneasy sleeps. I guess I was wrong because right now my head is tired after another night waking up from another dream or nightmare filled with emotional distress. Again, no story. Just distress." His voice had increased in volume, revealing his frustration. He stopped and sighed, letting the steam out of his voice, "I do have a slight impression of something; an image of clusters of people bumping into each other in a crowded space. People moaning. I am left with grief about something I must have dreamt. That's all I remember."

Genia said, "I find your experiences progressively odder. It worries me. Do you want to change rooms? Maybe the energy is negative in that room. Although all rooms are taken right now there are some bedrooms in the attic. The servants' quarters I assume. I haven't done much with them. Probably a cold and miserable place to sleep. Or hot under the eaves. Take Diane's room after she leaves. Or stay at Dimitri's." She looked over at her friend and smiled.

Daniel said, "I feel like I am channelling some strong emotions but I will wait. I'll stay for now." He looked a little shamefaced when he said to them, "I have been reluctant to tell you that sometimes the bedroom door is open when I wake from these dreams. One night I woke up because my bed had been shaking. Well, I think it had been shaking. I'm not sure now. My door was open so I decided to investigate. Intruders I wondered? I stepped through the door into the dark hallway and came downstairs. I saw the front doors open and the foyer was filled with fog. A human form seemed to be taking shape. And there was the perfume of roses. Dimitri, that was the night I surprised you when you were working late in the library."

Dimitri was startled, "That's why you were standing on the step? I remember you weren't moving which I thought odd at the time. I closed the doors." He stopped speaking to recollect those moments. He repeated his words slowly with effect, "I closed the doors. I walked through the vapour to close the doors. Good grief." He looked more intently at Daniel, "I didn't notice any form but I was coming from the left of it. You were facing it so your perspective was different. I didn't feel any hatefulness or ugliness. I don't remember the scent of roses. But since then? Has your bedroom door been open since?"

"Yes, a few times. I have followed it each time to the open front doors. I haven't seen the fog again. I lock the doors tight and go back to bed. One night the doors slammed shut as I was walking down the stairs. I stayed awake the rest of that night. It was probably wind currents but violence was implied. We really should get an inspector to look at the air flow within the foyer since we have so much trouble there. Yet there was a brutality in both doors slamming shut at the same time. Much like last night. That sounds funny to say but I sensed violence. Maybe remnants of the dream that woke me up or something else. Maybe it isn't an inspector we need but a priest."

Genia asked, "Followed what?"

Daniel asked, "What do you mean?"

Genia said, "You said, 'I followed it'. Followed what?"

Daniel said, "That's odd. I don't know why I said that."

Genia asked, "What are you feeling as this happens?"

Daniel mused for a moment, "I feel curiosity. But if I have had a bad dream I feel the lingering emotions of the dream. The unremembered dream. Nightmare."

Just then Petra and Fel walked into the room. Fel took a stance in front of the fireplace. They could hear Cordelia's voice somewhere near.

Petra said, "I am popping my head in to say 'Good morning'. I'd like to join you to hear the mystery unfolding but I'm meeting with Gerald to discuss the draft of my new play and get his expert opinion. Fel said she would give me a summary of your meeting later."

Diane entered the library as Petra turned to leave, "Fel and Petra can I join that conversation with you later? I really need to put in a few undisturbed hours on my character development this morning. When are you meeting?"

Daniel interrupted, "Diane, I have been meaning to ask you about your process of creating a new character. How about we take a walk along the beach later. I can probe your brain about your process and update you on our research."

Diane said, "That's a date young man. It really bugs me that I will have to leave early before the mystery is solved."

Daniel grinned, "We'll email you updates. How about we meet at 5pm for the beach walk to work up an appetite for the excellent dinner Genia is providing?" He looked over at Genia. "It's your turn tonight, right? I have the number of some great take-out joints if you need help. I know how you love pizza."

She laughed at him. "No need to worry. Fiona is cooking up a delight as we speak. I think we'll have turkey to honour you."

Gerald, Cordelia and Dave came into the library.

Cordelia asked, "Who's a turkey?"

Genia said, "My mocking nephew."

"Why?" asked Cordelia.

Fel said, "Can we get started? It is already past ten and I am driving to Wicklow to do some research."

"I'm outta here," said Diane. "A warning though. I tend to emotionally pace when I am thinking out a character so if you see me acting erratically in the garden, ignore me. I also go over my lines so avoid me if I am screaming, crying, laughing. You've got the idea and I suspect you all do it yourself."

Petra waited for Gerald to greet everyone and then led him out the front doors.

Cordelia and Dave sat down as Fel began to speak.

Cordelia interrupted, "Oh I see Genia has some coffee. I assume there is a fresh pot in the kitchen? We just got back from a long walk on the beach and I could use the warmth of a hot cuppa. I'm going to get one. Anyone else?"

Dave said, "Great idea. I'll have one. No sugar."

Dimitri said, "I'll join you Cordelia. Fel, don't start without us."

Fel's response showed her impatience, "I don't have time to wait for you to get coffee. Why didn't you get it earlier?"

Genia spoke, "Fel, no need for rudeness. I should have had some coffee and tea here already. Dimitri, since you are on your feet, could you go to the kitchen and ask Fiona to bring in a tray? That way we can get started."

He responded, "Will do. One-minute Fel. I will be right back."

Daniel said, "What is on our agenda today?"

Fel listed them, "The graveyard on the estate, the cellar on the estate, information about the manor, information about the Loth family, information about the O'Donovans, my research of Wicklow Gaol, and the local graveyards and a nearby village. Information about a Cork connection. Oh and the letters and the markings on the stone."

Dimitri walked back into the room, "Fiona wants to know who wants toast or cookies or muffins?"

Fel said loudly, “Stop the interruptions.”

Dimitri was laughing, “Sorry Fel, I couldn’t resist. I told her to bring some muffins and fruit. She’ll be a few minutes.” He sat down and looked at Fel, “You were saying?”

She responded, “Focus. Daniel anything from the translator?”

“Yes. I spoke with him yesterday. He gave me a partial report on the stone. One side of the stone, the side facing the sea with the amateur carving simply has the reference ‘Psalm 33: 18, 19’. I looked it up in the King James Bible, assuming it was the only viable translation for the time. It reads, ‘Behold the eye of the Lord is upon them that fear him, upon them that hope in his mercy; to deliver their soul from death, and to keep them alive in the famine. Our soul waiteth for the Lord; he is our help and our shield.’ Heavy stuff.”

Fel said, “Is that it?”

Daniel said, “I guess you are suggesting we don’t debate the meaning now. Below the psalm reference is a symbol which my friend says may have been used during the Famine as a warning to others. It is a circle with a sideways cross through it. Below the image are the words, “Beware. God does not dwell here.”

“Well that message is clear enough,” said Cordelia.

“The other side of the stone?” Fel persisted.

“It is simply a carefree poem about ocean tides and the wealth that comes across the sea. Generic, vague. Bad poetry. The meter is off. He said it was unusual to be in Gaelic since it seems like an English sentiment. He has no idea why it would be. He’ll send me the complete translation of it. It doesn’t seem to have any deep relevance. He was thinking it was put there when the place was built to signify a connection across the water to England.”

“So, nothing worth pursuing there. The letter?” pushed Fel.

“He will send something tomorrow evening,” said Daniel.

“Genia? Anything to report?” asked Fel.

"The art conservator from Dublin is arriving tomorrow to look at the portraits. He or she, I'm not sure now who is coming from the museum, might have some information for us. I am interested in the dates of the portraits. And if the conservator knows the artists who painted them."

"The graveyard?" asked Fel.

Just then Fiona arrived with the coffee, testing Fel's patience further. Feeling cowed by Fel's disapproving demeanour everyone jumped quickly to get their coffee.

Fel said to Genia, "Continue."

"Just a minute Fel. Let people get seated," Genia said.

When that happened she said, "Niall was away for a few days. He took his wife north for a family wedding."

Dave said, "I wonder what an Irish family wedding would look like? Are the traditions different? I suspect lots of music and dance. I must ask him..."

Fel silenced him with a glare, "Enough! Genia continue."

Genia gave Dave a sympathetic pat on the knee as she answered, "Niall returns tomorrow. He'll finish clearing it. Top of the list he told me. We have had to wait for Dr. Brandy Bothwith. She brought in inspectors to get permission to touch the area. Ireland protects these old sites. She will be here as well to get the rubbing off all the stones. Most of references on the stones have an older script. All in Gaelic. Should be a few days before the graveyard is fully documented. I have asked her to add some background research into the names, for her report. The chapel is completely cleaned and furnished now. The wall plaque needed some special care. I will look there this afternoon to see if that has been done. I will also be looking again for any loose stones near the altar."

She turned to her friends and said, "In her letters she writes about hiding letters from him under a loose stone near the altar. I couldn't find any loose stones when I looked before but now I am thinking the altar might have shifted after the fire and be in a different place. Or the years of dirt might have clogged the seams between the stones and they are no longer loose. So, I'll be on my knees looking at all the stones. The carvings on the floor are near the altar where it sits today. I hoped they would give us some clues but I'm told they are a bible quote, 'The Light shines in the darkness and the darkness has never put it out.'"

Dimitri said, "That's an interesting choice of scripture. I suspect any letters will probably have rotted away by now or been burned in the fire. I hope we'll find some of your family names on the plaque. That would make our task easier. Let me know Genia when the conservator shows up. I'll join you. Are you finished your report?"

When she nodded Dimitri continued, "I guess I may as well give my meagre report. My task has been to look at the books and documents in the library that relate to the history of this estate. The place has changed hands a few times. There are many documents. I suspect some were lost over the years. Some records relate to when it was a commune. Some lists of sales of cows and the like. So far nothing startling other than the book I spoke about before that talks about a son murdering his father."

Fel asked, "What about the Marquis of Loth? Any information?"

"Was that my task?" asked Dimitri.

"No, it was mine and I have been lax," said Daniel. "I have nothing yet."

"Daniel, you've had a week since we saw the letters," said Fel. "Anything about his presence at Oxford? And did you look in the cellars?"

"Oh no!!" He was laughing defensively when he replied, "I have been carousing with this theatrical bunch. Blame Cordelia for my negligence. She forces me to drive her around the countryside to explore the towns and villages. But I think we have done more shopping than exploring. I will look at the cellars as soon as we finish here."

Fel said, "I seem to be the only one who does any work around here." She kept talking despite the protests, "I found our O'Brien in the records of the Wicklow Gaol. Cian O'Brien was charged with sedition against the Queen. I think our letter said he had been meeting with a group with a plan to go to Dublin Castle to ask the English for help during the Famine, the poverty of the people. But I guess that was considered sedition. I found a book in the local library that had a few paragraphs. It said he died trying to escape. He came from a family with a few pennies and they tried to help but he died I guess before they could bribe anyone. I didn't find a Daniel Irial O'Donovan in the records. So I tried the surname Loth. Nothing there either."

Genia said, "Great try Fel."

Dave who had been listening with a fascinated look on his face said, "If you are referring to the son who lived here and killed his father wouldn't the last name be different from the aristocratic title? Do you know if there was another name beside Loth?"

Dimitri said, "Do we? I don't think so. I can't remember. Daniel, you'll look for it?"

"Or the family erased his name," said Cordelia.

Fel said, "something to consider. Daniel, let me know if you find any more names. So back to O'Brien. He lived in a village called Rosalee outside Wicklow."

"Our village?" Genia asked excitedly.

"Our village? What do you mean by our village? Did the estate come with a village and someone lost it?" asked Cordelia chuckling.

"No," said Genia smiling, "her letters say she walked to the village. It couldn't be Wicklow. It's too far from here. Even though there are no local villages now, we have wondered if the village ceased to exist. Over a million-people died and another million emigrated during the Famine so I suspect entire villages disappeared. A local village means she could have lived here."

"But," said Fel, "it doesn't say where this village was located. Could be north of Wicklow not south east. More research. I'll keep looking for the village. OK what else? Oh, I drove to Cork yesterday and looked around the library and the historical society for any Famine history. Especially looking for a kind landlord who helped people. Not much. Until we have her family name there is no point in continuing to search."

"Anything else?" Daniel asked. "No? Then I am heading to the cellars to look for a room, possibly used as a cell which has carvings on the wall. Anyone want to join me?"

Genia said, "There is electricity down there and I think it is dry. Mostly stone walls, stone floors. I think Gerald wanted to join you. But catch him later."

Dave and Cordelia went with Daniel.

Dimitri said, "If O'Donovan is an aristocratic name then there would also be a surname for them. I'll look in my books. Genia, do you have some time this afternoon?"

"OK. But our mystery is getting very complicated," Genia said.

Chapter 20

"Who keeps blowing out my candles?" Cordelia shouted as she walked from the dining room into the kitchen, "You're ruining the ambience I'm trying to create in the dining room."

Daniel and Genia just stared at her.

"Will no one admit to the foul, foul deed?" she complained.

Dimitri entered the kitchen through the back door just then. A little current of air flowed around him. He was obviously in a great mood as he said, "Good evening dear friends. To quote the great Bard I say, 'I would give all my fame for a pot of ale and safety.'."

Diane came through the hallway door into the kitchen at the same time. She responded, "Shakespeare's As You Like It, Act 3?"

Cordelia said, "Wrong play, right act. Henry V, Act 3, Scene 2 I believe? How about 'Tis an ill cook that cannot lick his own fingers'?"

Petra joined them, as well, in time to say, "Romeo and Juliet, Act 4, Scene 2. Studied it in school. Am I right?"

"Hmm, yes. I think so," said Cordelia. "Here is another Bard quote, 'If music be the food of love, play on.' Twelfth Night. I remember playing Olivia to Justin Carter's Orsino. Many years ago of course. I love the Bard's comedies."

Gerald came into the kitchen, "I didn't get the memo. Did we need a Shakespearean quote to get fed tonight?"

Daniel said, "I hope not or I will starve."

Genia said, "To the dining room everyone. Cordelia are you in charge of the drinks? Yes? Fiona made cucumber water. The jug's in the fridge. Thank you. Everyone follow Cordelia. Dimitri can you help me with the meal? Daniel will you check on Fel and Dave. I think Fel is back from her travels. Let them know the salad will be served in seven minutes. Precisely. No laggards. Gerald find some music to play during dinner. The player and CDs are in the cabinet in the dining room. I have a new Stravinsky CD in the cabinet. Though pick what you like. It's a diverse collection."

~~~~~~~~~~~~~~~

Later, as they gathered in the library, Gerald said, "I'm glad I walked the beach again this afternoon. That was an excellent meal Genia."

"Thank you," she said. "I'll tell Fiona you liked it. I hope she never leaves me. Oh Fel you're on the list for dinner tomorrow night. The past owners are coming to dinner. Do you want Fiona to handle it?"

"No," she answered. "I'll figure something out. They aren't vegetarians, are they? I don't like vegetarians. I doubt most of them care about animal rights. They just want special attention. Too picky."

Genia burst out laughing, "Dear sister, sometimes your judgements are ..... hhhmmmm what's the word? Disgraceful. I don't think they are vegetarians. They didn't mention it when I called to invite them. Now, changing the subject. Daniel did you go into the cellars? Find anything?"

"Yes, we went to the cellars. No, we didn't find anything," he looked at Dave and Cordelia for comment. "Just some stone rooms. One with a wine cellar. No carvings or marks in the walls."

Cordelia spoke up, "I went down again to show Gerald. Nothing remarkable."

"Surprisingly dry cellar. I wonder how it was built? Who designed it? I expected it to be a damp hole," said Gerald.

Dimitri responded, "I found some information about that in the records today. The original building was built circa 1770 as a hunting lodge for the Marquis of Loth. His family had acquired the land during the first potato Famine of 1740. I assume, from
~~~~~~~~~~~~~~~

historical accounts of the time, that the land was used for cattle and by-products. Even then the people had only potatoes. I think there was some grain. I assume Irish labour was used to build the manor; labourers who would have understood the challenges of building a stone cellar in this soil and climate. I agree, they did well by him. It was the third son of a later Marquis of Loth, who transformed the hunting lodge into the grand manor it became in 1822. Some of the building, closer to the sand dunes, fell down a few years ago leaving this central core."

Genia asked, "When was the chapel built?"

"There was only a line about the chapel in the records. It was a stone chapel built the same time as the hunting lodge became a manor. Same stone. It was built on the ruins of an old monastery. That was all that I found. So circa 1822."

"Dr. Brandy Bothworth is in charge of restoring the chapel and the graveyard. She was puzzled about the foundations. She suspected the chapel walls and roof were set in place about the same time as the manor but the foundations were earlier. She couldn't find any historical reference. I'll tell her to connect with you. A monastery. That's interesting."

Daniel said, "So I have other news since our meeting this morning. My friend emailed me his rough translation of the letter my father hadn't translated. It's a letter Father Doyle wrote to our ancestor in Montreal. I had asked him via email today to hurry up. And he did. Apparently, I owe him a meal next time I travel to Dublin."

Daniel stopped, showing some hesitation. "I know we have been waiting for this. I have it in my pocket and I'll read it to you but be prepared. It's not a happy letter."

He took it out of his pocket. "The letter was written September 30, 1848." Daniel looked at Genia, "It reads,

'Dear Danny,

My news is sad young Daniel. Your beloved Mother died this past week on September 24th. May she rest in peace. It was a tragic accident. The accounts are from witnesses who were too late to save her. I have been told she had been lighting candles in her chapel and had fallen asleep. A candle must have fallen over. The altar cloth caught fire and ignited some wood that had been piled in a corner. The wooden support for the roof above the window gave way and the roof and the stones fell on her. The local police suspect she was overwhelmed by the smoke and had died before the stones fell.

She had been to see me in Rosalee the day before. She was distressed because your aunt had ordered a servant at the estate to cut down and burn the roses growing over her beloved chapel. She often spent long hours there in prayer. I gave her a letter from you that very day. She wrote you a response immediately. It may not have reached you as yet. She was concerned you were returning to Ireland. No need now. You were her deepest joy.

Her Father and sisters came up from Cork to see her buried beside her sons, the wee ones who died so young.

Bridget Mary Betha Dimond will be at peace now. May God rest her soul.

She was a true and obedient child of God.

In the service of our Lord,
Father Doyle,
Wicklow,
September 30, 1848'"

"Read it again Daniel?" Diane asked quietly.

He repeated it.

"He must have been heartbroken," Genia said. "Nineteen, maybe twenty by then, in a strange land without family or money. Accused of murdering his father. I know it has been more than one hundred and fifty years but still what a loss."

Fel said, "And he was a fugitive. In her last letter she was trying to clear his name. Probably no longer a viable option. Would the grandfather in England have given him aid?"

Petra looked at them with a thoughtful expression on her face, "I probably write too many mysteries but it all sounds suspicious. Do you think it was an accident? I read the copies of the letters Daniel left here. In her last letter she said she was listening to her sister-in-law for clues to the real murderer. It was the cruel sister-in-law who gave false witness against her nephew, turned away the poor, locked her in the cellars, followed by the most spiteful act to cut down the roses she cherished."

Genia looked at her and nodded thoughtfully, "What a horrible thought."

Dimitri said, "But credible considering the description of the sister-in-law in the letters. There probably wasn't much respect for Bridget Mary, an Irish Catholic. Maybe they didn't know she was Catholic. Even if her husband loved her when he married her there might have been a prejudice against her. The Irish were much maligned by the dominant English. Maybe he married her for money. She must have had some money in her background if her father was able to feed people during the Famine. Also notice, dear friends, the name is not O'Donovan but Dimond."

Fel said, "I'll look for the name Daniel Irial Dimond in the gaol. I have my computer here. I can look it up now." She pulled it out of a desk drawer and took it over to a corner chair and sat down. "I hope it works. The battery keeps dying. But I have kept it plugged in all day."

"I love the 21st century," Dimitri said. "Instant information. Can anyone look up her full name and see what that brings?"

Daniel said, "Well I just happen to have my phone here as well. Let me see."

Genia said, "I am stunned by her death. Well, the manner of her death. She died in her chapel. Possibly the only place she felt safe and cherished. The only place she could feel was all hers."

Dimitri asked, "Were you able to read the plaque in your own chapel today?"

"Yes, there is little on them. In old Gaelic. Brandy was with me and she said they were both a dedication of the space to the glory of God."

"I found it!" Fel said, "I found Daniel Irial Philip Dimond in the Wicklow Gaol records. He was incarcerated for murder, 1847. It says he escaped. That's all. Good grief we found him."

Dave startled them all, "Hey! Hey! Hey! I got it. I got it!" He was so excited he was stumbling through his words so he slowed down and enunciated, "This Marquis of Loth had or has the surname of Dimond. See even the seal is the same as the seal on the fireplaces." He turned the phone for them to see. "There is a website for the family. The manor is featured and there is some history written here."

Dimitri began to laugh, deep stuttering laughs came from him, "So as I mucked through these smelly, dusty old books, all I had to do was some internet research? I am feeling incredibly old now."

Genia said, "Our ancestor started here in this house? The quiet, kind old guy my grandmother talked about walked these shores, slept in this house and ran away from this house. He walked these halls. I wonder which bedroom was his? Hers? That is a little difficult to grasp. Oh and that is the chapel she spent so much time in as she grieved for him. Those are her roses." She paused for a moment and then said with a tone of wonder, "She died there."

Daniel stood and walked over to the fireplace. He traced the name carved into the stone with his fingers. "Dimond," he said. "He used O'Donovan to fool the authorities who looked for him. Our family name is not O'Donovan."

Petra said, "This knowledge conveys a much deeper and more dramatic story. So he escaped from the Wicklow Gaol. He must have had help. Who bribed whom? There must be more to the story in local history books."

Fel said, "I can look for it with another library search."

Petra said, "I'm intrigued. I'll help you Fel."

Genia spoke again, still caught in the amazement of what they had discovered, "It was his father who died by the stone, the fairy stone. Our fairy stone."

Daniel sat down again and said, "Her full name is not getting any results on the internet. Hey, wait: I'll try O'Donovan."

Fel said, "You probably need an Irish heritage website."

Genia still bemused said, "He was beaten and kept in the cellars here. This is our family home. He was locked up in local Wicklow Gaol where tourists walk about taking pictures and discussing the horrors of the place. I just can't grasp the idea that we have these roots. I didn't have time to look more closely for loose stones in the chapel. How amazing it would be to find one of his letters to her."

Chapter 21

The front doors banged open. Daniel heard Cordelia give a brief scream from behind him in the sitting room, followed by an embarrassed laugh. Their guests were feeling some tension.

"George. Jonah. Come in, come in. The rain is just lashing down and the wind is fearsome," Genia said. She looked beyond them. "The storm is making the sky darker than usual this time of the evening. But I confess I love it because the rain is just lovely for my plants although not as comfortable for us humans. Come in where it's warm. There's a fire in the sitting room. Give Daniel your coats first."

George and Jonah gave up their coats and followed Genia. They sat close together on the sofa. It was obvious they were not comfortable. Dave, Diane, Cordelia, Fel, Gerald, Dimitri and Petra were also in the room. Some standing and some seated. Genia introduced the middle-aged couple to her house guests although there was little need since they were mostly familiar faces from film and theatre. Except Fel.

"Drinks, for either of you?" Daniel asked. "We have colas, some great Irish wine, beer, and Irish whiskey. Probably some other choices if we search. Diane makes an excellent margarita."

Both, still subdued, chose wine.

Genia sat beside them and sought to relax them, "There are some nibbles here. Dinner will be a tad late."

"But only by thirty minutes," Fel said. "I don't think the oven is working right therefore the roast needs more time." She looked over at Dimitri. "Stop muttering," she snapped.

Genia smiled a bright smile at George and Jonah. She had warned her sister and Dimitri to be civil this evening. "I am so glad we were able to arrange this time together. I understand you have been away, travelling in other lands?"

Jonah answered, "Yes, we were on our honeymoon."

There were many expressions of congratulations.

Jonah laughed, "It is actually our tenth honeymoon. We decided when we got married we would have many honeymoons to celebrate being together. This time we went to Greece."

Dimitri came at once to sit on the couch beside them to question them about their time in his homeland. The next forty-five minutes was a comfortable exchange about places, experiences and events by everyone present. During the wait, more wine was served, easing the tension of all Genia's guests. George looked a little glassy-eyed.

Cordelia gave them a hilarious account of a taxi ride in Wales, "I thought I was having a conversation with the driver about the challenges for a New Yorker of driving on the other side of the road. I told him the narrow roads were charming but fraught with hazards. I thought he was responding to me. His accent was thick. Welsh. It wasn't until I heard him say something about his leg and Montreal that I realized we were not speaking the same language, if you know what I mean." She pointed towards Gerald, "My husband had followed the insane conversation with some amusement. He laughed for hours."

By now Jonah had relaxed but George still seemed tense. Extra wine was not helping him relax.

Dave, who had gone to the kitchen to help Fel with the meal and to set the table in the dining room, returned to them in the sitting room.

"Ladies and gentlemen and most honourable guests," he announced in his suave French accent, giving a dramatic wave of his arm and an exaggerated bow, "your dining experience awaits. The table has been set. Most beautifully, I must say. The candles have been lit and the wine poured. Our chef, Felicity O'Donovan, is serving tasty spring potatoes and carrots fresh from Genia's garden, local lamb with a mint sauce, salad and Fel's specialty: warm Canadian sweet rolls with local butter. A feast to be sure."

Gerald, who loved his food, stood first. He looked at Dave quizzically, "OK Dave I am guessing we are again in Shakespeare land." He looked at George and Jonah and said, "This crowd seems determined to reveal my poor knowledge of Shakespeare but I will give it a go. Dave, I am guessing you are giving us an imitative performance of Launcelot, the clown in the Merchant of Venice?"

"No!" Dave answered.

"I know the answer," said Daniel. "Mopsa or Dorcus, one of the tartly shepherdesses in The Winter's Tale?"

As everyone laughed Dave answered in a droll voice, "*Merci* Daniel. *Merci* Gerald. Neither of you is correct. I was portraying a hungry person inviting his friends to dinner."

The laughter moved them all towards the dining room.

After they were seated Dimitri raised his glass and said, "With gratitude to She who gives us life."

Amen was the response with a click of glasses.

"If you believe in that stuff," Petra added.

"You object?" Dimitri asked.

Petra responded, "I don't object but every dinner you say something like that. All I am saying is I don't believe in it."

Dimitri smiled and raised his glass as a salute to her, "A conversation for another time but I will say for now there is a big difference between faith and belief. They are not interchangeable in their meanings. Faith is a supernatural gift."

"Yes, at another dinner, please." Genia said quickly, turning to George, "I understand you are an interior designer and I should thank you for much of the excellent restoration of the manor."

George had spoken little since he arrived. His voice was tentative. “Thank you. I see you have chosen light colours as well.”

“Was that your choice? A light colour palette?”

“Yes. The rooms seemed dark and cold. I tried to lighten them. I don’t know that I was very successful.”

Cordelia leaned forward to speak. Her friends tensed. In the discussion, at dinner last night, they had decided not to speak of their strange experiences to the past owners. They still weren’t sure it wasn’t an elaborate hoax; or shadows or wind and cold.

Dave had also named a need to present an unbiased context in which to hear the past owners’ experiences. Sometimes, he had pointed out, an objective audience invites a less exaggerated description of an event than a subjective audience. They needed objectivity.

But they all knew Cordelia’s impatience. She had argued with them for a ‘cards on the table’ approach. Her husband had cautioned her about exposing her reputation to fake media outlets. He had said, ‘Imagine a trumped-up headline that interprets our experience as occult worship and séances.’ When he said the word ‘séance’ they saw her face perk up in response.

‘No!’ He had said emphatically.

‘No!’ Genia had said emphatically.

So, remembering her reluctant assent to their plan, they all waited for the words she would use to honour that plan, while manipulating the conversation towards the topic she wanted to discuss: ghosts. Oh, so subtly. They hoped.

Cordelia said, “Genia, is that why you painted the kitchen white with light ....”

But George interrupted her abruptly, with feeling, “You do know your home is haunted, right? That’s why it’s so dark in here.”

Cordelia’s voice trailed off, “.........accents?”

Jonah laughed, "Sorry folks." He looked around the table at every person, some with food on the way to their mouths, some chewing and some with mouths open, such as Cordelia. Gerald was chuckling.

Jonah continued, "We didn't mean to just name this in such an abrupt manner but the truth is we are both uneasy just being in this place. We had some weird experiences here."

Cordelia was delighted and in an exaggerated simpering voice she said, "Oh really? I just need to know more. What weird experiences?"

The rest of the group were giving encouraging nods except Fel who was rolling her eyes unseen by their guests who had been seated beside her. Genia looked intense.

Jonah expanded, "As you may know we had invested in this place as a hotel. We thought with the lovely grounds, the access to the seaside, the history and the closeness to the towns and the gorgeous Wicklow county we had a winner, especially with all the prosperity of the Celtic Tiger. Our troubles began when we couldn't get staff. Sure, the construction crews, sturdy men and women, happily took our money and did a fine job but they would never stay past four in the afternoon. We thought it was just a cultural thing. We both grew up in Wicklow. We know about the social life, the need to gather with others in pubs and community groups during long rainy bouts to keep spirits from being flattened by the rain."

Dave laughed, "And to argue history and politics," reminding them of a recent pub visit.

Jonah smiled and kept speaking, "They were always here promptly at seven every morning. The work was excellent. But once the work was finished and we planned a date to open as a hotel, no one applied for the positions. We increased the wages. Nothing and no one. We queried the locals for the reason for the difficulty. We were told people felt the place was haunted. We didn't live here in the house, so we had no inkling. We couldn't imagine what could be so bad that some choice positions for local people were being ignored. We dismissed it as nothing. We Irish are brilliant at seeing wee people and ghosts. Many ancient places in Ireland are considered haunted. It has become a tourist industry."

Petra laughed, "We people? Is that a commune or a new religion?"

Jonah said, "I think it's spelt 'w-e-e' as in small magical creatures. Many countries have these legends: elves, fairies, gnomes. It's a fascinating topic. One person told us there were fairies who danced with lights over the chapel at night. And the graveyard."

Genia asked, "Yes, the graveyard. Did you have a chance to explore that area?"

George answered, "It was thick with grass and bushes. Ireland has some strict rules about disturbing old gravesites so we never got around to clearing it. We put up a temporary barrier to keep people out of that space. I think there are eleven, twelve graves. Some stones had fallen over or sunk into the ground."

Genia said, "It's a family cemetery, I believe."

George responded, "I think so. We found some records and books in one of the attic rooms. I think the commune group packed them away. George had put them in the library as atmosphere. I flipped through a few. A fascinating history. Someone was murdered here. A man. Another person, a woman, was found dead in the chapel."

Jonah frowned, "It might be a dusty hunt. We put the records and books back in the attic when we moved out, to protect them."

Genia said, "Thank you for your care. We brought down some of the boxes and four of the portraits from the attic today. The art curator said they need to be cleaned of a hundred years of grime but otherwise they're in good condition."

Cordelia, impatient at this digression prompted Jonah sweetly, "Ghosts?"

Her friends laughed at her impatience.

Jonah returned to his reflection, "Not being able to fight the local superstition, we eventually hired students for internships from other countries. We had to move in ourselves to cover some evening shifts. I was able to shift my office and work here. We converted the attic into employee bedrooms and storage. The cellars became office space."

Gerald interrupted even though his wife frowned at him, "You spent some serious money on creating that fine wine cellar."

"Yeah, it was a small room, just the right size for the racks, but a strange room. It had bolts on the outside of the door like it was a jail cell. There were, and actually still are, dates and names carved into the walls behind some of those wine cabinets."

He looked at Genia, "Have you had the chance to explore the cellars? We can show you the marks."

"But not tonight," George said quickly.

Genia smiled at George, "Are you feeling anxious right now? Do you feel comfortable talking about your experiences here?"

George said, "Frankly, despite the excellent food and company, I want to get the heck out of here. I sit here waiting for It to show up."

"It?" Cordelia had jumped on this word. They all looked startled except Dimitri, Fel and Genia. For the theatre guests, the intriguing spooky mystery had moved from some banging doors and a chapel aura to a more substantial 'It'.

George answered, "I feel if I speak about it, It will make itself known. It is not very nice." He looked to his partner for support.

Jonah said bluntly, "There are two ghosts."

Diane and Dave both tried to speak, "What?!"

Fel stood up and started clearing plates. “I think I’ll just get dessert.”

Dave said, exaggerating his lovely French accent, “I’d help, but my butt is stuck to the chair right now.” He wriggled and everyone laughed at his ruse to stay in the dining room to hear more.

Daniel said, “Fel, just delay a few minutes and we’ll help you.”

She sat down again with a mulish expression on her face.

Cordelia, who was sitting across from the couple, was leaning forward, ignoring the byplay. “Two ghosts?” she asked.

Jonah looked at Genia apologetically before he responded, “We were reluctant to sell you this house after our experiences. But as time slipped by the memories faded and it didn’t seem so startling. Your brother was quite insistent about buying the place. We selfishly justified the sale and needed little encouragement to yield. In fact, your brother thought the idea of ghosts intriguing.”

Fel spoke dryly, “He would.”

“Now as we sit here it’s all vivid again.”

Cordelia repeated with a raised voice, “Two ghosts?”

Jonah responded, “Yes, one inside, the dark one we call It and one outside, the misty one. We have made some assumptions about them, possibly extremely inaccurate assumptions. We felt the dark one was preventing the white one from getting inside because the front doors were always slamming. We never experienced the misty one inside. Or maybe that one just didn’t want to come inside. Once in a while a face would appear in the library window looking into the room. A female countenance we were told. We never saw it. The first time we became aware of it, a guest, who had been reading late in the library had fallen asleep and woke to see the face in the window. He yelled for the entire twenty minutes it took for him to pack and leave. We had to mail some of his clothes to him which he had left behind in his haste to be gone. At the time we dismissed it as a scam to get out of paying his bill because he was able to linger long enough to demand a full refund as he was leaving."

George said, "But later there were other similar experiences. One guest said she felt compassion for the misty ghost because the face looked sad, lost. She had the impression it was looking for something. It seemed benevolent."

"The dark ghost?" Daniel asked.

"It?" George asked. The tone of his voice was tinged with anger, "It lives in the house. Downstairs. It is ugly. You know when It is present because of a feeling of hate and ugliness entering your space. I only saw the dark one once but I had felt it near in various degrees a few times. I never want to feel it again. I likened it to a snake. A swirling, venomous, vicious hate that touches your soul and lingers."

They all sat quietly feeling the emotional impact of the description.

Fel stood again, "Someone stack the plates and I will get dessert."

George said to her back as she was leaving the room, "It mostly appears in the kitchen, the dining room and the foyer near the front doors."

Fel grimaced at him and headed to the kitchen. Alone.

The faces around the table revealed fear, humour and scepticism. No one was heading to the kitchen to help Fel.

Genia took charge, "Let's have dessert and coffee in the sitting room. Dave, can you unstick your Paris derriere from the chair now and gather the rest of the plates? Petra check the fire in the sitting room. Cordelia and Gerald, please help Fel get dessert. Dimitri can you make some of your excellent coffee? Decaf I think. Does anyone want tea? No? Daniel, collect some cups, milk, sugar from the kitchen and take them to the sitting room. George and Jonah come with me and let's continue this discussion in the comfort of a warm fire, bright lights and deep inviting chairs. Diane can you blow out the candles and join us?"

Everyone moved.

Chapter 22

In the kitchen Daniel slowly gathered the coffee cups, the milk and the sugar for the tray. He listened to the interactions of the small group gathered there. He was amused by Genia's wisdom. Into the kitchen she had sent the fallout from what they had just heard. Cordelia was whispering loudly. It was obvious she was agitated but he didn't know if her emotion was fear or excitement. Her husband Gerald didn't know either because he had a perplexed look on his face as he watched her.

Dimitri was standing by himself, quietly watching the coffee perk. He wasn't engaging with anyone. In fact, he had been quiet most of the evening. Now that is strange, Daniel was thinking, since Dimitri often had some comment to offer. At the moment Dimitri's expression was one of worry. Daniel tested that impression in his mind. What would Dimitri be worried about? Tonight's topic? Or something personal? He decided to pay attention to Dimitri's reactions. He felt, of all of them, Dimitri was wise about the topic of the supernatural. It was clear to Daniel this ghostly adventure had lost its humorous feature.

He looked at his aunt. Fel was agitated as she jammed the dishes into the dishwasher. She was telling Dave that this nonsense was just feeding Genia's fragile emotional state. Dave had an incredulous look on his face. Daniel watched him processing Fel's assertions. As a former paramour of Genia's, Dave knew Genia better than most people. He knew her as deep, sensitive, thoughtful, empathic, kind, generous, fey, winsome, funny but never would he have used the word 'fragile'. Daniel was hoping Dave would challenge Fel but he simply gave Fel the dirty dishes he had collected from the dining room table and turned away, moving in the direction of the sitting room.

Daniel's attention shifted back to Cordelia as he heard her say, "Genia stopped the conversation just as it was getting interesting."

Her husband mused, "I was glad of it. We needed a reality break. I had begun to look for It to appear."

Cordelia laughed at him and put her arms around him. She said, "I'll protect you, big boy. Let's go listen some more." She took his hand. "Sit beside me and squeeze my hand if you get scared." They left the kitchen.

Fel turned to Dimitri and Daniel saying loudly, "This is wrong. We don't know these men. We don't know their backgrounds. I don't think this is a safe space for Genia."

Dimitri exploded, "Why the hell don't you just knock off the 'fragile Genia' shit. You know that isn't true. You peddle these insinuations like ...." He sputtered into silence.

Daniel spoke as Fel opened her mouth to respond to Dimitri, "No. Stop. Fel, no! This showdown between you two is not happening now. Is the coffee finished, Dimitri? Let's go then. Fel I want you in the room to hear any more disclosures." In the face of her hesitation he said, "Please? We have to figure this out."

He left. They followed silently with coffee and dessert.

~~~~~~~~~~~~~~~

George was saying, as they entered the sitting room, "We tried a séance. We held it in the dining room. It was awful. The lights went on and off. Dishes smashed. The doors banged. Some invisible presence was laughing. A horrible cackle. The room was filled with hate."

Cordelia had contained the agitation they had seen her express in the kitchen. She spoke with polite interest, "Who performed the ritual? What was your intent?"
~~~~~~~~~~~~~~~

Jonah said, "It was intended to entertain the guests. A guest, who had stayed with us for two weeks, said he was a medium and wanted to connect with the strong energy he felt in the manor. We didn't know we were playing with fire. It isn't like you imagine it as being more than atmosphere or an old house or ...?"

George continued for him, "Or a potential scam. But a ghost!? We were naive."

Cordelia again, "George, you said you saw the dark ghost. What does it look like?"

George responded slowly, "It looks like a thick dark nothingness. It feels like hatred and malice. It has some form of a body but the best way to describe its shape would be to imagine a dark aura around a body; like a distorted outline of what had been."

Diane asked, "Where did this happen and when?"

"It appeared in the kitchen one day."

"In daylight?" Cordelia asked, startled.

"Yes. Strange how we think the supernatural only appears at night. I understand now there is a thin veil between this reality and the next. Beyond the veil are our loved ones, often visiting us from that other reality. I think maybe at night, when we are relaxed, we are more receptive to see what is always there."

Dave said, "*Mon Dieu*, I remember reading something about that once. But I didn't ever think it referred to hateful darkness."

"Let's not delve into mindless heaven and hell chit chat right now," Petra said. "George, I am a writer with a great imagination but I find this all a bit far-fetched. I am probably the most sceptical person in this room," she looked over at Fel. "Except Fel. All I am hearing is a description of your own shadow. Something you imagined. Perhaps you were mistaken in what you saw and felt. Sorry to be so frank," she laughed. Then she added, "Rude."

George smiled, "I think you have already intimated you are not a person of faith. To be as frank, talking to a person without faith is like talking to someone in a box who thinks the only reality is in that personalized box. Faith is the certainty, the complete concrete knowledge, that there is something more. Faith makes the invisible visible. With an atheist the discussion always ends with a negative judgement after the atheist has reduced the experience to their limited sight. I have been told, 'It is something you imagined.' or 'It is all in your head.' I have always wondered why the blind dictate to those who have seen. Why those who see only in black and white dismiss the observations of those who can see in colour. I saw, I felt, I experienced a dark vicious soul standing beside me in the kitchen. It moved towards me. It surrounded me with the dankness of its soul. I cried to the One you decry, for release. It moved away. It smashed plates and turned over the table in the kitchen. The bully moved to the doorway between the kitchen and dining room and watched me. I was frozen in grief. Eventually it disappeared through the door. The foulness of its presence disappeared as well. The smell of rot abated. It left me defeated. I am not insane. I am not crazy. It was as real as you and me sitting here. 'It' is real." He had leaned forward in his intensity. Now he slowly moved backward in his seat and released some of the tension with a deep breath.

Dimitri responded first, thoughtfully, "Let's hope we don't get the proof you seek Petra." He turned to George and said, "Your experience sounds horrendous."

Genia spoke warily, "George, tell me about the white one. Why did your guest experience it as benevolent?"

Jonah replied, "George had been away the week that particular guest stayed with us, so only I benefited from that conversation. She said there was an expression of longing in the face that she saw peering in the window."

Genia felt her friends switch their gaze from Jonah to her with speculation. She knew there would be questions later, testing her impression.

Jonah was still talking, “She, the guest, also spent time around the chapel ruins and felt a positive energy there. I confess I never saw either of the ghosts. I was dismissive of the accounts until the séance. That night, in the dining room, when the medium began lighting candles as a few people gathered, expressing their excitement, I was wondering if I could market the idea and have a monthly fright night. Good for business. It was actually bad for business. We had to refund every guest that night and find alternative accommodations. Except the medium who wanted to invite some ghost hunters.”

George said, “I can still hear the unnatural laughter from that evening.” He looked over at Jonah, then continued, “I think it was feminine. Do you remember it that way?”

Jonah agreed, “A horrible mocking cackle.”

George continued, “The trouble began with this low cackle. I thought it was the medium seeking effect. When the candles blew out and the door between the kitchen and the dining room began banging, the cackle was drowned out by the screams of the guests. Some man, named Douglas, had a piercing high-pitched scream.” George laughed. “OK it isn’t kind to laugh but it was the absurd within the unusual, within the bizarre.”

Cordelia asked George, “Your experience with the dark one, was it before or after the séance?”

“The next day. Early morning.”

“Did you feel the séance had unleashed it or made it stronger?”

“Who knows? The medium and others had spoken of experiences they had in the hotel. I thought they were making it up. Up to that point I had felt some uneasiness. I would hear creepy old house sounds and see some ‘corner of the eye’ movement. There was often an odd rotten smell in a room. The staff talked of seeing dark shadows and a feeling of being watched. It worked in our favour in one instance. We had a student chef who had an eight-month internship contract with us. A lazy bully. We were always mediating between him and other staff whom he had annoyed. He had an experience in the kitchen one day that caused him to run out the back door, the kitchen door, in a panic. He wouldn't come inside again. We never got the details. He tried to sue us, but since his case involved a ghost, the court laughed at him." He looked at Petra and smiled, "They asked him for proof."

Petra laughed, acknowledging the irony.

George said, "After the séance and my experience in the kitchen, we made our plans to close the hotel when all internships were honoured. Some of our guests were experiencing uneasiness. It was impossible to keep staff. The medium had spread the word and some crazy people were showing up as guests to surreptitiously hunt for ghosts. It became unbearable." He looked over at his partner. "Do you remember that crazy old bird, Reverend Primrose?" He looked back at them. "The Reverend, who probably didn't do the eight years of ordination training, but got his qualifications over the internet, was presiding at a wedding party that had booked all the rooms for an entire weekend. Primrose heard about the ghost and decided he was a match for it. He turned the weekend into a spectacle by inviting a spectral photographer to follow him as he 'fought' the demons. Nothing supernatural was in evidence so he decided it was because of his holy presence. Frankly it was disgusting."

Jonah added, "He was one of those leaders you find in all religions who think they are demi-gods. Every situation becomes about their ego and their importance, expecting people to bow before them. There was nothing spiritual or loving in his depths. I agree it was quite disgusting."

Dimitri interrupted the flow and in a droll tone of voice said, "He would be known as an ass-holy person in religious circles."

Jonah paused, startled by Dimitri's simple statement. He then moved on without responding, "There were some guests who would camp outside because they said the stone at the beach and the chapel ruins both glowed some nights. I never saw it happen. But by then we were living in crazy land. I closed my senses and just moved forward with our plan to shut down the operation."

George said, "Then there were the ghostly figures that would appear at the back door. I was told they disappeared when people approached. Though why anyone would want to approach is beyond me."

Cordelia said, "More than two ghosts?"

George answered, "I guess. Though reports were that they were unresponsive and passive. Like someone frozen in time."

Jonah looked at his watch and with some relief said, "It's time for us to leave. As much fun as it is being in a haunted house and all, I would like to leave before It turns up." He laughed at the expressions on their faces. "Sorry to laugh. Don't worry. Just don't have any séances. Or OJ boards. I think that exacerbates the energy." He looked at George. "Remember the guest who brought her own board? She was almost creepier than the anticipation of a visit of It. Almost."

Genia stood as the round of goodbyes began. Daniel joined her as she walked them to the door. "Thank you for allowing us to hear your experiences."

George said, "We never asked you if you've had any events?"

Genia lied, "Some minor uneasiness. Nothing like you've described."

Just then the front doors opened quietly.

Genia smiled, "Those doors just won't stay closed. Daniel is getting a stronger bolt tomorrow."

George and Jonah left immediately without inquiring further.

Chapter 23

When Genia returned to the sitting room Diane and Dave were at the piano. Diane was playing the blues because she was leaving in the morning. She was making up lyrics to suit her sorrow,

"The mornin' is a comin',

the mornin' is a comin' and I must leave you my dear friends.

Only darkness and woe will be my friends now.

Oooooo. Oh baby."

Dave pushed her over and joined her on the piano bench and took control of the piano. "But no. No. We need a hopeful tune." He morphed from Diane's blues mood to a poor imitation of *Non, je ne regrette rien*, Edith Piaf's anthemic folksong. In his lovely French accent, he sang,

"Oh, the morning is a comin',

Oh, the morning is a comin',

but *ma chere amie*,

will return another day.

That day will have sunshine

and little fairies floating above our heads."

Diane put her hands on his to stop him. The music was tipping towards raucous.

Gerald said, "Dave, I didn't know you could play the piano."

"He can't. That must be obvious. Banging the same few notes is not 'playing' the piano," Diane answered. "He is destroying one of Piaf's signature pieces. She'll be waiting for you at the pearly gates, my friend."

Dave grabbed his chest, "Oh my heart is wounded." He lifted both his hands to his head, "My head and soul are wounded." He banged his head on the piano keyboard. "Oh woe. *Non, je ne regrette rien.*"

Diane began to laugh at his dramatic response as he began to moan loudly, "I thought I was faking it very well."

Petra had joined them at the piano. She patted Dave on the head as she said, "Diane, I hate that you are leaving in the morning. I will miss you."

Diane gave her an affectionate smile and replied, "Yeah, me too. But I am committed to start costume fittings in two days."

She pushed Dave off the piano bench and they walked together to the sofas. "Genia, you'll let me know the end of our mystery here? Those guys had some scary stories."

Cordelia was whispering in wonder, "How many ghosts does that make now? Gerald honey we have to stay outside some night. I want to see these apparitions. I want to see the glow around the stone and the chapel."

"Cordelia my love. No. Never. No," her husband replied. "I am not that curious. Ask another."

She turned to Petra who responded to the look of inquiry by saying, "To quote a wise friend of mine, 'No. Never. No. Ask another'."

Dimitri spoke up, "How about I host a late night ghostly quest at the cottage. It has a lovely porch with cosy chairs. I am curious as well. We can sip champagne, nibble on some Greek canapés and if it is a clear night be inspired by the universe."

Cordelia said, "That is an excellent idea." She turned to her husband whose head was shaking no.

Gerald said, "I am away the next two nights. Do it while I am away please."

Cordelia looked back at Dimitri, "Tomorrow night?"

"OK. Anyone want to join us?"

Genia, Dave and Daniel accepted the invitation.

Fel rejected the idea with a negative shake of her head.

Petra was shaking her head as well, laughing, "I don't like champagne so I'll pass."

Fel said, "Did we learn anything new this evening from our meeting with two guys with great imaginations?"

Cordelia said, "That sounded like more than imagination to me. That dark figure in the kitchen would have given me a heart attack."

Fel said, "Yes, but we have been here months and we haven't seen it."

Genia responded with a grimace, "And let's hope we never do. He said it enveloped him? And then trashed the kitchen?"

Dimitri said, "Genia and I both feel negative energy in the kitchen. Maybe George and the unlucky student were more sensitive to it than we."

Fel said, "We really don't know these people well. You are both susceptible because you accept the notion of ghosts as fact. You would be more easily fooled. No one else has seen or heard ghosts this past week. No one suspected ghosts until you two talked about it." She looked at Genia and Dimitri. "Some light around the chapel and stuck doors are not supernatural events."

Gerald intercepted, "While I agree the idea of ghosts was not on our radar you cannot dismiss what Daniel saw or the face in the window that Genia saw. To ignore their evidence discredits your argument."

"A ghostly imagination is not evidence," said Petra.

"The experience of a person is evidence," replied Gerald. "It is arrogant and limiting to say that because you don't believe, it can't be possible. Help us interpret it to suit you. Why did the doors bang so forcefully without wind or human agency? You were there Petra."

She answered, "I don't think it was some angry ghost."

"OK, then what was it? Who laughed behind Diane?"

Fel took over, "You believe it was a supernatural event?"

Gerald smiled at her, "I am saying you are both condescending in your arguments. And limiting. It is not good enough to deny something because it is not in your experience or beliefs. I am saying there was a time when the earth was believed to be flat and people were killed who disagreed. I am saying the same about air flight, the telephone and many more absurd notions. 'There are more things in heaven and earth, Horatio, than are dreamt of in your philosophy.'."

Dave joined the conversation, "Ah, our man Hamlet. Well done Gerald to bring the Bard into the conversation. He has a quote to win any argument."

Petra gave a snort, "Who is arguing? You're wrong. All I'm asking is that we consider other options."

Gerald said, "Exactly my point. What other options? But maybe our discussion needs to address what you imagine as God."

Petra said, "I was told as a child there was an old guy in a nightgown hanging out in the sky with thunder bolts. Not what you're thinking?"

Gerald said, "No, not at all. I think most atheists, if they listened, would realize those old images have little to do with faith."

Daniel changed the subject, "We seem to heading down a dead-end road. Forgetting the supernatural for a moment, I am still thinking about ancestors. I notice they mentioned marks in the cellar walls. We didn't find any because they are behind the wine racks. A definite task for tomorrow."

Gerald said, "Remind me why the marks are important."

Daniel said, "We have been trying to figure out where the ancestors lived. The letters had some clues about where our ancestors lived. She mentions marks on the wall of a room in the cellar where our ancestor, and his mother as well, were kept by the evil aunt. So tomorrow I will look behind the wine racks. We suspected this was the house and I guess we have basically decided this is the place where our ancestors lived. Just doing some extra verification."

Genia said, "I have something to show everyone. Daniel, Dave, Petra can you help me?" She led them to the library, returning in a moment. Each of them was carrying a portrait. Genia carried an oval wooden frame with the image of a beautiful, young woman with sparkling eyes and a suppressed smile. Dave carried a large, heavy wooden frame with a portrait of a grim-faced young man. Daniel carried a heavy, wooden frame with the image of a middle-aged woman with heavy brows and a disapproving face. Petra carried an image of a young boy. Genia, Daniel, Petra and Dave faced the troupe holding up the portraits for them to see.

Genia said, "The curator was here today. We brought down these portraits. There are a few more but these caught my eye. They are all painted circa 1830 by an English painter. The name is not well known. In fact, the curator said he must have been a family friend because the work is shoddy and only a family friend could get away with it. Strange reasoning, I know." She paused before saying, "Do you notice anything curious?"

Cordelia came closer to examine the images. Diane followed her.

Dimitri was chuckling and it was annoying Fel, "Out with it Greek man."

He said, "Don't you see? It is as plain as the nose on your face." He was now laughing, full of merriment.

The women by the portraits were looking at him standing beside Fel.

Diane gasped, "I get it. It's Fel. That beautiful young woman looks like Fel. Or rather Fel looks like her."

"Gracious," said Cordelia. "That's true. Same hair colour. Same shape face. Same shape of the eyes. Same green eyes. Put your hair up in a bun Fel. Smile just a little. Let's see."

Petra agreed, "Fel this could be you."

"No. That is nonsense," Fel objected. She began stepping back, away from the portrait. Away from them. She was becoming distraught.

Genia set the portrait on the floor, leaning it against the wall. "What's wrong Fel?"

"That does not look like me. How dare you suggest it. That is a tragic figure. A victim. I am nothing like that. How dare you." She looked at Dimitri. "You're always trying to make me look weak and simple." Dimitri had stopped laughing.

He turned to her, "But don't you know how much I respect you and admire you? I admire your spirit, your fighting spirit. Fel, you are a worthy opponent."

"Fuck off all of you," spitting her words at them as she started for the door.

Daniel spoke quietly, "Aunt Fel, I don't think our ancestor Bridget Mary Dimond was a victim. You are like her, beyond the physical similarities. She has fire in her letters. She was a rebellious woman. Look, she has a little smile despite the fact they disapproved of smiles at the time. She looks defiant. A look I often see in your eyes, like when you tell us all to fuck off. How shameful of you, young woman!"

Fel laughed.

Daniel continued, "I see strength in both of you. You were both caught in a place that didn't give you an opportunity to explore your life; your depth. For her it was a struggle to survive the evil of a sister-in-law who sought to control and brutalize her spirit. She held on to her love. You had all the love but sometimes that can be a trap in itself. Your parents and your paternal grandparents loved and overprotected you. You were the last in the nest and so they loved you and that love became a very comfortable cocoon. When it disappeared, your whole identity disappeared. So, you sought another cocoon and couldn't find it. That is sad but not tragic."

She was watching him. Everyone was silent. He continued, "From her letters I think she was a strong and resilient woman. A strength she found in loving deeply and believing in those whom she loved."

Fel said, "You are reading a lot into her letters and her image."

Daniel grinned at her. "Well I have been thinking about her a lot. And you. I know I am your annoying nephew, not much younger than you, but I also know you love me and you are proud of me. It just isn't your way to show it."

She grimaced at him and in a schoolmarm voice she ordered, "Everything you just said is bullshit. Let me see the portrait again."

They all crowded around her as she stood in front of the image. No one remarked again about the similarities, giving her time to adjust to the idea. Yet they crowded her, waiting for her reaction. Fel stared into the face of the woman she resembled, taking some time to see what they saw. She ignored them as she took her time. When she set it down she said, "If I look like her then we are probably related." She looked at Genia and Dimitri, "It looks like you have your proof."

Relieved, Genia said, "All the pieces of the puzzle are most definitely fitting together. This is the home of my, our, great, great grandfather. And I suppose, his mother, our 'great' times three. It is an amazing turn of events that we are here. I wonder if our brother had an inkling or had felt a spiritual connection when he came here. He certainly was insistent we needed to claim the place."

Everyone but Fel and Dimitri had moved to seats. Gerald poured some whiskey in a glass and sat down and began to sip it. His wife leaned against him. Dave put more turf on the fire. Diane and Petra joined Genia on one of the sofas. Daniel stood. Dimitri picked up the other portraits and stared into the faces. He held the portrait of the stern-faced man. "I don't see much of a resemblance here." He looked at Daniel's face. "Daniel could you frown for me? Give me a good grim look? Maybe I'll see you in here."

Daniel just smiled.

Dimitri then pointed at the child's portrait. "There are similarities between this one and the beautiful woman. Genia, didn't the conservator tell us to take them out into the sunshine tomorrow and compare features? I'll do it tomorrow, when the sun is at its brightest."

Cordelia said, "I believe I am emotionally exhausted. How many ghosts did we count? I wonder if it is your ancestors who haunt the old timbers? What are you going to do about it?"

The question was unsettling to Genia and her answer revealed the strain, "I wouldn't know. Is there a book? A 'How to Get Rid of Ghosts for Dummies' book?"

"Maybe it will be a wait and see scenario," said Daniel.

"But what will we see?" asked Dimitri. "I don't want to see the dark ghost."

"And I will miss the fun," Diane said standing. "OK, it may not be fun. I have to admit I don't share your courage and I feel quite spooked. I'm off to bed because I will be leaving early in the morning. They're sending a car for me before nine. I think the director is afraid I am too cosy here by the sea with my most excellent friends so the car will make sure I don't delay. Thank you Genia for this break away. I feel incredibly rested and blessed; except for the spooky aspects." She turned to Cordelia, "My gratitude to our entertainment director for not making me play Bridge."

Gerald laughed saying, "I think that's on the list for another night."

Diane turned to the others individually and expressed her joy for their friendship. Before she left the room she said, "My character for the next few months is an angry, embittered old hag who has ruined the lives of two people. She must find ways to make amends. So enough now with being nice as I move into my mean woman persona. Farrah Hadid is directing. I have never worked with her but I have been told she is deeply insightful. I need to up my game or go deeper into my scary inner self, to match her intensity. I might need a long break after the film, to get my dark side back under control."

Genia stood up to hug her. "It has been such a joy to have you here my dear friend. You are always welcome. Call any time if you need a reminder of how nice you are and how we love you. I will see you in the morning before you leave."

Everyone hugged her before she went to bed. Petra and Fel followed her up the stairs. The conversation they left behind in the sitting room, settled into the warm desultory mood of friends who are comfortable and happy to be together.

Chapter 24

Hours later a loud crash woke Daniel. He could hear the wind had not abated. He heard the thump the heavy waves make a second before the water turns into spray and splashes up. But there was another crashing sound and it was from downstairs. He guessed the front doors were open again and were banging in the wind. His bedroom door was closed. Reluctantly he threw back the warm covers and stood up. When he stepped into the hallway he saw Gerald, Dave, Genia and Cordelia had also been disturbed enough to leave their rooms. The foyer light was on which was odd. He knew he had turned it off before going to bed. But maybe someone had been up. Maybe someone was still up. The front doors were open, not so odd. A regular occurrence. One door was banging widely while the other was moving slightly. Odd that one door was more affected by the wind than the other. The cold and wet was blowing into the manor, the marble floors will be slippery. They all moved down the stairs. Daniel reached to close the doors but found one of the portraits at his feet. The right door was smashing against the portrait, which was jammed under the door. He pulled the door wide, bracing against the wind pushing back at him. He pulled the frame out from under the door and handed it backward to Dave. He turned and secured the doors.

He heard Genia gasp. She was looking at the oval portrait of Bridget Mary Dimond in Dave's hands. The painting was wet. The frame was damaged. No telling if there would be damage to the paint.

Genia went into the library to check the other portraits. The stern portraits were safe and dry. The child's portrait was missing. Daniel went back and opened the front doors to look around. He found it just out of reach of the doors with mud on the face of it. He brought it to the library.

Genia took it and said, "I'll let it dry before I wipe off the mud. I guess we have upset something with these portraits."

"The ghost?" Cordelia asked, her eyes wide.

"Unless someone in the manor did it. That is difficult to imagine. I would think ghost before I would ever think friend," said Genia.

"The doors were open and the lights on. There could be an intruder," said Dave.

"I locked the doors before I went to bed," answered Daniel.

"Then someone could have already been inside. I'll take a look around the downstairs," suggested Dave.

"I'll come with you," said Daniel and followed Dave out of the library.

Cordelia sat down on the sofa. "What do we do with the portraits this evening? This could happen again as soon as we go back to our rooms."

"I will take them into my room," Genia said. "Tomorrow I will put them in the chapel. I have a sense they will be safe there."

Cordelia looked worried, "Are you sure?"

"Yes, I think a point was made this evening and there won't be any more commotion."

"What point?" Cordelia asked.

"I think our dark ghost didn't like them and let us know just who is in charge. As either George or Jonah suggested, Bridget Mary is not allowed inside and I suspect the portraits would be included in that mandate. We'll talk tomorrow. I'm tired and a little pissed off. I need some sleep before I explore the antics of the spooky any further," said Genia.

Gerald said, "I was sitting here considering the same notion; a point has been made."

Dave and Daniel entered the library. Dave said, "Nothing downstairs and we checked the locks on the windows, the cellar door and the back door. All is tight."

"I'm heading back to bed," Genia said defiantly. "I have had enough nonsense and I need sleep." She took a portrait into the hallway, "You hear that Madame? Enough!!" Dave followed her with the other portrait, showing some support for her bravado. Cordelia turned to follow her but stopped to look back at her husband. She lifted one eyebrow.

Gerald answered the question implied by the lifted eyebrow, "I'm too awake to sleep. I think I'll stay here in the library and have a look at the letters. I haven't read them yet."

Cordelia nodded and went to the stairs, her voice trailing behind her, as she asked Genia, "So you've never seen or felt the ghost upstairs? I can sleep peacefully?"

Daniel spoke to Gerald, "I'll join you Gerald. My bed is not inviting right now. I'll just run upstairs and get a sweatshirt. My t-shirt is wet from the rain."

When he returned he walked over to the drinks tray in the corner. He picked up the whiskey and waved it at Gerald, who accepted. Daniel sat down opposite Gerald using the arm chair and matching ottoman Genia had used the previous morning.

Gerald laid aside the letters he had just read, "I am a little worried I will be away for two days. Do you think we could convince everyone we all need a break in Dublin?"

"That is an excellent idea. A change in perspective is needed. But I suspect Fel won't go and if Fel doesn't go, Genia won't leave her here alone. I can't leave Genia. But again, an excellent idea. Cordelia?"

Gerald simply shook his head, "Same scenario. Cordelia will not leave Genia." He swished his finger of whiskey inside his glass and then sipped. "What do you think is happening? I'm interested in your point of view Daniel."

"I'm not sure I have an intelligent point of view to offer. There is nothing in my experience to compare. I also think Fel and Petra have some valid points."

"The portraits tonight? You didn't find anyone downstairs and the two controversial portraits were the ones set outside. Who has been listening to our drama and would be clever enough to stage it?"

"If I was directing this nefarious drama I would have the villain sneak inside this evening as we were dining. The villain would be listening at the doors, moving surreptitiously about the downstairs. Maybe even looking in our bedrooms. Setting the portraits outside is a good scare tactic. I would have the villain sneaking out the front doors and waiting for our reaction."

"OK," Gerald nodded, "very good. Would you let the audience see the context/motive ahead of time and watch the planning unfold through the eyes of the villain or would you film it through the reaction of the victim?"

"Oh, the victim. Fear sells better than cunning."

"Do you think a human villain is causing the trouble here?"

"I might be more afraid of the 'who' than the 'It'; a human villain rather than a supernatural villain. Some spooky wisps of a ghost do not seem substantial enough to scare for long."

"And you think it can all be explained away without the supernatural ingredients? By Fel's reckoning we should have some investigators and bodyguards here. Yet when you and I examined the chapel we didn't find any trace of special effects. Same with the front doors and the back door. The gates at the end of the driveway were still locked."

"Yes, but ghosts?" Daniel took a sip from his glass. "I'm not ready to reach that far."

Gerald smiled at him, "I remember producing a film a few years ago in Spain. It was a very old castle. Lots of atmosphere. Strange noises. There were many legends attached to it. It had a reputation for being haunted. Nothing ever happened. No ghosts appeared. No scary howls. But strangely the film from the five days we were there was useless. We had checked it every evening as you do. Some great shots. Clear colours. Lovely balance of shadows and light. But back in London, at the studio, when we viewed it, we found it was a mess of strange sounds and wobbly lines with shadowy figures."

"You didn't blame the cameras or the camera guy?"

"No because I have worked with Faulkner many times. And we had viewed each day's work in Spain and been pleased with the results. Maybe one camera could be broken but not all five. He could not explain it."

"Someone may have sabotaged it?"

"No sabotage. Faulkner always had tight control over the product. Maybe there is a cause we don't know but the reason why I am leaning towards the supernatural is the content on the finished film. What we were fearful of encountering while there because of the stories we were told, was actually in the film; shadows, orbs, guttural sounds, even a violent scream which gave me shivers. So, my point is I am not closed to all options."

"Dimitri made a good point recently complaining that the entertainment industry seems consumed with all things supernatural lately and therefore controls the definition of the supernatural; usually violently evil. What does the supernatural look like really? What are your thoughts about it?" asked Daniel.

"I think he has a valid point. You and I have a responsibility to make films our grandmother would watch but that is not what the public buys. It's difficult to satisfy the public's need for fear and stay within our own values. Also, grandma's taste in films won't make blockbuster profits."

Daniel said, "My grandmother liked anything James Cagney starred in from dancer to gangster. Why does escapism need murder and fear? Some of the best films have depth. What is your favourite film?"

Gerald said, "Easy. Anything with Spencer Tracy. Especially the latter years. The director, Stanley Kramer, knew how to give Tracy his space and let him act. A great team. How about you?"

Daniel relaxed into the question, enjoying a conversation about making films with a respected peer. Sixty minutes later they both decided it was time to return to bed. The manor was quiet.

Chapter 25

"It speaks of rain and let's hope that's all it's doing: speaking. If it starts to even whisper to us we can go inside." Dimitri was chuckling as he welcomed his friends to his cottage. "Such an unusual turn of phrase, 'It speaks of rain'. I have often wondered about the origin of it. Come, find a cosy chair. There are pillows and quilts if you feel a chill off the water."

Genia, Cordelia, Daniel and Dave chose their seats and relaxed into them. Genia stretched out her legs with a groan, "I was in the graveyard today carefully pulling weeds. I had asked Niall if I could help him and he took me quite seriously. No quarter given. I suspect I will regret my offer in the morning when my back muscles begin to creak awake."

Cordelia responded, "So you're warning us you might fall asleep. We'll ignore you if you start snoring, but we'll listen if you start talking in your sleep. You might reveal some interesting delicacies about your hidden self."

Genia waved both hands at her, dismissing the teasing, "I live a boring life, except for when my lovely friends come to visit, so I think my hidden self would be boring. I do have a haunted house though. Which is unbelievable. It defies imagination."

Daniel said, "Unfortunately the one person who would have loved this ghost hunt isn't here."

Genia smiled at him, "Your dad, probably your mom as well. My brother was such a character. Always ready for an adventure."

Cordelia turned to Dimitri, "Thank you for hosting this little ghostly adventure and thank you Genia, Daniel and Dave for joining the fun. I am so very excited about seeing a ghost."

Dimitri said, “My pleasure. What could be more blissful then sitting on the edge of the Irish Sea, on a warm summer evening with people you adore, watching for ghosts after the stroke of midnight?”

“You’re funny my friend, but I agree,” said Dave. “I wonder if we will see anything on this cloudy evening? As you said it speaks of rain. I see the moon has been obscured by the clouds.”

“Do you believe in ghosts, Dave?” asked Dimitri.

“I am not so arrogant as to rule out the possibility of the supernatural. The universe is far greater and more mysterious than my pitiful life or my imagination.”

Cordelia asked, “And you Dimitri? What are your thoughts?”

Dimitri smiled, “I have no doubts at all.”

Genia interrupted, “Now it’s bugging me. What is the origin of that expression you used about rain, Dimitri? Is it a local idiom, a Greek idiom or a bit of old dialogue? Has anyone heard it before?”

“It’s vaguely familiar from my childhood but I don’t know it,” Cordelia said. “But I have heard another odd expression, ‘The devil is beating his wife’ to describe light rain on a sunny day. If the sun is vibrant in the sky and it starts to rain the devil is causing the wife’s tears to flow on humanity. Freaky heh?”

“Ugly heh? *Mon Dieu*,” Dave responded. “What a horrible thought. Violent. Vile really. I had an idiom I wondered about until I visited the childhood home of Shakespeare’s wife, Anne Hathaway: ‘It’s raining cats and dogs’. Someone was asking the tour guide why the beds had canopies. Oh, and by the way only rich people could afford canopies or even beds. The tour guide replied that bugs and mice and rats burrowed into the thatch on the roofs and sometimes fell through onto the bed. If it rained the straw would become slick and cats and dogs, who also snuggled into the thatch, would slide into the rooms.”

Cordelia roared with laughter, "No, that cannot be true. That is outrageous. What a thought; to wake up to a startled wet cat clawing at your face trying to get away."

Genia was laughing as well, "That's plausible Dave but I can't imagine a dog crawling into the thatch on a roof. What if it was a mastiff and it landed on you? A canopy wouldn't protect you. It could crush you. Ok, I have another version. I had heard the expression was related to the heavy rains in London and the open sewers in the 17th century. When the rain caused the sewers to overflow the dead cats and dogs that had been put into the sewers would be washed into the streets. It was a measure of the amount of rain that had fallen."

Daniel was laughing when he said, "I think today's speech lacks creativity. We have become pedestrian in our daily communication. Cats and dogs are more interesting as a measure of rain than to say, 'One inch or two inches of rain'. Imagine a weather man or woman predicting the rainfall as per a cat deluge. I suppose people would be phoning the TV station asking for exact predictions." He imitated the sonorous tones of a male TV reporter, "A cat deluge, ladies and gentlemen would be three inches deep and a dog deluge would be five inches depending on the breed."

Cordelia laughed, "Daniel, I agree we are a lazy generation when it comes to words. I hate to hear people use the word 'fuck' because it is a lazy word. It no longer has shock value. It's vulgar because of the laziness. When our children were young Gerald and I would give them rewards for finding the most interesting word to replace the word 'fuck'. They came up with some hilarious options. Gerald had the idea when Sam was twelve. Sam had come to his father in his study and said, 'I dropped my fucking bike.' Gerald said, 'What a strange way to describe your bike. What does it mean? They looked up the meaning and my twelve-year-old Sam was so horrified he became the one who challenged his brother and sisters to select new words. Some of their adjectives were bizarre. And it is interesting that Sam is now a playwright with a great fondness for words."

"I'd like to meet Sam. He sounds like a charmer," said Dave. "So here is an idiom that makes me cringe because of its origin: 'rule of thumb'." Dave looked at them, "I'm sure you've heard it before. Urban legend has it that it was spoken by an English judge circa 17th century, allegedly, when he ruled that it was perfectly legal for a man to beat his wife if the rod was no wider than his thumb."

Genia said, "I heard that as well. I suspect it relates to that monstrous proverb, 'spare the rod, spoil the child.' How much violence has that caused over the years? People often take the sacred word literally instead of using some common, compassionate sense. Do they really think a loving God would condone torture? On a child?"

Dave spoke, "Unfortunately my dear, people often are just that stupid. The sacred scripture, from all religions, has been used to justify the foul deeds of humanity."

Dimitri waved his hands to get their attention. He said softly, slowly, "Friends, look at the back door of the manor. The kitchen door. I turned out the outside light and the kitchen lights, yet there is light there now. A frail light."

Cordelia whispered, "Maybe someone turned the kitchen lights on."

"I have been watching the area. It didn't come on suddenly as a house light would do. It has been forming weakly, right there. Shapes." He looked at them. "Can you see? Move gently, over to me. I have a clear view."

They all saw a light which seemed to be getting brighter.

Daniel whispered, "I suggest we all watch and not speak so we don't disrupt the apparition. Later we will compare our impressions? Agreed?"

Everyone nodded.

Daniel watched as shapes formed. He was curious to see if he had remembered accurately. And he wanted to hear the impressions of others. He saw the same shapes as before. He still had an impression of two small figures sitting and one taller figure standing. Yes, he definitely believed he saw human forms. They were too defined to be anything but human forms. Again, he felt a sense of tragedy, as though they were seeking help. The postures conveyed defeat. The figures didn't move. He peered at their clothing. The cloak on the tall form was torn at the ankles. The smaller figures wore rags. Their poise looked like they were comforting each other.

The light around the figures was brightening, permitting even more clarity. From vague black and grey images, the light around them now revealed colour: a blue cloak, a tattered green shirt on one small figure, a dull brown on the other. Definitely, there was a woman standing and two little boys sitting on the step. The bones in their faces were clearly defined. Yes, desperation, Daniel thought. So thin. The woman's hand lay on the shoulder of the child closest to her. A high-pitched cry could be heard. The figures didn't move. The cry increased in intensity. It was a sound that penetrated his heart. Keening? The sound was pure, piercing grief. The figures made no such sound. No movement. The piercing sound was coming from the direction of the chapel. He noticed, as he looked for the source of the sound, that the chapel beyond the trees was all light now: a soft pure light with a blue tinge. It shimmered. Slowly the light swirled out of the chapel, oscillating above it. He could clearly see the outline of the chapel that had been obscure behind the trees, within the darkness of the evening.

He heard someone gasp. The delicate diaphanous light, was moving from the chapel towards the back door where the figures stayed motionless. It had a graceful swirl as it moved; an elegant beauty. The woman and the two boys were enveloped within the beauty of the light. Embraced. The keening softened in intensity. It changed to crooning. Then the light appeared to shrink slowly back to the chapel, rescuing the pitiable figures; taking them to the peace to be found there. The radiance dimmed and hauntingly faded.

All was dark again. All was silent.

No one spoke. Someone was weeping. Daniel felt a tightness in his own throat. He looked over and Dave was holding Genia in his arms, crooning to her in French. Dimitri was murmuring to himself, under his breath. Probably a prayer. Cordelia was standing, staring at the scene. There were just no words.

Eventually Genia and Dave sat down. Dave shifted his chair closer to hers and reached for her hand.

Cordelia whispered, "What did we just witness? What did we have the privilege of seeing?"

"I think we saw a deep compassionate response to a deep experience of suffering," Dimitri whispered with reverence in his voice. "A suffering that has left scars in time." He breathed deeply. "I don't know if I can discuss this right now, my friends. I am feeling overwhelmed. We were allowed to see something so sacred it defies words. We saw beyond the thin veil. I want to go inside, say my prayers and then write how I am feeling. I can't be objectively descriptive right now. Does anyone mind if I just leave? I need to hold the sacredness of the moment. Feel free to stay here."

Genia said quietly, "No, I am feeling the same. I think I will go to my rooms." She hugged each of them and walked off across the lawn. Dave went with her. They avoided the back door and walked towards the front of the manor.

Cordelia looked at Daniel, "Would you mind walking along the beach with me. You don't have to talk but I just can't go inside. I shouldn't have picked the night Gerald was away. I'd make that man pace with me if he was here."

"Of course," Daniel said. "Do you need a blanket?"

She took the blanket, silently hugged Dimitri and walked down the steps, turning towards the beach.

Dimitri retrieved a flash light from a table beside his chair. Daniel took it with a brief expression of gratitude to Dimitri. He followed Cordelia.

They walked silently within the darkness, using the small beam from the flash light, to guide their feet. Daniel was thinking over what he had just experienced. He realized, when he had approached the image the night he was returning from the beach, he had disturbed a scenario that must play out over and over again. The words hope and salvation roiled in his head. Love saved them? He imagined these were Famine victims turned away despite their pitiful states. Did they ever get food? Or did the tall woman in the shabby coat, have to watch her babes starve? And the light was ....? That was a more difficult question.

After thirty minutes Cordelia spoke quietly, pensively. "I didn't know it would affect me so strongly. It seemed like a lark to watch some ghosts. Eventually a story to repeat over a glass of wine and dinner when we returned to New York." She turned towards the calmed sea with her face turned upward. The stars were clearly defined now. The clouds had moved west. The universe was revealed to them; vast and mysterious. "I feel small in a very large, awesome universe."

Daniel didn't think a response was necessary. He knew his role was to walk, hold the flash light straight and listen as she mentally navigated her way through her thoughts and emotions. He was struggling with his own reaction. His first encounter with the figures at the back of the manor did not engender the emotion he was feeling right now. The world suddenly felt like a vibrantly sacred place for him. More dramatic. More intense. Larger. Mysterious. He felt .... peace in this moment.

Cordelia had turned around and they began the walk back. Daniel quietly matched her pace.

He saw the large stone at the top of the path. Someone was standing near the stone. They both stopped, cautiously peering into the night. They were a little spooked.

Genia spoke out into the night, in the direction of the beam of their flashlight, "Hello, I wondered where you had gone. I was pacing in my room and found I was too restless to stay there. I felt compelled to return. I feel drawn to the chapel. I'm going there, if you want to join me. Dimitri and Dave are at the cottage waiting for me."

Genia held out her hand to help Cordelia up the last few steps of the path, bracing her hand against the fairy stone.

Cordelia put her arm lovingly around Genia, "That's the best idea, Genia."

When they entered the chapel, Genia lit all the candles at the entrance, in the windows and on the stone altar. She said, "No electricity. I am debating the necessity of disturbing the ancient ambience with electrical wiring. Until then all the candles add a lovely peacefulness. And warmth."

There were two deep chairs in the sacred space and a wooden bench had been placed against one of the walls. Genia had begun to claim and define her favourite space with bright pillows, as well as some beautiful hangings in rich fabrics and bold colours. Daniel, Genia and Dave took some of the thick meditation pillows and piled them to use as a padded back and butt support, when they sat on the thick rug covering the stone floor. Daniel leaned back against the cool stone wall. Cordelia huddled in a deep chair with her quilt arranged around her shoulders. Dimitri took the other chair.

They sat silently for a long while, feeling the comfort of one another.

Dimitri said reflectively, softly, "I think the source of the expression I used, 'It speaks to rain' may relate to the writings of St. John of Damascus who wrote that the Creator speaks through Creation. There are messages in the rain, the wind, the sea and the trees. In all of nature. In light. We just need to learn the language. I think that notion resonates with most faith traditions."

There was a long silence as they pondered Dimitri's words.

Eventually Cordelia whispered, "I felt, as I walked on the beach, that the sand between my toes, the splash of the water and the chill in the air were all a part of me. I feel like I have been touched by the universe. Included in the universe. I know that sounds fanciful but I can't exactly express what is happening within me at the moment."

Daniel spoke softly as well, "That's interesting. I felt the same way. Feel the same way. As though I have been sleep-walking and just now woke up to see a surprising reality."

Cordelia spoke with some fervour in her voice, "Can someone explain to me what happened? I cannot describe the moment as seeing a ghost. I did not feel fear. I felt wonder. I felt beauty."

"I think we saw and felt a love that is eternal," responded Dimitri. His voice was soft, peaceful.

"Did I just see the Spirit of God?" asked Cordelia, trying to reflect his tone.

"I think what we saw was deep love in action. In some sense we did 'see' the Spirit of God."

"So, you think it was a ghost? Ghosts?" Cordelia asked.

"I go back to a conversation with Genia and Daniel some time ago. What is a ghost? Not what we see marketed on film to titillate the emotions and sell tickets. I think a ghost is a soul that lingers."

"What is lingering in my home?" asked Genia.

"A soul that doesn't know its way Home. A soul that fears defeat in death. A soul that created, through egoic self-determination, a complete blindness to Grace," replied Dimitri.

They were all quiet; pondering his words.

Cordelia said, "I was raised in church. I remember dressing up with little pink gloves on my hands, a pretty dress and sometimes a dainty hat. I remember being told to be good. I remember something about lambs. I don't remember my heart being engaged."

"Hmmm yes, Cordelia. That expresses it well. My heart is engaged," said Genia.

"*Mon Dieu*, is that what faith is?" asked Dave. "My mother is Muslim and my father claims to be Jewish. I have believed if I didn't kill anyone, steal, lie or cheat, etc., I was in line with the sacred teachings. That I was living in faith. No one mentioned this depth of feeling, this sense of connection with all that is around me."

Dimitri voice was still soft, peaceful, "We are often told faith is being 'good' and a punishing God defines what is 'good'. Human made laws regarding the practical application of being good have regulated most of our religions. I think the many religions have it backwards. Faith leaders should create sacred space so we can see God ourselves. Faith doesn't need to be taught. Ask for faith. It is given. Goodness doesn't need to be taught. Faith encourages our goodness. Faith reveals the invisible. We cannot explain it to one another. Or preach it." Dimitri stopped suddenly looking at them. "Sorry, I have some faith baggage."

Genia replied as thoughtfully, "I want to experience the divine, not be told about it in wise theological attempts at proofs."

Cordelia took a deep breath and said, "I cannot shake the 'story' we saw this evening. Who is the light?"

Genia said, "Let me be unscientific and speculate. Good thing my sister isn't here. I think it's my ancestor who died in this chapel and I think she continues to save people. I wonder if that scenario is played out every night or just some nights."

"Our ancestor? You think that was Bridget Mary?" Daniel asked in surprise. He looked out the window thoughtfully. "Yet now that you say that, it seems to make sense. A compassionate face in the window looking for something or someone. A compassionate response to the poor outside her door. Light rather than darkness. A compassion that comes with a perfume. Her roses? Her precious roses?"

Dimitri spoke, "I see you have put up the portrait of her and her son. That must have caused some change in the energy here."

"Yes, I hope so. I hope the portraits brought her some peace," said Genia. "I want her to find peace."

"Yes, but I feel she is somehow connected to the one inside so maybe she can only find it when they both find it," said Dimitri.

"Let's hope it's soon," replied Genia.

Chapter 26

Daniel realized he was rubbing his eyes and it wasn't for the first time in the last thirty minutes. He looked up from his laptop, pulling his attention away from the manuscript he was reading on the screen. His agent Samuel had sent it to him soon after he had arrived at Genia's but he was just now reading it. Samuel had been right. It was a good script. A very good script. It had certainly kept him riveted for the last few hours. He looked down at his scribbles on the note pad under his elbow. He had subconsciously begun to map out how to 'shoot' the story. He thought he might show it to Gerald tomorrow. Gerald was back from his trip to Dublin and its environs.

Checking his watch, he saw that midnight had long passed. The manor was quiet. He needed a break and a munch. He quietly left his room and headed to the kitchen to explore the leftovers in the fridge. He found the ingredients for an abundant sandwich: lots of cream sauce, layers of old cheddar from the local farm, thick cured ham and as a nod to health, a lettuce leaf and a tomato slice. Ah, maybe a pickle too. He grabbed a sink cloth and wiped the mess of cream sauce off the counter while gathering his few utensils to be cleaned. Knife, spoon and the extra plate went into the dishwasher and the food back to the fridge. With the smile of a hungry man he turned back to his sandwich. It was on the floor and the plate was broken. How on earth? Bemused he stared at the mess on the slate floor. How did he not hear the crash? He laughed at his tiredness and heard an echo of his laugh behind him. He swung around quickly seeking a familiar face but there was none. He was alone. The laugh was repeated but it sounded like a stifled crackle. He looked at his feet thinking he might have stepped on something that would crackle. Paper? The lights dimmed as he attempted to rationalize the sound. He shook his head. Tired eyes. Tired mind. Tired ears. He stooped to clean the mess before starting the process of recreating the perfect sandwich.

As he stooped he saw it. In the doorway between the kitchen and dining room a velvet dark shape had appeared. It looked solid. Nothing vaporous about it. Slim. Less than two meters tall. It had a vague human form. There was no movement. No sound. No eyes or mouth. Just a deep dark void. This was not a shadow.

He stood watching the void a few feet from him. He was trying to find an explanation for what he saw. Was it a mirage like what he and the others had seen by the back door two nights ago? A harmless mirage? He caught movement to his left and realized the cupboard doors above his head were opening and closing quietly. How odd. Then he was struck by a wave of mental sewage washing over him. He began to gag.

The kitchen lights went out.

Cold, roiling fear hit his gut. He had no response to this experience. He felt hatred filling him, a feeling that came from outside of him. He knew the darkness had moved towards him because the foul feeling of hate increased. He felt enclosed. Chilled. Its presence was squeezing out all hope, all joy from him. It was a total absence of good. A curious smell invaded his senses: dirt, mossy damp dirt. Graveyard dirt. He felt a tightness in his chest. His breath was clogged. It was a cruel foul embrace. Was he having a heart attack?

He heard a scream behind him as the muscles in his legs slackened. The squeezing stopped suddenly but the hate remained. The vile presence turned its concentrated attention away from him. Fel was standing in the doorway with the light from the hallway outlining her. The dark shape hovering over him must have been obvious to her because she responded with a commanding voice.

"Daniel," she yelled, "get up. Move over here." She shouted upstairs, trying to wake the people sleeping upstairs. "In the kitchen," she yelled. "Wake up Genia. Come to the kitchen. Dave. Gerald. Help!!"

The entity slipped away from Daniel and moved towards her. He felt intense relief. He fell to his knees and drank in the fresh air; all his lungs could absorb in large gasps. The hall light went out and the kitchen door snapped closed. Fel screamed. Daniel was trying to sort out in his mind why she was screaming. He knew he needed to get to her. He was laying on the slate floor in the dark kitchen. Reluctant to move, unable to move. But he had to move. He slowly twitched a finger, then his hand and his arm. His energy had been drawn out of him by the dark entity. Pushing against the cold floor he got on his knees. He crawled toward his aunt. She was moaning now. The foul hate must have captured her. He struggled to open the kitchen door that opened inward, towards him. He had to lift himself higher to reach the door knob. He was sucking in air. He crawled up the door, fingers grasping the decorative moulding and then the door knob. He had to pull it open to crawl through. All movements were needing the energy he had lost. God, he was cold. He could barely see. Where was she? He heard doors opening upstairs. Still on his knees he was now through the kitchen door reaching for his aunt. Where was she? Was the dark around her? The moans were moving away from him. He felt a cool breeze and knew the front doors at the end of the hallway must have opened. Why? What? Unbelievably Fel was being dragged down the hallway, away from him, towards the doors. He tried to speak but his throat released only guttural sounds.

Fog entered through those same doors bringing a sweet perfume. The fog was blue translucent light. It had a vague human form. He could see the dark entity move back, away from his aunt who was lying still on the floor. It rose up to face the light. He heard

Genia gasp above him on the stairs and someone cry out. The light surrounded Fel who lay motionless. He heard a soft, soothing croon coming from the light. It was a gentle sound in the midst of his terror. He saw the dark entity growing in size as it moved towards the comforting sound. It was without sound as it hovered above them all. The beautiful light left Fel and rose to meet the darkness. Both light and dark mingled, becoming a swirl above Fel. Daniel held an image in his head of a childhood ice cream cone with a vanilla and chocolate ice cream mix swirled together in a cone. This swirl was a surreal energy acting out a storied relationship. The two parts of the swirl struggled for dominance; undulating around and around. The light began to dim, reduced to a milky fog. The swirl moved to the open doors and separated. The light was pushed outside. The doors slammed shut.

The dark remained, hanging above them in the foyer. All the lights came on and the velvet shape was clearly outlined. It twirled around to face them. It was still large. The foul had won a battle for supremacy, Daniel thought. This was his impression even though there was just a vague human form without a face to show expression. It hung in space, triumphant. Slowly, taking its time to leave them, it faded. The smell of dirt and the thoughts of hate trailing behind. He heard the cackle of laughter.

Genia ran down the stairs and stumbled to her knees beside her sister. She lifted Fel's shoulders against her chest and began to rub her sister's face, "Fel honey, wake up." She kept repeating the anguished words. Petra joined her on the floor on the other side of Fel and rubbed Fel's arms.

Daniel stood with the help of Gerald and Dave who had appeared on either side of him. He felt trashed. His body was exhausted by the experience; his life force sucked dry.

Gerald said, "Let's take you to the library. Cordelia pour some whiskey for shock. Can someone light a fire?"

The front doors opened again starling them. Daniel cringed backward in fear. But this time it was Dimitri. He looked at Fel at his feet with Genia bracing her and saw Daniel being supported by the two men. He reached down and helped Genia lift an unconscious Fel to standing, then he simply lifted her into his arms.

"Library," Gerald pointed. Dimitri moved in that direction. He laid Fel on one of the sofas and pulled the bright comforter off the back of the sofa to tuck around her.

"What happened?" he asked with a whispered urgency. "I was sitting on my porch when I saw the chapel light up and that light move towards the front of the manor. I could hear keening and then a scream from inside the Manor. What happened?"

Cordelia was passing out sips of whiskey to everyone. No one refused. By now Daniel was sitting down. His head was bent over his glass and he was using it as smelling salts. He lifted it to his lips. He needed the heat of it, the fire of it to clear his throat. His throat was tight. He didn't know if he could talk. It wasn't just the physical weakness. He wanted to weep. He had been completely helpless and demoralized in his helplessness. He wanted to howl to break up the chunk of fear stuck in his chest. Petra came over to him and began to rub his shoulders. That simple act of compassion seeped into his spirit, warming him and lessening his despair.

He heard Genia whispering an answer to Dimitri, "I was asleep. The screaming that you heard, Dimitri, woke me up. I struggled to get to the hallway, recognizing my sister's voice. She was yelling at us to wake up and then she just screamed. An agonizing, horrible scream." She crossed her arms across her waist in a self-comforting gesture.

Dave fit his arms tightly around Genia. His voice was strained, "We almost knocked each other over as we responded to the screams. At first the foyer was cold and dark. I noticed the doors opening. No one was there to turn the locks or the handles and yet they opened by themselves. Fel had been screaming but she had stopped. There was silence. I started down the stairs," he looked over at Gerald and Cordelia, "and someone was beside me." He nodded a question in Gerald's direction, "You?"

Gerald nodded silently in agreement. His face strong and calm.

Looking back at Dimitri, Dave said, "I yelled because it was now quiet which was scarier than the screaming. And darkness was .... there was a stench." His voice trailed off as he shook his head silently.

Petra was now rubbing Daniel's temple. She said softly, "I screamed in response. An unconditioned response to fear I guess. I couldn't see anything but I was feeling violated by something; like something foul was rubbing against me. Then the mist entered the foyer. It became luminous. That was beautiful. I began to feel hope in a drama that I didn't understand."

Dimitri walked over to look out the window towards the chapel. "There is still a faint light there. Anyone want to go look?"

They all turned towards the window but no one stirred in that direction.

Dave sighed, "I guess we have all had enough of the supernatural for this evening. What time is it anyway?"

"It's past two," Cordelia said.

Genia walked over to check her sister on the sofa, "Should we call a doctor?"

Cordelia asked, "What would we say?" She bent over Fel. "Is she asleep? Did she faint from the experience? Or get knocked unconscious when she fell?" She felt for a bump on Fel's head and shook her head no when she didn't find one. She began to rub Fel's feet.

Daniel cleared his throat and answered in a cracked whisper and abbreviated sentences, "Fel saved me. I was in the kitchen. Making a sandwich. It appeared. It attacked. It was just suddenly ....

But maybe it had been watching me. No warning. The kitchen light .... out. Surrounded by hate. Couldn't move. Squeezing me. My knees, shaking." His throat clenched and he had to breathe deeply to release his voice.

They waited.

He leaned forward, and in a rush, said, "Fel must have been coming to the kitchen herself for food. When she opened the door from the hallway and saw it around me she yelled for you. It turned away from me and went after her. It was dragging her to the front doors. Did you see that? How? How could it do that? The thing leaches your energy. It masters you. I think Fel's in shock and may need to recover her body heat and her energy before she wakes up." He leaned back against Petra's warmth.

Dimitri turned abruptly from the window. "I'm going to go out to the chapel. We have felt only goodness and hope from the light, right?" They mostly all nodded but cautiously. "Then I think I will walk over and just hang around. Anyone else?"

Petra held out her hand to him, "The ex-atheist will join hands with a faithful man and take her chances. Let's go."

"No," both Genia and Cordelia said forcefully.

Cordelia continued, "Let's just wait a moment. Please. Let's take a moment and consider this. Dimitri you didn't experience what we just now experienced. For certain these past few days have taught me that we should yield the darkness and the light more respect. The dark might be provoked to return if you go to the chapel. None of us can cope with any more of that tonight."

Genia added, "Let's look at this in the warmth of the sun tomorrow. Actually, later this morning. I think some plans will have to be made because we can't linger in a place where we are attacked by invisible forces."

"Sunshine is a great idea," said Dave. "Outside works for me."

"OK," said Dimitri. "Does anyone want to spend the night in my cottage? There is an extra bed there, a sofa and some comfy chairs on the porch."

No one responded immediately. His invitation had taken them a step further into this new reality, reminding them this was not over. They had no control of what haunted them. He had offered a practical response to the fear they were feeling, anticipating a desire to escape for a few hours.

"I'm worried about Fel," Genia answered. "Let's take her to your cottage. I'll come and sit with her. If she doesn't wake by morning I think a doctor should be called."

"A good idea," said Dimitri. "We can put some good energy around her."

Genia smiled and turned to the others, "How is everyone else feeling? Want to join us?"

Cordelia said, "I have never heard that the dark entity has been seen upstairs. I'll take my chances in my bedroom." She looked at her husband. "If you're coming now as well?"

He stood up and took his wife's hand, "Yes my love, let's go snuggle under the covers. How is everyone else?"

Dave said, his French accent strong in his emotion, "I'll go with Genia and Dimitri to help carry Fel. I also need to feel the good energy."

Petra asked, "Daniel can I share a bed with you for the rest of this evening? I promise I have no intention of seducing you. I am cold and afraid. It's a shock to suddenly be confronted by the supernatural. I might have nightmares."

Daniel stood and held out his hand to her, "I welcome the warmth. Do you snore?" They left the room as Dimitri picked Fel up from the sofa. Genia followed him leaving on the lights.

Chapter 27

Daniel heard voices below his window the next morning. He rolled over and looked at the clock by his bed. Almost nine. Petra had left the bed. Her side was still warm so she hadn't been long awake. He fell back against his pillow and let out a long slow groan as the memory of the early morning hours crept back into his head. He rubbed and rubbed at his face, attempting to scrub away the memory of the darkness, his weakness in the midst of it and his inability to even form words to speak of it. He really didn't want to go downstairs and discuss what had happened. He hadn't rested well. Petra was a restless sleeper and had kicked him a few times in the night, waking him up. Within seconds the memory would pour back into his head and he would feel the anxiety and fear, looking to see if the bedroom door had opened. He'd calm himself back to sleep and then Petra would kick him awake again. By sunrise he was resenting her. But he slept again and now, after two brief hours, he had to face his family and friends.

What had happened to Fel? Did she wake up? How would she feel today? Her final scream had rippled through his body. Still did. He hadn't been able to get to her. He felt shame because he hadn't been able to save her. He had been drained of physical strength. He remembered when he was a young boy, ten maybe, he'd been caught in an undertow just off shore. Fortunately, his dad had heard him cry for help after the current had sapped every bit of energy out of him. He could barely walk for hours afterward because his muscles had been so depleted by the battle against the undertow. Last night had been the same and there had been no preparations for that battle. If Fel had not saved him what would have happened? Concern for her and the smell of coffee moved him out of the bed.

Everyone except Fel was outside in the sunshine. Genia had a pot of coffee, sweet rolls and jam on the table in the gazebo. They welcomed him and fortunately they were listening to Dave's memory of the first play he headlined in Paris, a play that had received bad reviews.

Dave was saying, "One reviewer commented that it was my fault because my French sounded fake and I should have spent more time practising. *Mon Dieu*, I am French. It is my first language. I left that reviewer a long response on his answering machine, in French."

They laughed at his passionate look of disgust.

Cordelia said, "Speaking of language, my worst review was my attempt at an Irish accent in a film I starred in many years ago. I still cringe. I don't know how I have the gall to be in Ireland. I imagine people pointing and staring at the American who butchered their lyrical language. If it had been a play it would have been over and gone, leaving behind only sad, regretful memories but that film still plays on. I see it on late night television and I suffer through it occasionally to keep my humility." She lowered her head in a pose of a humble woman.

"You aren't fooling anyone, my dear," her husband said.

Dimitri was looking over their heads towards the manor, "Genia, have you seen Fel since she left the cottage?"

Genia said, "Yes, she told me she wanted to do some research in Cork and wouldn't be back until late."

"So, she's alright?" Cordelia asked.

"She woke up after a few hours, got into a fight with Dimitri when he asked her how she was feeling. She left the cottage upset at all of us. Later she came to me in the kitchen as I was talking to Fiona about the day's chores and told me she was taking my car for the day. She wasn't receptive to questions," answered Genia.

Cordelia looked at Daniel and he felt his stomach tighten. His head was screaming no, don't, please don't ask. She asked, "How are you?"

Daniel forced a laugh and said, "I'd feel better if I had more sleep. Petra kept kicking me and she talks in her sleep. Long orations about her scandalous life."

Petra objected, "I do not talk in my sleep. Do I? Did I say anything interesting?"

"Yes, a most definitive yes. I will reveal all someday if you bribe me. Otherwise I could get a few bucks from the gossip papers. Imagine the headlines: 'Famous playwright has a potty mouth in her sleep'."

Petra protested, "I'm sure I do not! No way!"

"Maybe you were talking out a new salacious play? Wow, that will be some play, is all I can say."

Petra laughed at him, "You're making all this up. I hope."

He had successfully turned the attention away from himself, "You'll never know." He turned to Dave, Genia, Dimitri, Gerald and Cordelia, "I want to run an idea past the wisdom of this gathering. Last night I had the impression we saw a story being played out. In fact, I think Petra said something about it as well. Let me tell you my impression of a story line and you can tell me what you think." He looked to them for consensus. "OK then. I saw the dark entity pulling Fel to the open front doors; our Fel who looks like our ancestor who had suffered in this house but died in the chapel. When the bright entity came in the doors, I assume from the direction of the chapel, the dark released Fel. The light crooned over Fel. I think we all felt relief when the bright entity entered the story. Then the dark and the light struggled. The light was pushed out. The doors slammed. I think, and I am being careful, I think the dark rules the house and prevents the light from entering. I know we are very careful about facts and not making assumptions but I don't know how we find facts about a ghost story. An ancient ghost story. So, I suggest we speculate. And remember George and Jonah suggested a similar story."

Genia was frowning, "I think, and I am also being careful here, I think the night we found the portraits of our ancestors outside in the storm we were given a huge clue that there was conflict, considering which portraits did not get put outside."

Dimitri said, "For the sake of argument, maybe it hadn't had time to put out the others."

Dave agreed, "You have some good basic points Daniel. Dimitri I think it has had the last few nights to put out the other two portraits and it hasn't."

Gerald asked Genia, "You put the other portraits in the chapel?"

"Yes and so far they're safe," she responded. "I have put some family pictures in the chapel as well. If it is my ancestor, the mother of the early Daniel, she might like to see his pictures."

Dave nodded, "Pictures of your ancestors from the farm, set in the library would be interesting as well. To see if there is a response."

"It might be a negative response. I don't know if I want to pull the tail of the dark one. But what are we going to do?" asked Cordelia. "We can't live like this in fear of such a dark presence."

They all looked at each other silently.

Gerald spoke up, "I guess we now know it isn't paparazzi or someone with a grudge stalking us."

"I wish it was," answered his wife. "I never thought I would consider those hounds a better torment than something worse."

"But what do we do?" asked Genia.

Daniel spoke thoughtfully, "We know a séance is a bad idea."

"Good grief, no." Genia responded.

Daniel again, "A priest?"

Dimitri said, "I have some seminary training," he nodded at them as all but Genia reacted with surprise, "yes, enough to know better than to attempt any rituals other than prayer. Genia has spoken of trying to pour good energy into the manor and failing. We have seen just how powerful the dark entity has become after years of hate. We undeniably felt it last night."

Cordelia said, "Yes, in my bones. As one of the past owners said at dinner It, and I use the capital 'I', It, will not be easy to forget. I respect their courage in returning here considering what they had experienced."

Dimitri nodded in her direction, "With such intense hate we cannot address this lightly or without some planning."

Gerald said, "So you think there is a chance to defeat it?"

"I think we'll need to do some serious research. I can discretely contact some respected spiritual leaders and probe their thoughts. I'll tell them I'm researching for a film," said Dimitri.

"So you think there is a possibility?" asked Genia with some vulnerability showing.

Dimitri said, "Just keep singing your happy songs, my friend and thinking good thoughts. We'll see how the divine responds."

Chapter 28

Daniel stood within the darkness of the night looking up at his bedroom window. He could feel the breeze off the sea, wet on his neck. He was so tired. He had been pacing for four nights, unable to sleep, leery of the darkness inside the manor, wary of his dreams and mostly afraid to be in the kitchen. He was taking morning naps in the hammock. He hoped he was hiding his anxiety from the others. Yet, everyone seemed subdued now, fearful. It seemed like they were waiting for something undefined to happen. He could see Genia was worried. Dave was hovering and protective of her. Daniel wondered if their past intimacy was being rekindled. Cordelia was trying to keep spirits high by introducing games. Her husband stayed quietly close. Petra and Dimitri spent a few hours, each day, on the cottage veranda in conversation about faith and the divine and the veil. Petra said she was experiencing space in her life and needed to know more. Dimitri told her his words would just build more boxes and she needed to avoid boxes and explore her new and brighter space. He mostly taught her how to meditate and develop a gratitude attitude as a precursor to wonder. She railed against his unwillingness to give her form and substance. Dimitri argued that faith meant learning to live within the freedom of the spirit. 'Go to the source,' he told her, 'and be ready for some surprises'.

Daniel had pretended he had some work to do and had either stayed in his rooms during the days or created reasons for some solitary walks through Wicklow county. Fel was still absent. When she woke up at Dimitri's cottage, after the encounter, she was vehement about rejecting the care and concern that was being offered to her. She had sent word she was staying in Cork to do research. He suspected she was struggling with the same feelings that kept him standing on the beach at midnight staring longingly at the windows of his comfortable bedroom. Fel was less likely to reveal her vulnerability than him.

He heard someone calling his name and saw Dimitri standing by the fairy stone. Yes, Dimitri the night person, would be awake. He walked towards Dimitri urging a smile on his face to replace his look of anxiety. “Hello Dimitri. You’re up late. It must be past midnight. I’ve been getting some air and looking at the stars. Lovely night.”

Dimitri braced one hand against the fairy stone and reached towards him with the other. He took Daniel’s hand and pulled him up the last two steps of the pathway. “I always find these last steps a little tricky, especially at night. They have a slight slant.” He let go of Daniel’s hand and answered Daniel’s question, “I’m up because the night gives me peace and my creative energy is free to soar. Tonight, I have been watching you pace the beach. You stop often to look at the manor, more than you look at the stars. Tell me what concerns are behind your fake smile.”

Daniel started to laugh. An awkward laugh that released some of the tension in his gut. The laugh dwindled into a slightly desperate wheeze. When Dimitri invited him into the cottage Daniel hesitated. He didn’t want to talk. But he felt a nudge at his back from Dimitri and reluctantly stepped inside Dimitri’s home for the first time. The entrance opened directly into a cosy sitting room. The walls were painted white with the blue of the Aegean Sea as an accent colour. A Greek key design artfully outlined dozens of framed photos of moments on stage, as well as groupings of family and friends. There was a small library in one corner of the room where two large deep chairs were arranged under the light of a reading lamp. Daniel sat there. Across the room from his chair, he noticed two religious icons hanging on the wall, at waist level, above some pillows. A candle holder rested on a nearby side table. He imagined it was the place where Dimitri meditated.

"Dimitri, you mentioned once that you had left the seminary after a few years of study. Why did you leave?"

"Ah, Daniel: a distraction. OK, I will give you some time to gather your thoughts. But we will talk about the anxiety I have seen in you."

Dimitri looked over at the icons and sighed. A huge sigh. "I left the seminary because I felt organized religion had lost its way. My great grandmother, my *Progiagia*, taught me wonder when I was very young. She was my principal caregiver. My parents and my grandparents were busy working, trying to exist through the hard times in Greece. Besides teaching me how to appreciate all Greek food my *Progiagia* told me if I ever wanted to see the divine I should use wonder as my looking glass. 'Look for beauty,' she would say, 'and let your heart be enraptured within it.' I grew up knowing the divine communicated through love no matter which religion you professed. I was inspired to study to be a priest and share that simple message with everyone. I couldn't believe most people didn't know their own truth: their value, their beauty as revealed through the holy. But what I found as I studied, the fault for that lay in the organized religions. I became disillusioned and one day I woke up with tears in my eyes realizing I had lost the wonder, the awe my *Progiagia* had taught me. I had lost the possibility of seeing the miraculous. So, I left to find it again."

"Why the stage?"

"The stage gave me and still gives me an opportunity to live in creative wonder."

"You never married?"

"There are few real people in the world. Your aunts are real."

"Felicity?"

"Yes, she thinks deeply, feels deeply but doesn't trust anyone to love her. She hides behind the negative walls. Your Aunt Fel has not had the advantages of Genia; to be tested and honed by the world, finding her own power, her beauty. Everyone comments on her physical beauty but her real beauty is buried deep so no one can see it and attack it. Genia has been able to shine because she has been honed by the fire of life. Felicity has had only the protected love of parents and grandparents on an isolated farm. After the death of those she could trust to love her, she left the farm and followed a successful sister, still not finding her own strength and inner beauty. I have great love and respect for her."

"But she hates you."

"No. She hates my ability to see her vulnerability. I don't let her hide. But Daniel let's talk about the hidden you. It has been a few days since you encountered the darkness. What are the residual effects? This is between us so don't worry. I won't repeat what you say."

Daniel gave him a quiet smile, "It's interesting that you name that concern about confidentiality. I am feeling closed off from the others and I haven't wanted to discuss my feelings. But confidentially? Man to man? I am terrified of encountering It again. I am not physically fearful. I am not worried about being physically hurt. I am fearful of how it made me feel, to the depths of my soul. I was," he stopped and struggled with the next words, coughing to mask the potential tears choking him. "I am still feeling demoralized, degraded. As well, I feel like I have gone through life falsely believing I had control of my life and now I realize it was a mendacious security I was taught from birth. Does that sound odd? That I no longer feel secure about who I am?"

Dimitri said, "Not really. A great theologian, an Ulster man, wrote about the dilemma of fear. He posed the problem of being ordered to enter a room with a tiger in that room. You have fear but already you're thinking of how to cope with it. You're planning strategy and taking stock of your physical strength and capabilities. If you're smart you'll say a prayer asking God to put the tiger in a good mood. The damage will probably be physical. But life has given you coping mechanisms.

But what if the room you are ordered to enter holds a ghost? How do you prepare for that? How do you prepare spiritually to encounter what is behind the veil? Especially if your life has never understood or considered even the possibility of another reality beyond the veil?

There is a third room: the divine. Are you ready to meet the divine? That was the work of the religious leaders over the centuries but instead they taught and planned in reaction to the first room instead of the second or the third, telling us to follow all the rules. Most of the rules were dictated by culture rather than spiritual awareness.

Nothing in life has prepared you for anything more than the common place challenges. You are a man. You can fight off a physical assault. But nothing in human history has prepared you or any of us to meet the supernatural. We are at a place in history where that divine wisdom is slowly being reintroduced to us."

Daniel sat in silence pondering Dimitri's words and then gave a brief negative shake of his head.

"Was it evil I encountered?"

"No, you encountered the remnants of a life lived without love or compassion, justice and a wishing well for others. Basically a bully. It is just a void without a compass Home. It can't let go of the only place it dominated and derived power, so it lingers and continues to bully. A bully dominates through fear and control, finding the vulnerable within us and mocking it."

Daniel said, "I don't have your spiritual background. How would you prepare for the scenario of the ghost in the next room that your Ulster theologian posed?"

"Well maybe by not assuming what I will meet is something out of a horror novel. Not all ghosts are scary. Some are benevolent beings bringing warnings or comfort. Secondly by being prepared spiritually; prepared no matter the light or darkness of the supernatural you will meet. You saw the light and the darkness battle. The light dimmed in the face of so much hatred. Hatred, a foul hatred, which attacked you, is truly wounding. What do you have within you to fight it? A strong belief in yourself? Faith? Is your soul strong? A soul is made strong by an awareness of the holy. How aware are you of this other powerful, amazing realm that surrounds you? How often have you wrestled in faith to understand eternity? Your soul?"

He paused to let Daniel absorb his words. "Let me continue the theologian's analogy. The first room is the tiger. The second room is the ghost and the third room is the Spirit of God. Enter that room with silent humility and wait. Don't have words or expectations. Wait and listen. There is nothing within you that can begin to understand the mystery of the Spirit of God. That comes from God.

Dimitri paused to let Daniel respond. Daniel was silent, considering his friend's words. Then Dimitri continued, "How do you prepare for a bully ghost? Much the same as in this reality: prayer, positive response, projection of your own strength and coping with your own fear. Our fear saps our power. Fear is a common ploy used by governments, advertisers and bosses to control the masses. We all fall for it. Conquer your fear and you will have your freedom back. But pray as you battle. You have spiritual power. Find it."

"Conquer my fear against a darkness that attempts to dominate?"

"What is really bothering you Daniel? Is it how you feel demeaned and weakened by the entity? You have to forgive yourself and shake it off. Move on. You have encountered your worst challenge. You know fear. You've met something that scared you into feeling useless. Now get control back. But pray first. Be spiritually prepared. Find your spiritual power."

~~~~~~~~~~~~~~~

As Daniel walked back to the manor after his meeting with Dimitri he mulled on the last words, 'Now get control back.' Why not now? He decided he needed to address his enemy. He could not walk in fear any longer. It was limiting him. He no longer went into the kitchen at night. He knew It had also appeared in daylight but somehow the daylight made him feel more protected. He had to stand up to the bully power. He wanted to sleep in his own bed.

It was way beyond midnight now. He opened the front doors and walked into the foyer. He stood at the foot of the stairs, arms wide, stance strong and said in a quiet, mocking voice, "Come on witch. Now. Here. Let's give your haunting a second act. Let's see what you can do. Dropping some pictures from the walls, slamming doors and night time creaks are all amateurish. Some squeezing and some ugly laughter is weak. Hey, a mouse could do better. Are you a mouse? Let's see some real action."

The air stirred slightly. The wind around the doors sent in a draft. Or was it her? In insolence he waited pushing down the fear inside. "So you have nothing, no imagination? Let me help you, let me direct you. How about some howling? Some spine-chilling howls? Being a bitch, I suspect some barks would suit you better. Just a little bark, bitch, or would mouse squeaks be your limit?" Daniel felt his knees tremble a bit but he didn't back down. He further mocked his opponent with a laugh. "You have failed. You
~~~~~~~~~~~~~~~

have been defeated. Get out, go wherever darkness goes and just disappear."

The heavy doors crashed open behind him. The cold was fierce. The air foul. Daniel stood strong, defiant, his hands on his hips. "So more slamming doors is your miserable response?" He lifted his hand to pinch his nose, "And the stench of your presence with it."

Daniel felt pressure against his back. "Is that your cold snout pushing me, bitch?" A frigid claw dug into his hair, scraping and pulling. The cold pushed him towards the open doors. He grabbed the banister with his left arm, the other twisted within the spindles. A force slammed into his right arm while ice ripped at his head. He swung that arm backwards, twisting from his shoulder, arching his back. His dark enemy took advantage and slammed cold into the centre of his back, shoving his chest into the banister. Daniel's knees collapsed and he fell bashing his head against the oak post. Angry, he rolled over quickly, pulling away from the icy grasp on his head.

Gasping he said, "Come on bitch. More? A little pushing and cold? Or should I call you beloved Aunt Alice? Alice Flora. Did no one love you?"

His words had caused a reaction. He sensed the invisble entity had retreated suddenly. Maybe a sign of shock?

He pushed his advantage into it. "Yes! I - am - your - nephew. I am Daniel Irial Dimond's descendent. I am Bridget Mary's great, great, great, great grandson. I have come to claim Daniel's house. I will open the doors for his mother to return. She will rule here."

His body was slammed into the floor beneath him. He passed out.

When he awoke he was still on the floor and the front doors were still open. He could hear someone crooning. A white mist was floating above him. The glorious perfume of roses filled his nostrils.

He heard someone speaking. It was Genia speaking softly. "Bridget Mary, I see you. You are welcome in this home." She was repeating the statements over and over again. "Bridget Mary, I see you. You are welcome in this home." As Genia spoke the mist developed into human form. Arms appeared. Hands appeared. A face appeared. It was the face in the portrait. That face lifted towards Genia. The expression was impossible to decipher but the feeling of well being was real. Then Bridget Mary gently disappeared.

Genia came down the stairs and sat on the floor beside him. "Daniel, what happened? Wait, let me wake up some of the others to help you."

"No, please don't. I don't want any attention," he sat up as he spoke.

"But what happened? I felt the cold and knew the doors were open. I came out and saw you on the floor."

"I had just come back from Dimitri's and I decided to tackle Aunt Alice on my own. Foolish I know." He rubbed his head where it had hit the marble floor.

Horrified she said, "But Daniel she's dangerous."

"Yes and I was stupid," he stood up and held out his hand for her to grab. "I have just been feeling so, so, so, so ...... powerless: and I guess I was trying to regain my power by yelling at Alice. I was tired of being afraid. I guess I have proved that my power is not enough to tackle the darkness. Dimitri just told me I needed some spiritual support and I didn't listen. I think I will go to bed. Aunt Alice has established once again who is in charge. I'll take a headache pill first."

Genia lifted her hand to touch the bump forming on his head. "Let me see. There's a bump. Did you hit your head? The skin isn't broken."

"Yes, I hit my head," Daniel said without explaining more. He was slowly realizing Genia was not aware of the extent of his battle with Alice and he didn't want her to know. "I think I slipped on the marble. The grass is wet and my shoes are wet."

"I wonder why Bridget Mary was here?"

"She looks like the portrait. Strange to see a very distant relative appear long after death. We know where Fel gets her beauty." He tried to make a joke now. He urged her to start up the stairs. He wanted to be alone.

"Let me lock the doors."

Chapter 29

Felicity unexpectedly joined them in the dining room after a six-day absence. Dimitri had just spoken the words of thanksgiving and all spoons were raised and mouths were open, ready to taste the soup he had prepared when she entered the room. Dimitri stood immediately, dropping the serving spoon into the soup tureen with a splash. His actions revealed his relief at her return.

She said sardonically, "I swear all you people do is eat and drink. How do you stay in shape to be kings and queens of entertainment?"

Dimitri pulled out a chair for her beside him while Genia went to the kitchen for dishes.

Daniel was relieved to see her spirited attitude but he knew walking in the doors must have been difficult. He and some others, had not seen her since Dimitri carried her to his cottage after the encounter with the dark entity. Aunt Fel would not want sympathy. Humour was needed so he answered her comment by saying, "I am yet a humble prince of entertainment but I need lots of food for the strength it takes to carry my ego around."

Fel winked at Daniel. Good grief was she still in shock? Fel in a playful mood? He looked around him. No one else had seen the wink. She calmly tasted her soup and said, "Obviously Dim was the chef tonight. Too much garlic."

"My dear if I had known you were joining us I would have added onions as well. Your personal favourite, I understand." She grimaced at him. Looking at everyone she asked, "So what is the topic on the table tonight? Let me guess. Ghosts? Ghouls?" She looked at them all and waited for a response. She smiled. A happy smile.

Genia answered, with a little worry line creasing her forehead as she considered her sister's strange mood, "Actually we were discussing whether to play Bridge tonight." She looked across the table at Cordelia, "But no one seemed interested."

Cordelia had been studying Felicity's face silently. She now pounced, pointing her finger at Fel. "You know something!" she said accusingly. "You're like a cat wiping cream off its face."

Felicity raised her eyebrows and bent over her soup saying coyly, "Cats should never be given cream. It's not good for their digestion. Makes them fat."

Petra said, "Out with-it Felicity O'Donovan. The last time I saw you, you were unconscious. Since then you have been away. We saw a ghost. You and I, the atheists, the doubters, the deniers, in this crowd saw the supernatural. You had two ghosts around you. Talk sista'."

Felicity laughed, "OK, I'll talk." She looked at Dimitri beside her, "Have I told you how much I respect you?"

Dimitri turned to pudding, smooth rich chocolate pudding, in response, "No, but I have always known." He lifted his glass of wine and said, "But tell me more."

Fel moved her face close to his, "At another time Greek man." She then turned to the rest of them, "You all look gobsmacked. I have some wonderful things to tell you. But first can we have the main course Chef?" She looked back at Dimitri.

She refused to respond to their curiosity until after dessert. Instead she created an intimate space with Dimitri at their corner of the table. She encouraged him to tell stories as the others listened. They were fascinated and confused by her vibrancy.

Daniel wondered at her strength.

Genia looked bemused.

After her last bite of the velvety caramel pudding with cream Fel said, "We need to go to the chapel. I have some things to tell you which should not be heard here. Everyone comfortable to join me there? Or are you playing Bridge?" She was laughing at them.

Of course, they agreed to follow her.

Genia asked Dave and Daniel to grab some chairs from the gazebo and meet them in the chapel. She asked Dimitri to collect some of his quilts he kept on the chairs on his porch, to offset the coolness within the chapel. Felicity went with him. Cordelia, Gerald and Petra cleared the table and stacked the dishwasher. Genia gathered candles from the kitchen drawer. In the chapel she lit all the candles placed on the rock shelves near the entrance, the altar, the window sills and in the lanterns. The little bits of light, shaped shadows on the stone walls, creating an intimate, sacred ambience. Slowly everyone gathered quietly and found their comfortable place, either on the carpeted floor with pillows or in the chairs. There was a slight perfume of roses from outside. They waited for Felicity to begin.

"So, a few things I need to get out of my head first." She turned to Genia. Her mood was quieter; serious. Her eyes held a slight shimmer of tears and her voice was hesitant, "I am sorry for the ugly way I have acted since I came to live with you many years ago. I know I have been resentful and hateful."

She shook her head as Genia started to speak, "No, I see the love on your face and it humbles me, but don't give me an easy out on this. It is true! I would sometimes hear the words come out of my mouth and see them hit you like little slaps. Although I knew I was being hateful somehow it was making me feel better. It gave me a sense of power. We will talk about this much more over the coming months but you need to know why I behaved badly. In fact, it is relevant for our experience here."

She stopped to wipe her eyes. When she started speaking again her voice was constricted, "I've been scared ever since I left the farm. I was ten years old when Genia left for London, eight when John left to study in Dublin. Our grandparents, Buppie and Nana, loved me and gave me lots of cuddles and kisses. Their home was also on the farm so I saw them often. My mom and dad were the same. I was the cute little girl with the curly Irish hair and the fair Irish skin. I was petted and adored. Then they were gone. All of them. Within three years." She had to pause to let out the breath she was holding. "The farm had to be leased so the land could be worked. I felt all alone. The farm had been my cocoon. I was twenty-two but I was not ready to fly. I came to you Genia, but you had a full life. I lived with John and Miriam for a while and watched Daniel grow up but I hated the big city living. I returned to follow Genia around the world. I have felt useless and aimless; always on the outside looking at everyone having a delightful time. I became angry. I know I have been hateful."

She put up her hand to stop Dimitri from speaking. "Wait Dimitri. Let my story of woe continue to flow." She gave a wobbly giggle and took the handkerchief he offered. "But these last few weeks with my research I have had purpose, power and I suppose a niggling of an identity. You were all listening to me instead of tuning me out. Well no wonder you tuned me out, no one likes to listen to constant complaint and negativity."

Dimitri began to speak again but she said with a smile in her voice, "Not yet Greek man. Let me hold the floor for a while longer." She gave a huge sigh. "When I was surrounded by the dark entity, who I will call by her name, Aunt Alice Flora, I felt the hatred, the ugly, the nasty darkness. Yet I was not as shocked by it as Daniel would have been." She looked at him. "I was not shocked because it was familiar to me. I have been feeling those emotions; that satisfaction of hurting another, scoring a hit and getting attention even if it was negative attention. I felt her resentment. In the past few days of reflection I saw how she had become so hateful. She had removed any obstacles that would have challenged her. Her hate just increased, layer upon layer. I must say I have wept for her now that I understand her."

Fel stopped to blow her nose. They waited.

"What shocked me, what totally disarmed me was the love I felt when Bridget Mary embraced me; healing love and acceptance poured into me. I was not unconscious due to shock. I was peacefully healing. I felt cuddled and kissed like my grandmother used to cuddle and kiss me. I went to sleep, feeling safe and protected for the first time in years."

She paused because her throat was clogged with tears. "I have missed my mom and dad. I miss Buppie and Nan. I have missed that adoring love that affirmed me. When John and Miriam were killed I couldn't weep. I just became angrier. I see now anger has been my shield. When I awoke at Dimitri's I had to leave because I wanted to hold onto the love and the peace I was feeling inside. I didn't want to talk and diffuse it. I also had to leave because both encounters made me look at the horror I had become. I was ashamed and I wanted to be alone to weep. A Robbie Burns' poem comes to mind, 'O would some power give me the gift to see myself as others see me. It would free me from many a blunder.' Or something like that."

She laughed at herself and said into the air, "Sorry Mr. Burns for corrupting the words. The point being, the darkness had helped me see just how ugly I had become. The loving embrace of our ancestor revealed understanding and forgiveness."

She smiled at them, "OK I can see you all want to jump in but I still have more to say." Her smile turned to a huge grin. Daniel had never seen his aunt grin. Maybe some giggles after a few glasses of wine but not much else.

"After I left Dimitri's I packed a bag, I took Genia's car and drove to the Glendalough monastery and walked the grounds. I had to make some peace with God; that One I have been denying. I don't want to talk about that because that is a private journey that doesn't matter here. Then I went to Cork. I went looking for Bridget Mary Dimond nee O'Donovan."

They all looked startled. "Yes, I found the records. Her family lived outside Cork, south of Cork. There was a good living there. They are mentioned locally in the Famine records. Her family are mostly remembered because of their great kindness. I won't go into detail now but there are a lot of her descendants we will have to meet someday. Well maybe after we master the Cork accent."

She smiled in memory of some recent interesting conversations. Then Fel said quietly, lovingly, "She is coming. Can you feel her? She comes with the perfume of her beloved roses."

Everyone reacted with gasps.

Cordelia gasped, "Where? What should we do?"

Felicity said, "Do nothing. Wait for her."

Daniel felt warmth but he thought that was from all the candles and the leftover heat of the day coming in the open windows. The scent of roses had increased.

Felicity said, "She is deeply loving. That's what you should be feeling."

Daniel felt the energy change in the chapel. The air thickened. Well that's a strange thought he mused.

From the corner of the chapel a soft light appeared. No form. Nothing scary. Just light. And perfume.

Felicity said, "She has been waiting to take Alice Flora Dimond, only daughter of Marquis of Loth, Home. She keeps returning for her because Alice Flora doesn't rest. She roams in anger and hate. Her father had abandoned her in Ireland because she had a relationship with the maid. He beat her, had the male servants brutalize her and then sent her to a brother who was equally brutal in his condemnation. He enjoyed humiliating her."

The light did not increase but the feeling of comfort and love intensified.

Felicity continued quietly, "Why do I know this? Partially from Alice Flora's anger that night but also because I have met new friends who told me more about the history of the manor: Father Henry Morgan and Sister Veronica Ramos. Several people have mentioned that this place used to be a commune. It suggests hippies and losers. Did you never think that odd? I did and so I researched the commune. It was actually a United Faith Meditation Centre. From all over the world, for many years, people came to this place to heal. Few people knew about it because it was controversial for its day as a multi-faith centre. They stayed low key. It survived because it was the 'love-in' generation. Although it was hosted by Christian leaders, if you understand that true Christianity is welcoming all people into a," she stopped for a minute, "let me remember how Sister Veronica said it, 'welcoming all people into a sacred space of love and compassion without religious divisions'." She smiled, "Or something like that. The Centre was financed by a trust fund from a very wealthy Muslim family. It eventually closed as the world turned away from faith and we entered our post-theist culture. God is dead? Sound familiar? Those who had maintained the Centre died or moved away. The trust ran out of money and there weren't any funds to fix the parts of the building that were falling down. The estate began to crumble further until Jonah and George bought it."

"This is a place of healing? But...," Genia asked, still bemused by Fel's description of Bridget Mary.

"You're about to ask about Alice Flora's presence in all this?"

Genia nodded. Fel looked at everyone. They were all silent, even Cordelia, who was looking towards the steady light in the corner.

"Do you mind if I just keep going and you can ask questions later?"

Silent nods were given.

"Father Henry and Sister Veronica live in Wicklow, in a Catholic Retirement Home. I had tea with them twice this past week. And, I invited them to dinner tomorrow night. I think it's Daniel's turn to be chef." She turned to him. "They don't like pizza Daniel."

Everyone softly laughed at the 'ah shucks' look on Daniel's face.

Fel continued, "No worries, we'll plan something together for the diet of two very senior people."

She twisted back to face everyone. "They told me amazing stories I want you to hear. They also gave me their impression of our Aunt Alice Flora Dimond. They had done some research of their own. Aunt Alice lived to be 85. She died in 1880. I suspect she is buried in the graveyard?"

Genia was able to nod yes since Niall had cleared the graveyard and Brandy had documented the stones. "Yes, she is there along with Bridget Mary, her husband, her two children and some other relatives. All Dimonds. Bridget Mary is buried closest to the chapel, in fact near the corner where she is appearing."

"Thank you Genia," Fel said. "Alice Flora never married. Why would she? No children of course. She was a hateful spinster. Her father had shamed her. She was sent in disgrace to live here with a cruel brother. The manor became her life. She protects it. Henry said they had initially thought the angry relationship between Bridget Mary and Alice Flora was about the ownership of the estate; the manor in particular. Bridget Mary would attempt to enter the front doors and Alice Flora would shove her out. But over the years, and many trusty bolts later, they realized she was coming for Alice. To help her. To take her Home. They felt only love and acceptance in Bridget Mary's presence and decided she could not be vengeful. So they had to rethink her tenacious purpose."

She stopped speaking to shift her body on the floor where she sat and said in a complaining voice, "Genia, the carpet is not thick enough to cushion my bones." She stopped over the last words and groaned, "See it will take some time for me to change from negative to positive."

Genia smiled at her and said, "We both have some growing to do."

Felicity cocked her head sideways, smiling shyly at her.

Daniel could see Fel was not comfortable with the shift within herself and her relationship with them. The addiction of acting in hate and anger, was not going to miraculously heal.

Felicity placed a cushion behind her back and another under her butt. "Back to Alice Flora. Father Henry and Sister Veronica dealt with Alice's darkness by always praying when they felt her hate. They had chants which calmed her. They said the first year there were some nasty disturbances but eventually, other than the occasional altercations between Bridget and Alice at the front doors, Alice gave them a break and didn't bug them. They acknowledged it was her house and they lived in some harmony. I suspect the trouble Jonah and George experienced was due to the interference of the medium and the ill-advised séance."

Petra inserted, "And maybe because they were gay?"

"Yes, that's a thought."

The light had not moved from the corner. Cordelia's eyes had not strayed from the corner either.

Dimitri said, "Wait. Wait. Too much information. Let's just stop for a little minute and reflect on what you've said. OK?"

Felicity nodded.

"Bridget Mary has been at peace but returns for her sister-in-law?"

"Yes."

"The sister-in-law who probably murdered her?"

"Yes."

"They are certain?"

"Yes."

"Why are they certain?"

"Bridget Mary told them."

"Ah. That makes sense."

Daniel said, "It does?"

"Yes, both entities communicate. Just not with words. Who killed her husband? Did she find out?" said Dimitri.

"Yes?"

"Who?"

"Alice Flora, during an argument with him. She pushed him down onto the rocks by the fairy stone. He hit his head. That might have been an accident. Father Henry thinks he's at peace."

"Did the priest and nun ever ask questions of Alice Flora?"

"Initially yes but she communicates garbled hate. There are only some impressions of her biography. They were happy not to disrupt the fragile peace."

"How did we disturb the peace?"

"I suspect because Danny looks like our ancestor. Both the light and darkness reacted. Sister Veronica and Father Henry will help with some answers tomorrow night. They will arrive after five and hopefully we can eat by half past five? They like to be home and cosy in bed by eight. Father Henry is frail."

"Why don't we just meet in the afternoon for tea instead?" Dave asked.

"Father Henry has a plan which involves evening," Fel responded.

"A plan?" several voices chorused.

"Yes, he thinks we should address the situation," Fel again.

"I don't know if I like the idea. I am certainly not prepared for it." Genia said. "We are sitting here with a ghost appearing near us and we have begun to accept that as normal. I don't care if it is a relative, even a tragic loving relative. It isn't normal. It could all explode into horror. I can still hear Fel scream that night. Just last week. It is embedded into my bones. I will never forget it. Do we think we can control that ugliness?"

Dimitri said, "I can see the need to confront Alice Flora but I don't know if we are capable of such a task. It could go very wrong."

"Or very right. Father Henry and Sister Veronica know what they're doing," said Fel.

Cordelia spoke for the first time since entering the chapel, "Genia, we all spoke recently about needing some final solution. We have been fearful these past few days after meeting Alice Flora again. This might be an answer to a prayer. Who better to help us than two spiritual leaders who lived with her for so many years?"

Genia's voice revealed her anxiety, "Yes but it is all too soon. I have hardly coped with the idea of a malignant presence let alone baiting it."

Felicity reached over and touched her sister's hand. "How about we listen to my friends tomorrow night and see what they propose? Then you can decide. How does that sound?" She looked at everyone. Everyone nodded except Daniel.

Daniel responded with a touch of anger, "I don't think it's a good idea. None of you except Fel and I have actually experienced the darkness. Giving it a name and an identity does not lessen the vile hate. Knowing we are related to a ghost that has killed two people and haunted this house for years does not diminish the danger. Do you seriously want to encounter it?"

"Again," said Fel softly, "we can address all this with the pair tomorrow evening. We have a whole day and night to consider the possibility. After we hear what Father Henry and Sister Veronica have to say we can decide what to do."

Daniel was keeping his eye on the corner and the light that appeared.

Gerald asked calmly, "Fel, could you tell us what happened to you that night? I understand the emotions you felt but could you relate what happened to you that night?"

Fel said to him. "Of course. I heard Daniel leave his room and head for the kitchen. I knew he was looking for food. At six feet two he must need a lot of food. Thinking about him eating made me hungry and after a bit I headed towards the kitchen as well. When I opened the kitchen door the lights were off but I could see Daniel crouching near the floor. He had one hand on the counter and he was gasping. I saw this through a thick darkness that surrounded him. I wasted a few seconds trying to figure out what it was that surrounded him. The supernatural has never been my first guess. Eventually I realized it was a definite, albeit see-through being, with intention and decision, surrounding Daniel. A threat. It was clearly attacking him. I yelled to wake you up. I don't even know if you heard me because as I began to yell the shape turned away from Danny. I saw him slip to the floor. I heard him continue to gasp. The shape moved towards me and I stepped back, away from him, hoping to run upstairs but it just enveloped me. I think the kitchen door closed between us."

She looked over at Daniel, "I know why you don't want to take the chance to feel that again. It was concentrated hate. Vile. Horrendous."

She looked back at the others, "I think I tripped on something and fell backwards. As soon as it touched me I think I started screaming." She looked at them for confirmation.

"It isn't a sound I ever want to hear again," said Genia almost weeping. "I still shudder when I remember it."

"I agree with you Genia," said Petra. "The screams reached inside me. I think I started screaming in response. And the hate that night. The ugly vicious hate was overwhelming and I wasn't getting a concentrated effort."

Fel said, "I remember the first scream but not much else. I agree the hatred was overwhelming. And then the love, that beautiful love surrounded me. More than the hate it affected me deeply. I felt cosy and at home. I either went to sleep or passed out, eventually waking up at Dimitri's." She looked at him and said, "Sorry for being such a pain in the butt when I did. As I have explained I was not in a great mental state and I had much to think about."

Dimitri just shook his head, negating any offence.

Gerald said, "Thank you Fel. I'm interested in hearing what Sister Veronica and Father Henry have to say. I can't imagine how this can resolved, especially when you consider both entities have been here for over a hundred years."

Cordelia pointed to the corner and said with a slight panic, "The light is moving."

Fel turned to Daniel, "Danny, when Bridget Mary surrounded me that night she poured into me healing love, a love that erased the effects of my encounter with Alice. She also conveyed some information. Bridget Mary has been in your room a few times since you arrived and she wakes you up. She can't stay long because Alice chases her out. She is fascinated by you because you look so much like her son. And you are staying in her room so she worries you feel residual pain from her anguished days and nights. As well she knows you have suffered from what happened the other night. She was able to give me peace but not you. She wants to embrace you. Will you let her?"

The light in the corner had intensified as Bridget Mary began to move.

In his head Daniel was screaming the word no. He hoped it didn't show. The conversation with Dimitri had helped but he wasn't ready for this. "Please tell Bridget Mary I thank her but I don't need to be healed. All is well."

"I can feel her beauty," whispered Petra.

"She brings the beauty of the Spirit with her," said Dimitri.

Petra said, "It's amazing. Is this what it really feels like beyond the veil? Is this what you talk about Dimitri? I can understand now why people of faith think atheists are deaf and blind. How does one convey this amazing feeling? Even as an author I struggle to find words. It's like standing in the middle of intense wonder. I feel like I have embodied that WOW that I feel when I look at a mountain expanse or the gorgeous beauty of a night sky."

Dimitri said, "Hmmm. Like you've been seeking this moment of sheer and complete satisfaction all your life and finally you understand why it has been elusive; it cannot be found on this side of the veil. It is our soul connecting to the Creative Spirit."

"And we are free creative beings made whole by the Spirit," continued Genia.

"Do you feel this all the time?" Petra asked.

"No, in fact it is often elusive because the world is noisy and distracts us," said Dimitri. "It's a way of living, thinking, seeing that can be lost in the noise. Meditation helps to turn off the noise and encourage the wonder and speak to the desire."

Daniel stood up. "Speaking of desire, I have a deep desire to pee and so I am heading to the bathroom and maybe a walk on the beach to look at the stars. See you all in the morning."

He walked out.

Chapter 30

Daniel went looking for Genia the next day. The air was warm. The ground was soaking up the noon day sun and the flowers were basking in the bright nourishment. Summer was well come in this corner of Ireland. He found Genia alone in the sitting room opening windows. She walked around the room fluffing pillows and moving chairs an inch left or right.

Daniel thought she was showing some nervousness. "Are you anxious about the meeting tonight, Genia?" he asked.

She stopped and looked at him with bright eyes, "It shows?"

"Yes. Do you want to talk about it?"

"Not much. I don't want you to worry about my trivial concerns. I am just a little overwhelmed by everything. A new home, family, guests and ghosts." She smiled then. "It just caught up to me this morning when I was listening to Dimitri and Dave discuss the menu for tonight. Somehow I have just kept coping and coping and tamping down the stress and then this morning I realized my pipe is filled to the brim and starting to smoke." She choked out a laugh, "A clear sign of my stress level is when I use inadequate metaphors to describe how I feel. Also, I feel like smoking which is another sign I am struggling. I only ever want to smoke when I am stressed."

"Genia, we have a few hours until Sister Veronica and Father Henry arrive. Dimitri and Dave have taken charge of dinner and I suspect Fel will help them. Why don't we take a walk along the beach? It can be a silent, zip the lips walk or we can natter away like crows. It might release some of the pressure for both of us by talking this through. Interested?"

She looked around her as though an objection or demand would need consideration before she could answer. Then she smiled and sighed, "That is a lovely idea. And I hope there is a breeze to blow out the mental cobwebs."

"There is a fairly strong breeze off the sea today so it's perfect. I'm heading upstairs for my sneaks and I will meet you back here in five?"

She nodded.

Ten minutes later as Daniel helped her down the first few steps by the fairy stone, he was saying, "Could we reach Wicklow walking along the beach? I guess it would be a very long walk but possible?"

"More than a fast day's walk," she answered. "And I think there's a golf course along the way."

Daniel helped her over a log. "We haven't talked about Fel's recovery? Do you want to chat about it?"

"No."

"We can talk about the warm relationship between you and Dave."

"No."

"We can discuss global warming."

"Really no, since I know very little except the fact that it's happening."

They walked in silence for a long space and then Genia said, "Let me introduce a topic. Why aren't you married yet?"

Daniel sputtered with laughter. He stopped to hug his stomach. "Fair enough dear aunt. A valid question which I will answer once you answer mine about Dave."

"OK. Dave and I are old friends. Your turn."

"I haven't found anyone as wonderful as my Aunt Genia."

"You are a silly man. There must be hundreds of women waiting for your handsome profile to turn their way and give a wink."

"I have 'winked' at a few women but few for long. I am looking for conversations deeper than the shallow versions I have found. I am looking for the woman who cares about more than the recent fashion items. Hard to find."

"But for sure she exists."

"I was definitely given a superb example in my mom. I miss them dreadfully."

"You don't talk much about them. Have you been able to find some peace?"

"I had wondered if my wakeful nights were caused by my lack of peace regarding their deaths. It was so wrong. So absolutely, unbelievably wrong. I had always worried about them when they travelled. You know how adventurous my dad was and how mom encouraged him. They would rent a car and just drive, often without maps. Remember the trip to Morocco? I got gray hairs from that trip when they were out of contact for two weeks. Dad talked to everyone. He trusted everyone. And yet one night in a quiet safe area of Vancouver they are hit by a drunk driver too stupid, too cruel to think of others. That haunts me. So yes, maybe it is the grief and rage I feel surfacing while I sleep."

"Fel said Bridget Mary has been responsible for your disturbed sleep."

"It's possible I'm channelling her memories. Last night I managed a few hours but I woke up disturbed by glimpses of people filled with sadness, grief. But I have found there is a lounger, under the shade of the old oak tree in the garden, that is perfect for an afternoon nap." His tone of voice lightened, "You are an excellent hostess. This place might be my new place to go between films; if the ghosts leave."

They were both silent for a while.

Genia said, "Will we ever get rid of the ghosts? I can't imagine selling the estate especially since it is our ancestors who are haunting the place. I feel a responsibility to do something. At least I know now I'm not going insane."

"Maybe the visit tonight will make a difference. If they were able to live here for thirty years they must have some wisdom for us."

"Dear God, I hope so."

"What happened after I left last night? Sorry to leave abruptly but I did have to pee and I wasn't feeling comfortable with the notion that a ghost wanted to touch me."

"Oh Daniel, I didn't think of it from your perspective. Basically, we stayed a while longer and talked about the visit tonight. But I think we were all a tad overloaded as well. Bridget Mary disappeared soon after you left."

"We have the most unusual problems now. Will I or won't I let a ghost touch me? How will we make Aunt Alice just go away?"

"Yes, I yearn for the boring life of difficult directors and difficult dialogue."

"Speaking of words, notice my brilliant segue away from your outrageous comment regarding directors, did you find the loose stone in the chapel? Did Daniel Irial's letters appear?"

"Yes, I found the loose stone and there was some rotted paper and a ribbon but nothing salvageable. I really wanted to see the words he wrote to his mom."

Genia turned around to start the trek back. "I am feeling some anxiety about this evening. I will feel better if I'm busy; maybe some gardening. Niall was here yesterday and gave me some advice for controlling the rose garden. Gardening will calm me."

Chapter 31

Father Henry was a short man with a huge amiable personality. Sister Veronica was a tiny bundle of friendliness. Her eyes sparkled and she never stopped smiling. As soon as they stepped over the door sill and greeted them, everyone was smiling. Except for Dimitri in the kitchen, they had all come to the foyer to greet them. Looking at their faces Daniel suspected this revealed the hope they were all placing on these spiritual leaders to fix the problem.

Sister Veronica clasped each person close as she greeted them saying, "I hope you don't mind being hugged. I know it isn't really done now to hug unless you are given permission but who would deny an old woman the simple blessing of a hug?" Daniel tried to loosen his stiff poise as he leaned down to be embraced. She paused after she hugged him and then lightly, without explanation, touched his face, only looking away when Genia spoke.

"We are so delighted to meet you. Please come into the sitting room so we can greet each other with more comfort."

Felicity led Father Henry to a cosy chair by the fireplace. It was a warm night so the hearth was left cold but she asked if he wanted it lit. He declined. Sister sat beside Daniel on a sofa. The rest took seats, not speaking just staring at the couple as Felicity began introductions. Genia reached for the tea pot on the side table.

Felicity said, "Dinner will be a few minutes. Would you like a cup of tea while we wait?"

Sister Veronica said, "Oh dear, I really don't like tea in the evening. Would you have any red wine? Irish wine is preferable."

Father Henry said, "Whiskey for me please, if you have any."

There was a confused pause as Genia's friends looked at each

Father Henry chuckled knowingly, "Did some huge walls of misconceptions just collapse? Will my sip of whiskey challenge your expectations of clergy? Weaken your faith? Even worse than my sip of whiskey, Sister Veronica likes a cigarillo once in a while."

Sister Veronica protested, "Henry, you know I hate it when you disclose my secret joy. I am always afraid it will encourage others to smoke." She looked around the room, "You won't be tempted to smoke now that you know I do? I only smoke once in a while when I can get away from the nurses. They tend to be quite stuffy and disapproving."

Felicity laughed, "Well served my friends. Of course, a whiskey and a wine."

Gerald stood quickly, "I have just the whiskey for you. A fine single malt that has spent some time in the black barrel. Some distinctive flavours were created. Ice?"

Father Henry said, "Only the devil would put ice in whiskey."

Gerald stopped what he was doing. He looked around at Father Henry and said in his usual steady tone, "I can see this will be an interesting evening."

Cordelia, who had been watching their every move asked, "Sister Veronica, I can't place your accent. Are you native to Ireland?"

Sister Veronica replied, "I was born in Ireland and as a young woman married a Spanish man. We lived in the sunshine and beauty of Spain until his death a few years later. What you hear is a Spanish influence I have never lost. Speaking of accents, I saw a film of yours recently in which you spoke in an Irish accent. It was a very good story." She paused and asked quizzically, "Why are you groaning?"

Cordelia smiled ruefully in the midst of her friends' laughter, "I was recently complaining to my friends about that role. It haunts me. It is one I would rather forget because of my poor attempt to speak with an Irish accent."

"But dear, look beyond the obvious. Your accent was a bit of an American stereotype of the Irish speech but the portrayal you gave of the blind sister searching for her brother was magnificent. We all wept with you when you found him. The anguish seemed real as though you had personally suffered the loss. You portrayed feminine strength and didn't fall for being a female version of how a man would react. I thought it was superb."

Cordelia looked startled now. Tentatively she said, "Why thank you Sister, thank you for redeeming a bad memory."

Sister Veronica said to them all, "By the way please call Henry and me by our first names. The titles of Sister and Father are really only used within a church setting or during counselling to elicit confidence."

Fel leaned towards her and said, "Veronica, could you share some of what you told me recently about the work you and Henry had shared in the manor?"

Veronica looked over at Henry, "How about I start and you jump in with your thoughts?" He nodded.

"Let me start with some biographical context. I had been raised in a religious home and I married into a religious home. When my beloved John died I turned to my religion. It didn't help me in my grief. I heard a bunch of hollow words. The only certainty was that I was a sinner and I must be obedient to the rules the priest daily named or I would suffer the fires of hell. I remember asking the priest where the love Jesus preached came into the teachings. I was told as a woman I should be more like Mary, obedient and silent, trusting in the church. But since only men were interpreting the teachings I eventually left and began a journey of faith. My husband had left me a hefty bank balance and so I was able to travel the world to hear the stories of faith from all religions. I was amazed at the many roads that had been carved into the landscape of life; similar in teachings and similar in mistakes. All religions began in love within the commitment of equality. Yet all eventually became institutionalized into rules and barriers and male dominance and power struggles. I eventually went back to the teachings of Christ trying to peer through the centuries of doctrine and dogma. One day, when I was wandering and wondering through Cork, I met a fascinating man called Father Henry Morgan."

Henry spoke up, "An intelligent and handsome kind of dude."

Veronica laughed, "I was going to say wise and witty but if handsome needs to be said then that's alright too."

Henry smoothed back his white hair and said, "I just thought our new friends should know I have a vanity problem. Shameful, I know."

Veronica shook her head and continued, "This fantastically handsome man preached some inspiring sermons about faith. He wowed me. He was echoing the lessons I had learned in my travels about faith, the divine presence and our relationship with the divine. Eventually we joined forces. I became a nun and we used my money and a huge donation from an Indian benefactor to set up the Centre.

Dimitri, the chef for the evening, who had been standing silently in the sitting room doorway, entered the room at this point, "I am anxious to hear the rest of the narrative and at the same time keep my food offerings from cooling. How about we all move to the dining room and eat while we hear more?"

Genia stood, "Henry and Veronica please meet a very old friend Dimitri Constantinides, whom we had sent to the kitchen to prepare the meal. He has been faithfully working all afternoon and we should honour his effort while it is hot. The dining room is this way." As they all turned towards the doorway she stopped and with a little laugh said, "Oh, but of course you already know where it is. Forgive me."

Henry offered his arm gallantly and said, "I've heard worse sins."

Everyone laughed.

Chapter 32

Over the meal Father Henry asked them questions about their lives. He was fascinated by the life of a celebrity. They both asked questions about privacy, creativity and celebrity parties. They were active listeners. They exuded kindness and acceptance. Daniel thought they sincerely wanted to know who they were at a deep level. Veronica encouraged them to tell stories about their families.

Gerald asked them, "When you found the manor and began to turn it into a base for people of all faiths, did you get much push back from others?"

Henry said, "Initially we were in the news, vilified at a time when people did not understand the unity of faith as lived out by many religions. We opened in the spring of 1960. At the time it was difficult to keep a smile on our faces. But we prayed and persevered. In the end the controversy worked to our advantage. When the media became distracted by other scandals we heard from people who agreed with us and began to come. We weren't trying to make a profit, just provide a place to talk about our connection to the divine."

Veronica said, "Our narrative is Christian, believing Christ was offering an invitation to experience divine power; a truth named in all religions and often outside religions. He didn't come to start an institution dedicated to restraining people. He was inviting flight. As do most religions when we grind off the veneer of centuries. Our common inner faith experiences here helped us to 'see' better."

Henry said, "Remember the story our patron told us? The one about the birds?"

Veronica looked puzzled and slowly shook her head.

Henry said, "The old creation legend. I don't know which country it was or which religion."

Veronica's eyes lit up, "Oh yes, the birds. Do you want me to tell the legend?" Everyone nodded so she continued, "The birds were sitting around in Eden after Adam and Eve had been escorted out of the garden. The crows were complaining about their wings. They asked God, 'Why did you give these to us? We can't do anything with them. We can't walk with them. They drag along the ground. We can't pick things up with them. And they're ugly and awkward to carry around. The feathers fall out.'

God answered, 'You can fly.'

'Fly? What is fly?' the birds demanded.

'Spread your wings. Spread them out as far as they will spread. Wider. Now move them up and down. Harder. Work at it. Faster. Now jump.'

'Jump?'

'Yes, off the cliff and into the sky,' God said.

'Jump? Jump?' they said with great agitation. 'Jump?' they squawked in chorus dancing around bumping into each other.

One robin emerged from the flock of crows and spreading her wings wide and vast jumped into the sky. She soared into the blue, through the rainbows and above the misty clouds. She soared deeper into her own light."

Henry added, "And the rest, having been shown the way, took flight." After a pause he added, "And that clearly described our ministry at the Centre. We met hundreds of amazing birds of all faith backgrounds seeking to learn how to fly. Thirty years of amazement and delight."

Veronica said quietly, "We have been privileged."

Henry smiled at her, "And then the walls came tumbling down and we hadn't enough money to fix them. Fewer people were coming to the Centre as the Divine became much maligned in the world and people shut themselves off from the spirit."

His words gave them all a moment's pause.

Into that pause Genia said, "This is a good time to return to the sitting room. Daniel grab the plate of cookies Fiona made for us. We'll take them with us. Anyone for coffee or tea? Hot chocolate?"

When they had all settled Felicity said, "Before it gets too late we should talk about our ancestors now. I have told Henry and Veronica about the events these past few weeks. They have a plan we should discuss. Discuss but not necessarily implement."

Henry said, "Genia, someday I would like to see the chapel as you completed it. It wasn't in our budget but we did make sure the stones were supported and wouldn't fall on people who wanted to explore it. One resident created a labyrinth in the woods, probably grown over by now. He was inspired by the light he would see from the chapel ruins some nights. People often sat outside near the chapel for prayer. Some believed there was a healing power radiating from the chapel."

Cordelia asked, "Have you seen the woman and two children by the back door?"

"Yes, a few times and the response from the chapel. It is an old story that needs to be healed in Bridget Mary. She could not save them in life but continues to try after death," said Henry. "I think the family has long been at rest and the image we see is either a residual imprint caused by the depth of suffering and hunger or it's an image created out of Bridget Mary's sorrow."

"How often did you see her?" asked Cordelia.

"Many, many times," he said.

"Fel said you thought she was returning for her sister-in-law."

"Yes," he looked at Veronica. "Would you like to talk about Bridget Mary? She seemed to connect with you."

Veronica nodded her head. "Bridget Mary is peaceful love. She just wants to finish a story of forgiveness and cannot totally rest until that happens."

"Rest? What do you mean by rest?" asked Petra. "I should confess that until the startling events of the last few days I have been mocking my dear friends' talk of the supernatural. I only learnt to 'fly' after that night. I love that story. Well not really fly yet but I am aware I will be able to fly. When you say rest, I hear only the old-fashioned images of bodies rotting in cemeteries waiting to rise up and lie with lions and sheep or some such metaphor of peaceful, boring afterlife that will come when the world ends."

Veronica gave her a thoughtful look, "Blessings on your awakening and your future flight. Thank you for asking for clarification because often we forget the baggage of images we use. By rest we mean a time when all the damage done to our souls by human living can be finally laid down. Rest from feeling guilt, anger, neurosis, shame, hate, especially self-hatred. Rest is when we realize in the baptism of death the soul can emerge in all its beauty. Recognize the baggage was human made and didn't need to be carried."

Henry added, "A great theologian once said, 'We are spiritual beings having a physical experience.' Imagine the day you get to take off the weight and fly fully into your own truth. That only happens after you have graduated from this human experience."

Dimitri asked, "I am curious about the plan. What are you thinking?"

"Veronica and I have been in prayer since we met Felicity and she shared the accelerated events here. We have also been praying since we stepped in the doors. The house feels different since we were here. The veil is thinner and I feel powerful hate and anger."

Petra again, "What do you mean by the veil?"

"It is believed that heaven is not up on some cloud but present to us and hidden from us only by a thin veil. If we had eyes to see or ears to hear we could see behind and beyond the veil. Sometimes the veil is thinner due to increased emotion within a space. That is why we tried to keep it peaceful for Alice Flora's sake. She is malignant only when her ownership of her home is threatened. The only thing in her life that gave her satisfaction is within these walls."

Cordelia was leaning forward in her chair, "How do you know this?"

"We figured it out over the thirty years we lived here. At first, we knew only that the place is haunted inside and out. Eventually a pattern emerged when both ghosts appeared. Someone did some research and someone else created a narrative and someone else wrote it down. It's in my notes somewhere."

Veronica added, "Bridget Mary conveys some of her story as she embraces you. She seldom noticed us though. She usually just showed up to find Alice. There would be a lot of door slamming and then silence again for a long time. We should have looked to see if there were specific dates such as anniversaries or full moons or likewise so we could prepare for the drama."

Genia said, "What is the plan we should consider?"

Veronica said, "Our thought was to invite Bridget Mary and Alice into the room and do some spiritual conflict management mixed with forgiveness."

"No!" Daniel said. "No, it's dangerous."

Veronica said, "Daniel they are going to come anyway so why not have the upper hand and control the situation? Alice does not know she can go Home. She has murdered four people to protect her home. Not to mention those who starved from hunger because of her hatred."

"Four people?" Cordelia exclaimed.

Henry's smile was pastoral, "Yes, the two babies born to Bridget Mary after her son was born. Not still births as written in the family history. Then she orchestrated a way to get rid of her brother's son after she killed her brother. She blamed the father's death on the son. Bridget Mary's son was supposed to die in the Gaol but Bridget Mary managed to get him out fast. The fact that he was still alive and could at any time come back and challenge Alice for ownership of the estate must have been a constant worry. I wonder if that is why she killed Bridget Mary? To discourage the son from returning?"

Gerald, the calm listener, asked, "Women could not inherit property. Did the distant father deed it to her?"

Henry nodded, "I don't know that part of the story. I agree it is curious. I suspect there are documents a good researcher could find to explain how she was able to live here and die here."

Everyone looked at Felicity and smiled.

Genia said, 'I think we have found such a researcher in our midst."

Dave was impatient, "Tell us more about the plan. I think Genia is at her wits end and moving out of the manor might be the only solution. The wicked aunt has increased her activity."

Henry looked at Veronica who nodded at him and said, "I think we are beyond discussing the plan. The participants are arriving. Alice Flora is here. The cold hatred followed us from the dining room. She is growing stronger and will appear soon. Hopefully by the fireplace so we can get Bridget Mary in the doors."

In response to the fear and anxiety on their faces he said, "We encourage you to repeat a chant in your head as long as she is here. If she manifests don't be afraid. Stay peaceful. Like all bullies she is empowered by fear and anger. The chant is simple, 'God reveal your unconditional healing love'. No fancy theology. But as you repeat the words you need to embody them in your mind. Feed the words with your heart and soul. Think of love in your life: your children, people you love, moments of love. The words only have power and intention when you actually recognize the Divine possibility in the room."

Veronica said in a deliberately casual voice, "We might be able to resolve this tonight and send Alice Flora Home. I think we must address this tonight. We can't leave it alone now."

Genia looked at all her friends and especially at Daniel asking, "What say you?"

Cordelia responded first as she grabbed her husband's hand, "I say we try."

Petra nodded.

Fel came and stood by her sister. She took Genia's hand, "I vote yes. We have no other solutions and it seems like the story is unfolding anyway." They both looked at Daniel.

Daniel didn't vote. He had stood when Father Henry said Alice would appear and had moved to the sitting room door that opened to the foyer. He stood as far from the rest of the room as possible. He noticed with some relief it was still light outside on this summer evening and Alice would not be able to turn off the lights and turn the world into darkness, as dark as her.

Father Henry said, "She is manifesting by the dining room door behind most of you. No don't make sudden moves or turn around. We'll watch her. Stay peaceful and loving. Oh, I see she is moving to the fireplace. You will all see her soon. That is surprising. She is as black as thick oily tar. She's projecting her rage as a defence mechanism against us. Return her rage with love. Look at her with love. It's a great power you have within you."

Veronica said casually, "Hello Alice. Thank you for letting us dine in your home once again. We have had many meals here. Your home has brought us comfort. I hope you have learned to trust our words over the long years that we lived with you."

Daniel could hear a murmur in the room as people saw her and began to whisper the chant. Petra's voice was louder than the rest; slightly hysterical. He allowed the chant to flow around him. He couldn't participate or project a loving acceptance to her. It was beyond him. He felt hate. Anger. She had destroyed lives. He could not share the optimism or hope. She will go straight to hell but let her think she will be received by a benevolent God if it will get her out of the manor.

Henry spoke, "Alice, you must be tired after all these years. So much hatred. So much fear. That is what I feel from you; deep fear. What are you afraid of Alice?"

The black silhouette of a human form hovered by the fireplace. The form moved from side to side as though surveying the people in the room. Daniel was curious to know if she could identify them individually.

Father Henry said, "Alice Flora, we know what you have sought to hide. We know you killed your brother. We know you murdered Bridget Mary and her wee babes. We know your nephew had to leave his mother and his homeland because you gave false testimony against him."

The figure swirled abruptly towards the Father.

Sister Veronica said, "Nothing is hidden, Alice Flora Dimond."

The form turned towards her voice but jerked back to Father Henry when he said, "We know your father sent you to Ireland in disgrace because you loved another woman."

They heard a muted scream of rage from the darkness.

"Your father was ignorant. That was not your sin."

Sister Veronica said softly in love, "Alice Flora, you have swelled in hate and made yourself as ugly and vile as possible to hide your secrets. All is known in heaven and on earth."

Daniel realized a face had begun to appear. It vaguely resembled the face in the portrait which Genia had brought down from the attic and now rested against the wall near where Alice had begun to materialize. The facial features were distorted. A horror show!

Father Henry said, "Alice it's time to leave this place and go Home to the One who anticipates you."

The face was less distorted but still a horror show because of the hate. The eye holes were deep and the empty depths revolting. The holes faced Daniel.

Father Henry said, "Alice Flora, it's time for you to find rest."

She was now grey. Clearer.

Sister Veronica said, "My friends, please continue to channel the love of God for her. Don't stop chanting."

Father Henry said, "Alice your final Home awaits you. It is a place of loving forgiveness." He looked at Daniel, "I am told you look like the nephew she accused of murdering her brother. You are a huge threat to her Daniel. Can you say anything to offer her forgiveness?"

Daniel spit out in a hard voice, "How can the bitch be forgiven for murdering children?" He stepped away from the wall, aggressively moving forward.

"How can the bitch, this vile disgusting bitch, be forgiven?"

Her profile was losing clarity. She was returning to her shadow form.

Daniel took another step forward, "How can the bitch know anything but hell, burning fire? That is justice."

Alice Flora began to swell in size.

Dave stood up in alarm and came to stand behind Genia and Felicity, who were together on a sofa. He hovered protectively.

Father Henry said, "Don't be alarmed. She has only a certain amount of scare tactics. Defence tactics. Your strength and shield is in your chant and your peaceful, loving response."

Daniel stepped forward and addressed Alice Flora, “You have caused suffering. You have caused others to starve to death. Children cried for a single piece of bread. Mothers held them as they died with tears on their faces. Do you think God is going to forgive you?”

Sister Veronica and Father Henry were silent, allowing this confrontation to happen. Maybe it was all part of the plan.

Alice Flora moved towards Daniel.

Daniel stepped forward to meet her, feeling very cold, “As an innocent and loving woman knelt praying to God in the chapel you had her killed. You purposefully let the fire burn her. Had you drugged her food so she couldn’t move to save herself? How long before the rocks crushed her?”

Alice was now swirling vibrantly above him. Ice.

“Did you sleep a good sleep ever again bitch? Or did your vile heart feed on the despair you caused?”

Alice Flora moved closer. Daniel was vaguely aware of Genia asking him to stop. He didn’t care. He felt murderous hate. He wanted this vile presence to acknowledge her sins and to suffer for them.

Father Henry said with a note of wonder in his voice, “This is amazing. I don’t think I have seen this before.”

He stood up and turned pointing towards the ceiling, “Veronica, do you see it?”

They were all trying to see what he saw while still watching Daniel and Alice.

Sister Veronica whispered, echoing his wonder, with one simple word, “Wow.”

Then they all saw it. A single clear orb with an inner oscillating rainbow was floating above them.

“Is that Bridget Mary?” Cordelia and Petra asked with awe in their voices.

"No," said Father Henry. "That is someone else visiting us tonight."

Genia said fearfully, "What? Who?"

Just at that moment Cordelia said, "There is another one."

Another orb, same size and shape moved around the room near the ceiling. Everyone shifted in their chairs or stood to watch the movements. They were like large bubbles that children blow through special wands.

There was silence as they watched them spinning gaily around the room. Daniel counted five orbs. As they passed he could feel their light. Their presence felt cool. Beautiful.

Genia whispered her question again, "What? Who?"

Sister Veronica answered gently, "I think it is your family coming to support you. Keep praying."

Daniel was mute. There were no words forming in his head. No thought was complete. He was shocked by the idea that his mom and dad might be in the room with him. He was confused. Alice Flora's looming presence was in his way as he moved his head trying to follow the circles of light.

Cordelia gave a shout, "What's happening to Daniel? Daniel move."

But Daniel couldn't move because he could feel the touch of another. Strangely not the horror show of Alice but a loving, familiar touch.

Father Henry said, "Daniel, two of the orbs are lingering near your head and another is in front of you. The one is front of you is increasing in size."

As they all watched, the orb grew in size and slowly took the shape of a human form. They could see Daniel through the shape as arms and legs emerged and a face appeared. A face with features much like Daniel's.

"Could it be the first Daniel, Daniel Irial, our ancestor?" Fel asked quietly.

Daniel was frozen in place. His anger was dissipating. His sense of injustice and pain decreasing. He was feeling oddly warm and comforted.

The full-bodied entity in front of him was his height. A voice spoke clearly in a beautiful tone, "Alice Flora Dimond, it is time to come Home."

Daniel thought the voice sounded like deep purple velvet. Smooth. Kind. Loving.

Alice Flora did not lose power but reared backward. In the kitchen they heard a violent eruption of dishes exploding.

The first Daniel continued, "All whom you have sinned against have come here to forgive you. Be at one and at peace. Join us."

Daniel could hear the murmured chants of the others.

Again, the voice spoke, "While you hated you were loved. A love has waited for you."

Alice Flora was reacting. She was shrinking in size and her features were once again appearing. She had retreated to the fireplace.

Genia said, "I can smell roses. Is Bridget Mary coming?"

Father Henry whispered, "Yes, but gently. She comes gently so she doesn't disturb her son. Keep praying and chanting everyone. Help them to reach Alice."

The orbs around the room grew in size and began to spin into brighter colours. Daniel saw that twenty, twenty-five more orbs were in the room. They were whirling and twirling. The words 'playful' and 'joyful' came to his mind.

The first Daniel said, "Yes, Aunt Alice you will face judgement just as we all did. For every slap you have given you will feel ten times the pain of the one you have slapped. For every hug you have given you will feel ten times the joy of that hug. That is divine justice. You will not escape the cleansing and healing of your soul. Come."

The room was now filled with the scent of roses.

Alice Flora was clearly revealed now. The face was scarred by years of hateful, vile thoughts. She was looking at the first Daniel with almost an air of vulnerability. Daniel remembered being enveloped within the darkness of her hate. He remembered the shock to his whole body; the icy cold.

The first Daniel spoke again, "We know you have longed for peace, for rest. The Holy One has known."

They could all see Bridget Mary now, as clear as Alice Flora. She floated beside Alice with gossamer hands reaching; a gesture that had been rejected often through the centuries. Daniel wanted to hear Bridget Mary speak as this simple loving gesture was made to Alice.

Daniel became aware of two orbs near his face, touching his cheeks. He was now sure he knew who they were. He knew they had come to give him peace as well. He felt cleansing tears on his face. The knot of hate and anger he had felt since their death was disintegrating. Healing.

He saw Alice Flora's wretched hand lift and reach towards Bridget Mary's. In that instant the room was filled with a bright light that encompassed them all. Blinding them. Binding them. And then all was gone. They were left alone with the lingering perfume of roses.

Epilogue

It had been a few weeks since Cordelia and Gerald had returned home to New York, leaving behind expressions of great love. Cordelia had cried over each of them. An experience, such as they had shared, had deepened their appreciation of each other. Petra's new love interest, Peter, had arrived the day before Cordelia and Gerald left for home. They had all been charmed by Peter. Cordelia had cried over him as well. Petra and Peter left to tour Ireland and to explore the burgeoning love between them.

Dave had left yesterday. He was returning for Christmas.

Genia and Felicity had taken long walks together. The sisters still had tensions between them but they spoke of them. Genia became aware of how often she had blocked her sister's need for love and acceptance, not able to cope with Fel's emotions. There had been many honest conversations; sometimes with tears, sometimes with anger but always with truth. They were grieving the loss of family. They were healing.

They never did play Bridge. Instead they had reviewed that night endlessly. Father Henry and Sister Veronica had returned often to share the wonder conversations and to help them unpack the knowledge they had gained after seeing beyond the veil.

Daniel was often pressed to relive the moment Daniel Irial had materialised in front of him to speak to Alice Flora. Daniel struggled to speak of his feelings; he told them about the initial resentment he felt as this presence prevented him from continuing his aggressive stance against Alice Flora. He had been empowered by his rage; some of it triggered by the memory of his parent's deaths and the injustice that had followed during the trial. Alice Flora was a target he could use to vent his anger and his feelings of being ineffectual and powerless as the farce of a trial had played out over those bleak weeks.

Despite his desire to hold on to that empowering rage, he had felt wonder creeping into his soul, dissolving the rage. He reluctantly let it go when he heard Daniel Irial speaking. He struggled to understand the shift in his thinking: somehow the rage and the injustice lost meaning in the face of the larger reality of life beyond the veil. Not much of Daniel Irial's words had registered but the recollections of everyone over the past weeks had filled in the spaces.

Genia had lamented the suddenness in which the orbs had disappeared. "Our ancestors," she kept repeating, "whirled around us in precious balls of brilliant colour. And then they were all gone. Pop!"

Dimitri had asked her what she had wanted to happen.

"I wanted them to stay and visit and have a cup of tea of course," she had said laughing at herself and him. "But really, I wanted to identify who they were. Father said they were ancestors. Which ones?"

Felicity said, "I think we know for certain about two of them; the ones who lingered near Danny's face. I almost want to say lovingly lingered but that is a subjective assertion."

Daniel said, "I felt loved." His voice was tight as he spoke and he had to take a deep breath to continue. "Thinking back, as the rage began to dissipate, I felt amazement. I kept asking myself if it really could be them and then I knew for certain it was them."

The home was peaceful now. The chapel no longer glowed at night, although Genia imagined some nights there was a faint halo of light around the sacred structure. The visitors at the back door, caught in time and sorrow, had not been seen again. Sister Veronica had agreed with Dimitri's notion; their appearance had been a manifestation of Bridget Mary's sorrowful memories; when she left they would no longer appear.

'I propose,' she had said, 'that Bridget Mary needed to heal as well. For a gentle and loving soul, the anger and hatred she must have felt against Alice Flora would have disturbed her rest.'

Tonight, Dimitri and Felicity, Daniel and Genia were sitting on Dimitri's front porch. The sunshine was gone, taking the butterflies with it. A slight breeze from the chapel was sending the perfume of the trailing roses towards them. All yellow roses.

A bright harvest moon was ascending.

Felicity said, "The sight of the harvest moon brings back beautiful memories. The sky is so large on the Canadian prairies, Dimitri, without any mountains to block the view. Just an endless beautiful horizon. When the wind blows the wheat sings. In the middle of this huge expanse of wheat and sky is a magnificent orange ball. The 'face' of the moon is clearly defined. Dad and grandfather would be in the fields working by the light of the moon harvesting the crops. Mom would dance. It was a family tradition. Grandad was quite strict about planting some crops in the moonlight as well. I wonder if it began here?" She looked at her sister.

Her sister said, "Wow, that's a thought. I have just taken those customs for granted but I wonder if Daniel Irial was the origin of those traditions. We will have to explore our childhood to see if there are more connections that have been handed down. The world is smaller than we think and we are more connected than we think. Imagine our ancestor dancing in the light of the moon. Daniel, I am glad you had your summers, as a youth on the farm, to make the family connection to this moment."

Daniel lifted a hand to gain their attention and whispered, "Look at the fairy stone. What's happening?"

They all watched in surprise as a glow appeared around the big grey stone that stood as a sentinel at the top of the beach pathway. Little lights appeared to be twirling and twisting along the width and breadth of the stone. The only sound was a slight distant hush of peaceful waves crawling up and back along the shore line.

Fel whispered, "One more piece of research I forgot to mention. There is a legend that the fairies are known to dance on the stone during some full moons."

She laughed with them, "Oh and my other piece of information: the writing on the stone that was deciphered for us about a yearning for England had been carved over the original words. The original Gaelic words simply said, "May you joyfully dance with the music that is soundless."

About the Author

Sally McShane lives in Vancouver, Canada. She has studied philosophy, Irish history, spirituality and drama and has written plays, short stories and meditative prose. This novel emerged after leaving her work within the inner city of Vancouver, an intense place of suffering, violence, struggle and infinite beauty where members of the community whisper deep truths if one listens well enough.

94982075R00146

Made in the USA
San Bernardino, CA
14 November 2018